PRAISE FOR THE MCKAY THRILLERS

"Soak it up! I love a taut plot, meaty details, and stone-scary heavies, all of which Hughes delivers express. But most of all I feed on language—crisp, alive, and juicy. From a kicked knee that pings like the last kernel in a hot-air popper, to the hero's haute cuisine, an Italian beef sandwich, doughy, soaked, slathered, with bright, deadly-hot peppers, Dirty Money is scrumptious crime fiction au jus!"

—Arthur Plotnik, author of *The Elements of Expression* and other language bestsellers

"Bone Mountain is a damn good book!"

—Doug Peacock, author of *Was it Worth It? A Wilderness Warrior's Long Trail Home*

"Bone Mountain is a hella fast-paced high plains thriller."

—Elwood Reid, Executive Producer and Showrunner for the number one hit CBS series *TRACKER* and other top television series, including *Big Sky* and *The Chi*

"Big sky, big bones, and big story—Robert D. Hughes' fast-paced debut mystery has it all."

—Michael Bracken, author of the novel *All White Girls* and more than 1,200 short stories

TWI$TED GREED

ALSO BY ROBERT D. HUGHES

BRIAN & DARCY MCKAY SERIES

Dirty Money

Bone Mountain

ANTHOLOGIES

Death and a Cup of Tea

Death and the Detective

Fedora II

Fedora

TWI$TED GREED

A Brian & Darcy McKay Novel

Robert D. Hughes

C J KEENAN Publishing

For Sally, always inspiring

There's the scarlet thread of murder running through the colorless skein of life, and our duty is to unravel it and isolate it, and expose every inch of it.

—Sir Arthur Conan Doyle, *A Study in Scarlet*

Chapter 1
(Day 1)

Terry Patchett trudged slowly up the steep mountain path, eyeing the crest of the ridge above. The route was made up of two parallel tracks on the hillside. Patchett knew that it was used by equipment and workers' trucks. A typical four-wheel drive vehicle with high ground clearance could make its way up. He didn't want to take a chance on damaging his car, so he walked. It wasn't that far. He picked his way along the rocks, placing his feet carefully with each step. It would be easy to twist an ankle on the loose stones. And yet, he was relieved finally to be alone.

The meeting he'd left a half hour ago had been a painful ordeal. Lawyers for both sides arguing as only lawyers can—sniping at each other in vitriolic legalese. The partnership in which Terry was a half owner planned to develop a "sustainable luxury community" named Paradise Preserve on this prime piece of Montana real estate. They claimed the project would benefit all stakeholders: the wealthy members, Geyser County, visiting tourists, and even the environment. That last one was a bit of a stretch, but they figured it would play in the target upscale market. Some rich folks liked to assuage their conscience when purchasing luxury vacation homes. The Paradise Preserve would mainly profit Terry and his co-investor, a mysterious silent partner based in Chicago, whom he had never met. Terry had invested his life savings in the enterprise and mortgaged his home to finance his share. An all-or-nothing gamble for a man with a wife and kid. But the potential payoff was in the millions, and within a year or two. The partner had a local guy representing him, a logging contractor named Seth Delmer who lived a few miles north. Terry had found Seth to be unreliable, hard to deal with, an all-around pain in the wazoo.

Terry wondered where Seth was. He hadn't shown up for either the lawyers' confab or the planning meeting at the county offices afterward. Terry hated meetings. Seth had been dropping out of sight recently, leaving Terry to represent them in public. This lack of accountability had caused Terry a hell of a lot of grief, especially today, when he attempted to answer pointed questions from the Montana Earthbarricade mouthpiece about compliance with state soil and water quality laws. He'd been hung out to dry, and he was pissed.

As Terry passed a grove of stubby junipers, he thought he heard a faint noise above him. He craned his neck to look higher. Nothing.

He worked his way upward. The smaller stones on the path rolled under the smooth soles of his street shoes, causing him to slide with each step. The first buildable lot was just over the hilltop ahead. This particular parcel was considered prime, salable at somewhere in the area of two million dollars, give or take. The surveyor had sent him a text that morning saying that the build site corners, well and septic had been marked with stakes and tape. He pulled his phone from his back pocket and brought up the satellite mapping app. The place where the terrain was scraped level by a bulldozer lay just ahead.

Ah, there it was, a roughly rectangular leveled off area of a few acres marked with wooden stakes wrapped with bright pink plastic tape. A future trophy second (or third or fourth) home of a mere 10,000 square feet for some megabucks pursuer of the Montana dream. Part of the philosophy of the project was to keep the homes relatively small, in keeping with limited impact on the environment. Though the average American home was only about 2,000 square feet, this prospective residence would be considered a modest retreat for a member of the Preserve. The home construction cost would be at least seven million dollars. Ten mil land and construction seemed like a lot, but would no doubt appreciate fast in the rampaging local real estate market. A mega-popular television series about a dysfunctional Montana ranching family had accelerated demand for this type of property. The TV series, though supposedly located adjacent to nearby Yellowstone National Park, was actually filmed hundreds of miles away.

A black Ram pickup sat on the far side of the build site, the cab apparently empty. As Terry stopped next to the first corner marker, a familiar man stepped out from behind the truck with a rigid smile on his face and a black handgun clutched in his right fist.

"What the hell?" Terry said.

The man stepped toward Terry and raised the gun, pointing it squarely at Terry's chest.

"Hey, let's talk. I mean, c'mon, man."

"No need for talk." The assailant pulled the trigger. Terry heard a loud BANG, then felt a brutal punch in the chest.

Standing as he was, with his heels lower than his toes, he fell over backward, his head slamming into the hard ground. A hole the diameter of a piece of construction rebar had appeared in his chest, but he was beyond registering such things. In fact, Terry Patchett was dead.

The man rolled Patchett's body up in a large blue vinyl tarp. He slung the parcel into the truck bed and slid the retractable bed cover over it, closing it tight. He inspected the ground where Patchett had fallen. No visible blood. With a boot, he scuffed the place where the body had landed, just in case. He figured his tire tracks would not be a problem, since the surveyor and the contractor's employees routinely used the road to access the various build sites. In any case, the gravel road surface was bone dry.

He drove slowly down the access road, lost in thought. He'd never shot a human before. An avid hunter, he'd harvested numerous deer and elk. But this was different. His hands began to shake on the steering wheel. He found it hard to get enough air into his lungs. But he couldn't falter. Had to get away. What if someone heard the shot and investigated? He took scant comfort in the fifty thousand he was to be paid for the hit. Hit? *Jesus.*

Two men worked their way up a steep hiking trail in the National Forest about a quarter mile away from the build site and a hundred feet higher in elevation. They heard the crack of a gunshot and abruptly came to a halt.

"Handgun," Jimmy Brownleaf said. "Down at that Preserve place."

"Yeah, that's what I thought, too," Doctor Phil Banham said. He was more used to treating accidental gunshot wounds than hearing handgun shots outside of hunting season. He raised his binoculars and scanned the rugged countryside below and to the east. A cloud of tan dust rose from the entry road to the real estate development known as the Paradise Preserve. He spotted a dark-colored pickup truck just before it disappeared around a bend. He couldn't identify the make, but the license plate was standard Montana blue. The numbers were unintelligible at that distance.

"Did ya make 'im?" Jimmy asked.

"Nope. Too far away and tearing out of there too fast."

"I sure don't see the point of that mess." Jimmy aimed his chin toward the development below and spat on the ground.

"Me neither. Think we oughta go down and have a look?" Banham said.

"I guess. That shot seemed outa place, ya know what I mean? Shit, I was enjoyin' the walk."

"Me too. Nice way to spend my day off." He sighed.

They headed down the rocky path, arriving at the trailhead a half hour later. They took Banham's Subaru Outback down the forest service road and across to the nearby gravel road into the Paradise development. They bumped along the narrow surface for a few minutes before rumbling over a steel cattle guard bisecting a barbed wire fence. There were no people around. A dump truck, bulldozer and trailer all sat empty in a flat area just inside the entrance. They walked around for a few minutes but did not climb up the rough track to the planned homesites.

Jimmy spoke up: "Let's get out of here. This place gives me the willies."

They boarded the car and Banham jockeyed it around toward the cattle guard. He headed down to the highway that would take them the fifteen miles into Clarkville. In town, they parked outside the city-county complex containing the offices of the Geyser County Sheriff 's department as well as the Clarkville town police.

Chapter 2

The two men approached the reception area of the county law enforcement offices. A young woman with unnaturally bright red hair sat behind a thick Plexiglas panel. As they walked up, she said, "Help you?" as if she weren't particularly interested in being helpful.

"We'd like to see the sheriff," Banham said.

"What about?" Red Hair said. She recognized the doctor and his scruffy companion.

"Um, we heard a pistol shot and saw a truck hightailin' it away up at that Paradise Preserve place," Banham said.

"So?" Red Hair said.

"Well, we'd like to tell the sheriff about it," Banham said.

She sighed. "Hang on."

Ten minutes later, Geyser County Sheriff Jim Reid came out a door off the lobby and approached them. A tall man of about thirty-five with a broad face, he was dressed in a khaki uniform with cowboy boots. "C'mon back, fellas," he said.

The sheriff dropped into a big chair behind his desk. "Whatcha got?"

The doctor and Jimmy briefly ran through their account of the gunshot in the valley, the doc doing most of the talking. Reid listened impassively until they stopped.

"Montana plate, black truck? That right?"

"Yep," Banham said.

"That's about as rare as quills on a porcupine," Reid replied.

"But still, something weird about it. A pistol, not a long gun. And the truck's movement was kind of…panicky. Anyway, just thought you should know," Banham said.

"Thanks, fellas," Reid said. He stood up, signaling the end of the discussion. "We'll check it out."

In the lobby again, Jimmy said, "He thinks it's bullshit. Well anyway, we did our duty. How about a cuppa coffee?"

After the two men left his office, the Sheriff dialed an extension in the building.

The Geyser County Attorney, Emma Whittier, answered her desk phone.

"Yes, Jim?"

"Doc Banham and that hiking buddy of his were just in here with a report that could turn out to be kinda interesting."

"Oh?"

"Yeah, said they heard a pistol shot and saw a black pickup leaving the Paradise Preserve in a big hurry a little while ago."

"They have any info as to ID, plate or anything?"

"Not a thing."

"What's your plan?"

Reid sighed. "I'll take Richard up there for a look." Richard Smith was the Geyser County Detective. He'd lost his job with the state police under cloudy circumstances several years earlier. Reid had inherited him as the sole investigative officer for the Sheriff's Department when he'd taken over and wasn't thrilled with the man's performance so far.

"Good. Keep me posted, will you?"

Reid and Smith arrived at the Paradise Preserve access road an hour and a half later. Smith shifted the county Dodge Durango into four-wheel drive high range and accelerated up the rocky route. They reached the first build site a few minutes later and got out.

Smith, anxious to appear knowledgeable, scuffed a few stones aside with the toe of a boot and said, "Looks like a vehicle was up here recently, I'd say."

Reid regarded the ground. "Yeah, but so what?"

"That story from Banham might be something. I mean, why small arms fire up here?"

"Maybe somebody shootin' at targets?"

"Construction's going on. So all kinds of guys working up here routinely." Smith shrugged. "It just seems a little strange, that's all. Let's look around."

Reid glanced at his watch. A little after four. "Okay, but I've gotta get back pretty soon."

The two men slowly paced around the area. No one else around—the contractor's people must have knocked off for the day. There was no evidence of gunfire, nothing out of the ordinary. But, on the way back down the access road, Smith said, "That's weird."

"What?"

"See the tire tracks on the left over there? Looks like somebody put a wheel in the ditch and swerved back up onto the road."

He stopped, opened the driver's door and stepped out. Indeed, it looked like a vehicle had recently careened through the shallow ditch just off the road surface. The grass was flattened, and a shallow rut had been carved in the dry soil. Like a drunk, or maybe someone in a big hurry. Smith scanned the ground, spotted something reflecting the late afternoon sun in a patch of scraggly grass. He found a small cylinder of shiny gold paper with a red and blue oval symbol. White letters spelled out: DUTCH MASTERS THE MASTER CIGAR. Smith picked it up and slipped it into his shirt pocket.

As he boarded the SUV, Smith said, "Hey, I maybe found a clue."

Reid regarded the deputy in silence. "I saw ya pick up some kinda cigar wrapper. If it's a clue, don't ya think ya should be just a little careful with handling it and drop it into an evidence bag?"

"Uh, yeah, okay." Smith blushed as he completed the suggested action. The ride back to town was carried out without further conversation.

The Clarkville Enterprise featured the following story on its front page the next day:

LOCAL LAND DEVELOPER MISSING

Terry Patchett, 32, of Clarkville has disappeared. Patchett, a principal in the Paradise Preserve luxury land development located 15 miles south of Clarkville, was last seen at a meeting with county officials early Monday afternoon. His wife, Melissa Patchett, said she last spoke with her husband by telephone round 2:00 P.M. Monday. He was due home later that afternoon but did not show and did not answer her texts or calls. She reported her husband's absence to the Geyser County Sheriff Department that evening.

Geyser County Sheriff Jim Reid said that two local hikers reported hearing a gunshot on or near the Paradise Preserve development a little after 2:30 P. M. Monday. The hikers, Dr. Phil Banham and Jimmy Brownleaf, told an Enterprise reporter that they were hiking on a Forest Service trail in the area when an apparent pistol shot sounded nearby, coming from the direction of the Preserve.

"It was weird, because that place is posted and nobody goes there except the builders," Jimmy told an Enterprise reporter.

According to Sheriff Reid, he and county detective Richard Smith investigated the Preserve property and found nothing unusual. Patchett is considered by the Sheriff's Department to be a missing person. Unconfirmed rumors have circulated recently that an out of state investor in the Paradise Preserve project has been imprisoned for an unrelated offense. Patchett's business associate, Seth Delmer, who resides on a rural property in the Crazy Mountains, could not be reached for comment.

Chapter 3
(Day 2)

Brian McKay sat at his desk and savored a sip of strong black coffee. On this August morning, he sat alone in his small office on the third floor of an old redbrick building in the River North area of Chicago. The day was already warm, but the thick walls of the hundred-year-old structure did a good job of keeping the steamy summer humidity at bay. He'd opened the double-hung window a few inches. Sounds carried a long way in the heavy air. Tires hissed along sticky pavement. Horns honked. Two men down on the sidewalk yelled a conversation where every other word was "fuck." An el train's steel wheels clacked along the tracks suspended high above State Street.

A year had passed since Brian returned from Montana, where the corporate fraud and murder case the media called "Dirty Money" played out. He and his niece, Darcy, had nearly been killed.

Darcy had recently completed her senior year at the University of Illinois-Chicago with a B.S. in Biological Sciences. She'd been a varsity softball player for the Illini her first three years and then quit the sport to devote more time to her studies in her final undergraduate year. She'd be pursuing a graduate degree in paleontology at Montana State University, starting at the end of the month. In fact, she was on campus in Bozeman now, looking for an apartment and registering for classes.

Brian's private investigations business had grown to the point where he was making a decent living, with an income approaching what he'd earned as an FBI agent in the Chicago Field Office until he quit a couple of years back. Single, he rented an apartment about four miles north of his office. He indulged his passion for classic rock—vinyl and CDs, as he had since his college days. The music was from the generation prior to his own, but he just flat-out loved it. CCR, The Stones, Dylan.

His PI clients were often insurance companies investigating false claims as well as individuals with problems like missing relatives or wandering spouses. He hadn't been in anything risky since returning to Chicago. He was getting a little bored. That was about to change. His phone rang. Caller ID showed area code 406, Montana.

"How's it going, man?" Brian recognized Bill Thorsten's voice. Thorsten, the resident FBI agent in Bozeman, had become a friend in the last couple of years as they'd worked together on cases.

"Making out okay. How about you?"

"Been quiet since we saw each other last year. Maybe something interesting now, though. SLC's got me looking at the Paradise Preserve. It's a so-called sustainable luxury development in the valley down near Yellowstone Park, not far from our old hangout, the 606 Ranch."

Brian remembered the 606 from the previous year. A corrupt cabal of executives from the Chicago-based Belcoe

Corporation had committed a series of crimes before turning the place into charred rubble. "How do luxury and sustainable co-exist? Sounds like an oxymoron."

"True, but the developers make the pitch that billionaires can buy a vacant build lot for a million or two and put up their very own Montana part-time dream home surrounded by gorgeous mountains while generating zero net emissions. Something about carbon offsets, xeriscaping, clustered development and such. It's a membership club, exclusive as an A-list Oscars party. Folks with liquid assets under ten million bucks need not apply. They're looking at guys who fly their own jets, TV chefs, NFL quarterbacks, Hollywood. Classes taught by some of the well-known members."

"Classes?"

"Yeah like gourmet cooking by some top chef, how to understand football by the Seahawks' quarterback, paleontology by Scott Noble Stevens."

"Maybe it'll work. Plenty of billionaires around."

"That's the target market. Initiation fee's four hundred thousand. Annual dues run another fifty k. The average residence construction cost is supposed to range from five to twenty million. Kinda like the Yellowstone Club but more uh, socially responsible, and no skiing."

"So why are you looking at it?"

"If it gets off the ground, it'll be one of the largest capital projects in the state. We routinely look at investments of this sort for possible money laundering, drug money involvement and so forth."

"Any indication they're dirty?"

"No, not yet."

"You've looked at the partnership agreement?"

"Nope. It's a private entity and we'll need to subpoena that along with financial information. Based on local rumblings, I wouldn't be surprised if there's somebody with deep pockets behind the two local guys. They appear to be just regular guys making a living before this deal came along."

"Who we talking about?"

"Terry Patchett came to Clarkville recently from the Oakland area, works as a real estate broker. Seth Delmer's a local boy. Interestingly, Patchett's wife reported him missing yesterday. This is per the local newspaper."

"Kind of early to jump to conclusions."

"Yeah, but there's another weird thing. You recall our two hiking buddies, Jimmy and that doctor?"

"How could I forget 'em? Those oddball guys we met on the trail near the 606 last year. They did a good deed there."

"Yeah. Well, they happened to be hiking near the Preserve yesterday and heard a gunshot just before Patchett went AWOL."

"Who's this Delmer?"

"Seth's got a reputation as a nasty drunk. Runs a logging and custom lumber operation. Don't know where he'd get the capital for a project like this."

"Which lends credence to the idea of a silent partner financing it."

"Yep. Anyway, what's my *favorite* McKay up to?"

"Darcy's doing fine. Finished up her bachelor's. Been accepted into the master's program in Earth Sciences at MSU."

"Cool. She'll be in my neighborhood here in the Bozone."

"Matter of fact, she's out there already. Glad you're around. Not to be overly protective, but…"

"Yeah, I know. She tends to get involved in stuff, kinda like you. I'll keep an eye out."

As soon as they concluded the conversation, Brian's phone rang again, another call from the 406 area code.

The familiar voice came on without preamble. "I've gotta see you. My ex is missing."

Brian remembered Arthur Sands from the Bone Mountain case two years earlier, near the town of Clarkville, Montana. A mercurial billionaire Chicago businessman, Sands also owned a huge bison ranch in Montana's Crazy Mountains. The ex he'd mentioned was Barbara Hardy, whom Brian had met.

"Oh man. What happened?"

"She was with me here last night. We said goodnight around ten. She slept in her own cabin but was gone this morning. I just got a call from some guy demanding a couple million dollars ransom. I need your help."

Brian knew Sands and Barbara remained close. She lived on the ranch fulltime, while Sands split his time between Chicago and there. "You report it to the sheriff?"

"No. I don't want to depend on those guys. My plane's at Chicago Executive. Hop on it ASAP and I'll tell you the rest when I see you this evening."

How damned presumptuous of Sands. Brian was tempted to put him off, but he listened as Sands told him how to find the plane at the private airport in Wheeling, northwest of the city. Sands urged him to get going pronto. After a little discussion, Brian agreed. He had nothing pressing for a few days, he knew Sands was good for a hefty payday and he liked the idea of returning to Montana. He'd been thinking about the beautiful mountains of the south-central part of the state that morning. Plus, he genuinely liked Barbara Hardy. As a bonus, there was an interesting woman in Clarkville he'd met last time out.

Brian drove home and packed a case. Before leaving his apartment, he called his girlfriend, Michelle, to let her know he'd be away for a few days. She didn't answer, so he texted her. Shortly after noon, he found a parking space near a small private terminal at Chicago Executive Airport.

Concluding the call with Brian, Arthur Sands set his cell phone on the desk with shaking hands. His normally impassive expression had transformed into red-faced agitation. The caller 's voice had a trace of western drawl. He remembered every word: "We've got your ex. You want 'er back, you will provide two million dollars, unmarked cash, in used hundreds. We'll be in touch. Meanwhile you'd best get the dough together."

Chapter 4

Barbara Hardy lay on her side on a soiled mattress atop an old iron bed frame. Her wrists and ankles were tied together tightly with black parachute cord. A blindfold blocked her vision. Duct tape covered her mouth. Foam ear plugs had been stuffed into her ears. Sensory deprivation, she thought. A term dimly remembered from a college psychology course. She could hardly breathe and had the awful sensation that she might suffocate. She had forced herself to calm down, lengthen each breath through her nose, forcing air into her lungs. She remembered an article she'd read recently on deep breathing: slowly breathe in while counting to five. Then exhale to the count of six. Keep going for two minutes. The exercise seemed to help a little, but she still struggled to get enough air. She was wearing the clothes she had on when she was abducted that morning: jeans, a peach-colored long-sleeved tee shirt and sneakers. She'd lost track of time but guessed it was late afternoon of the same day. She sensed she was in a small room. She could make out a slightly brighter area a few feet distant, through the blindfold. Perhaps a window—she couldn't be certain.

She tried to reconstruct the day. She'd dressed and made coffee at her cabin on Art's ranch around seven A.M. As she'd sat at the kitchen table drinking coffee and checking her phone, a knock sounded on the front door. She assumed it was one of the ranch staff. Art would have come in while announcing himself. She opened the door and was shocked to see a person a little taller and a lot wider than herself wearing a black balaclava that obscured the face. Before she could react, the person entered the room, grabbed her by the neck and placed a wet rag over her mouth.

She'd tasted and smelled a liquid sweetness, then gagged and fell to the floor, gradually losing consciousness. Next thing she knew, she'd awakened to the living nightmare she now inhabited.

She struggled to loosen her bonds, but they seemed as tight as ever. Frustrated, she wrenched her arms violently, causing her body to roll off the edge of the bed. She crashed to the floor on her side, helpless as a hooked fish on a riverbank. When she hit the floor, she let out a sharp groan. She could hear it okay, meaning the earplugs weren't very effective. Then she realized that the plug in her right ear had fallen out when her head struck the floor. She held her breath and listened, wondering if anyone had heard the noise she'd made falling. Nothing. Then, she heard the sound of a vehicle approaching the building. The engine noise stopped, and a door slammed metallically. She heard the outer door of the building being unlocked and opened. Footsteps came toward the room.

A person opened the door and walked in. From the creaking of the floorboards, she guessed the person carried some weight, likely a male. She noticed that the rhythm of his steps was resolute. She guessed he was the one who'd chloroformed her.

"Well, aren't you the clumsy one," he said, standing a couple of feet from her. "I told you to set tight, but you didn't follow orders. How would you like to have the skin on your back scraped off with a vegetable peeler?"

Barbara stayed silent. She was afraid to move or speak.

"Well, you seem to prefer the floor to that comfy bed. Some people just don't seem to know what's good for 'em."

Barbara tried to protest, but the tape over her mouth made her voice come out like a muffled exclamation in some foreign language.

"Don't bother. I don't care what you have to say. What counts is what your ex says. He'd better say, 'Yes sir, here's the cash.' If not, well, there's always that kitchen implement I mentioned." He barked a laugh, sounding like a raven caught in a trap. "But you're kinda cute. If your man don't pay the price, maybe we'll keep you for a while."

He walked out and slammed the door. She could hear the footsteps receding on the hard floor. Then all was silent again except for her labored breathing.

The man drank from a bottle and went outside. He walked with a barely perceptible hitch in his gait, as if feeling the effects of an old injury.

He boarded a Polaris Ranger side-by-side ATV, keyed the ignition and rode a short distance into a clearing in the woods. He dismounted and studied the ground. Next to a tall Douglas fir, there was a small pile of rocks, carefully arranged and looking like they'd been there for quite some time. He took off his cap and held it loosely in thick fingers. He stood silently for a moment, head bowed. His face wore a pinched look as if he'd bitten into a piece of spoiled meat that he could neither swallow nor spit out. He picked a couple of bright yellow arrowleaf balsamroot flowers from a nearby clump and carefully laid them over the rocks.

After a moment, he turned to face a nearby rectangle of freshly disturbed soil that stood out from the groundcover around it. The area was about three by six feet. He grabbed some fir needles, twigs and stones from the ground and scattered them over the rectangular space, attempting to camouflage it. Satisfied, he climbed aboard the four-wheeler and drove back to the cabin.

His phone rang as he hung his ball cap on a peg inside the cabin entry. A Chicago number showed on the screen. He frowned as he accepted the call.

"What's the status of our two projects?" A familiar male voice with a trace of a British accent.

"Everything's under control."

"Good. Anyone looking into it?"

"How the hell would I know? You think I hang with the local sheriff? Don't worry. Let me handle it. I know what I'm doing."

"Are you certain of that? You've got a mixed record in that regard. In fact—"

"You should fuckin' talk! Calling me from the graybar hotel. If you were so goddamned smart, you'd be out in free society like me." Seth's voice had risen in volume as he got agitated. He knew his cabin was isolated. Nevertheless, he should be more careful.

There was a long pause. "Ah, perhaps you forget to whom you are speaking."

He swallowed and tried to compose himself. He couldn't afford to let his temper screw things up with the man on the other end. The guy had a shitload of financial resources. And he was connected. Without him, the project in the valley would flatline and he would be out of a possible major windfall. And the current deal with the kidnapped woman could fall through. He cleared his throat and spoke, "Uh, sorry. I got carried away. You know, there's some pressure, doing what I've been doing."

"All right, then. Just don't mess it up. I'll be in touch." The man in prison ended the call.

The one in the cabin grabbed a bottle of Canadian whiskey from the table and drank greedily. He patted his shirt pocket, finding a torpedo-shaped brown cigar. He pulled it out, removed the gold paper band and fired up the cheap stogie. He tossed the wrapper on the floor. As the alcohol coursed through his veins and the smoke invaded his lungs, he felt better. He wiped his mouth with the back of a hand and capped the bottle. Couldn't afford to get drunk. He had plenty more work to do. But he needed to get outside for a bit, check out his property and equipment.

Chapter 5

Arthur Sands's sleek Citation Longitude waited on the airstrip, dual jet engines revving in preparation for takeoff. The plane was a glossy white with blue and gray stripes along the fuselage and tail wing. The side featured seven porthole-style windows. Brian guessed it was new. He remembered Sands owning a Hawker jet a year ago. Business must be good.

Brian had been whisked through security and given a ride on a golf cart directly to the plane's airstair. He climbed the steps to the cabin. A young blonde woman greeted him with a bright smile. She had the looks of a television soap opera actress. The only other occupant of the cabin was the pilot, who swiveled in his seat in the cockpit and waved at Brian while offering a toothy grin. Smiley folks.

"Sit anywhere you like," the woman said. "Buckle in. Once we're aloft, I'll check with you as to your needs."

Brian looked around at an array of plush seats upholstered in mocha brown leather. He selected one facing forward near the front of the cabin and settled in. The engines rose in pitch, the craft taxied onto a nearby runway and soon they were banking over Lake Michigan, turning sharply and heading west. Brian admired the cluster of shiny skyscrapers piercing the air more than a thousand feet above the Loop and along the lake to the north. Though he'd lived in Chicago nearly all his life, the richness of the city's architecture never ceased to amaze him. A few minutes later, the flight attendant served him a glass of cabernet sauvignon followed by a lunch of beef Bolognese over tagliatelle. The mahogany dining table was covered in starched linen and the silverware was real silver. The experience was about as similar to commercial coach as a Mercedes S Class to a donkey cart.

After lunch, he fired up his laptop. Thorsten had just sent him an email: a Clarkville private investigator was about to retire and was seeking someone to take over the practice. Maybe Brian would like to meet the guy while in Montana.

Brian looked up the P.I., name of Arthur Braswell, in an investigative database he subscribed to. Braswell appeared solid on the surface, licensed as an investigator for more than twenty years. No criminal record. Married, no kids. Member of the local Chamber of Commerce. Looked like a model citizen on the surface. But nobody really is. Interestingly, Braswell had been engaged by Arthur Sands the year before on an embezzlement situation at the ranch. The P.I. discovered the bookkeeper, a local woman, had been fudging the numbers and pocketing thousands from the bank accounts. Braswell interviewed the perp and elicited a written confession. She'd also signed an agreement to make restitution rather than face charges that would likely have put her in prison. Reminded Brian of his work in the FBI financial crimes unit, but on a smaller scale.

He wondered why Sands didn't just hire the guy to look for his ex-wife. Seemed like a long-time local would have the inside track. Maybe he'd contact the P.I. But the first priority was his current client, Mr. Sands.

Brian gazed out the window, but there wasn't much to see. Endless clouds edged toward the horizon like great boneless white birds. He thought of Darcy, now on campus at Montana State in Bozeman. Her text that morning said she'd been looking for an apartment to share with her friend Becky Stanton, who'd grown up in Bozeman and who was also pursuing an M.S. in Earth Sciences. Darcy wanted Brian to meet them for a campus tour while he was out.

He called James St. Claire in the Chicago FBI office and got his voicemail. He left a brief message, letting him know where he was headed.

His mind returned to the strange phone call from Sands. He remembered Barbara Hardy well from the time they last met, at the dedication of the dinosaur museum carved out of the northeast corner of the massive Sands property. Though divorced, she and Sands seemed as close as a happily married couple, possibly even best friends. Though her ex-husband lived in Chicago most of the year, she'd settled in at his ranch. Brian liked her more than Sands. She was an unassuming soul, one you wouldn't think compatible with the aggressive industrialist. She'd seemed a little lonely, a daytime wine drinker, he knew. Her son from a previous marriage, Scott Noble Stevens, was a nationally prominent professor of paleontology at the University of Illinois. Brian wondered whether Barbara might have a reason to intentionally disappear. And he recalled Bill Thorsten's mentioning Stevens as a planned celebrity teacher of classes at that luxury development, the Paradise Preserve.

Late afternoon, the jet passed over the snowy mountaintops of the million-acre Absaroka Beartooth Wilderness before curving north and gliding down into the

Bozeman area. At the airport, a white crew cab Ford F-150 pickup idled outside the passenger arrival area. A woman of about forty in long sleeved shirt and jeans stood next to the truck holding up a sign reading BRIAN M.

As Brian approached, she smiled and stuck out a hand. "Howdy and welcome." They exchanged names and she said, "Let me load up your luggage." Josie Wilshire then grabbed Brian's rolling suitcase and effortlessly threw it into the truck's back seat.

Aboard the vehicle, Brian learned that Josie had started working for Sands as a ranch hand a few months ago. Prefers the outside work, she says. A horsewoman all her life, she competes in regional rodeos as a barrel racer. Knows why Brian is there. Has no idea what happened to Barbara Hardy. Tells him that Barbara lives in a cabin near the big Sands house. Guesses that Barbara prefers her own space, though she and Mr. Sands are close and spend a lot of time together in the big house as well.

About an hour after leaving the airport, they turned off Highway 89 onto a gravel road heading into the high country. The towering wall of the jagged Crazy Mountains loomed above them, visible in stark silhouette against the darkening sky. Climbing up a steep road with substantial gain in elevation, they rolled through the ranch's big log entryway just before eight P.M. Josie entered a four-digit code on the keypad next to the sturdy metal gate, causing it to swing open. A hundred yards in, she dropped Brian and his suitcase off at a guest cabin near the ranch headquarters complex, then took her leave. As sunset approached, the clear high-altitude sunlight drained away like an outgoing tide. Brian's phone rang. Sands. They agreed to meet in twenty minutes in the main headquarters building.

27

Chapter 6

It was deja vu for Brian, waiting for Arthur Sands in the huge log-walled great room, with its western art and fifteen-foot-high vaulted ceiling. The bank of enormous windows facing the Crazy Mountains was dark, reflecting the dimly lit interior space. He flashed to the Old Faithful Lodge in Yellowstone National Park. A few minutes later, as Brian was considering dropping into a leather chair, Arthur Sands walked in. Dark hair, tinted glasses, medium height, wide shoulders, impeccably tailored clothes. He looked sad, not at all the confident businessman Brian remembered.

The billionaire strode over to him with a weary smile. "Brian, good to see you again." They shook hands.

"Yes, but unfortunate circumstances, Art. I'll do what I can."

In his office, Sands served them bourbon rocks and they took seats in cushioned chairs across a simple wooden coffee table.

"As you know, Barbara and I are very close, in fact, closer than when we were married," Sands said. "She's been spending the summer out here, while I'm mostly in Chicago or on the road for business. She's got the first cabin to the north, same as when you were here last time."

"She experiencing any problems you know of?"

"No. She's seemed happy as I've ever seen her. She's illustrating western history articles for print and online periodicals. One on Jack Slade recently published in *Wild West Tales*. She's proud and she has a right to be. Not everyone can do that."

"How's her health?"

"Good. She's cut way back on alcohol. So have I, for that matter."

"How did you find out she was missing?"

"Last night, we had dinner here and went out for a walk after. Talked about having breakfast together this morning. I went by her cabin around eight this morning to pick her up. The door was cracked open. She wasn't there. Her car was parked outside where it always is. Empty. I searched the cabin. Nothing. Talked with the staff. Nobody saw or heard anything. No strange vehicles entered or left the ranch. You saw the front gate. The others are also locked and Barbara had no way of unlocking them, far as I know. Fences are electric to keep the bison in, so unlikely anyone could climb them."

"Could she possibly be somewhere inside the ranch, away from HQ?"

Sands frowned. "Well, a person could disappear out there. But why in hell would she wander off when we were going to meet up?"

"I hate to say it, but what if she walked out a ways and got lost or injured somehow?"

"She'd call me."

"Assuming she's got her phone and there's a signal, right?"

He shrugged. "Appears her phone's not here. But yeah, the cell signal's sketchy. Works fine in some parts of the ranch, nonexistent other places. Hey, can you track her phone by the GPS?"

"No. Only law enforcement can do that. And they'd need a court order. What about her laptop?" Brian said.

"In her cabin, but I don't have the password. Doubt it would relate to her disappearing."

"Could you show me your recent emails and texts with her?"

"Sure. I'll forward all that to you in a little while."

"Are there cameras in that area, by any chance?"

Sands looked a little sheepish. "Actually, we only have cameras on the main gate and around this building. I should look into covering the cabins and other gates, I suppose."

"How about I check out her cabin now?" Brian said.

Sands shrugged. "Help yourself." He glanced at his Rolex. "I'm beat. But I'll be up for a while, if you think of anything I can do to help. Otherwise, let's talk first thing in the morning." He left the room, chin dipped, shoulders slumped.

Brian walked the short distance to Barbara Hardy's cabin. It was now fully dark, and stars were becoming visible in the clear sky. A blue Honda CR-V was parked out front. He entered the building through the unlocked door and switched on lights. The living room was neat and the southwestern style rug looked as though it had been vacuumed recently. A few magazines were spread out on the small coffee table near the couch, including *Montana Quarterly* and *The New Yorker*. A stack of papers turned out to be pencil drawings of landscape scenes. Several pencils and a clipboard holding a partially completed drawing of a coyote with a stark ridge in the background sat on the coffee table near the couch.

He explored the rest of the log structure slowly, taking in every detail. The small kitchen contained high-end brushed aluminum appliances and a coffee machine. On the marble countertop, a wooden rack held nine knives, no empty slots. He checked the dishwasher, which contained only a wine glass, coffee mug and a few dishes and utensils.

He went to the window, where an exterior floodlight illuminated a large pale gray-barked aspen tree, leaves fluttering like butterfly wings in the dry wind. The closed window was unlocked, not surprising in that remote location.

The dining table held nothing but salt and pepper shakers shaped like miniature stone obelisks. The refrigerator contained a bottle of Pinot Grigio and a few staples like eggs, lunchmeat, lettuce, butter and bread. After a quick perusal of the bathroom, he entered the bedroom, which featured a queen-sized bed, matching pine dresser and armoire and a small upholstered chair flanking an oversized window giving onto a flower garden full of penstemon and Russian sage. The bed was unmade, out of character with the tidiness of the rest of the place. His phone rang.

"Brian, it's Scott Stevens." The Chicago-based paleontologist's voice was tense and higher pitched than normal. "Any news?"

"Hey, Scott. Sands call you?"

"Yes, and I've been frantic ever since."

"Well, I'm just getting started. I'm in her cabin. Seems like she's a neatnik."

"Yeah, she sure is."

"When did you last communicate with her?"

"Yesterday, on the phone. She seemed okay."

"She mention her plans for the next day or two?"

"Not really. Said she'd be at home doing some drawings."

"Okay. I'll get to work then. Look, don't worry. I'll keep you posted."

"What? Man, I'll drop everything. I can be out there tomorrow."

"No, no, don't do that. Tell you what: go to her apartment in the city. Check it carefully for anything unusual, anything different than the way she normally keeps the place. Look at her computer, if there's one there. Her laptop is here in her cabin, but it's password protected and I haven't been able to get into it. See what her emails look like, if you can. And anything else you can think of. What exactly did she say yesterday?"

"Just catching up, you know. No drama. Mom seemed normal, glad to be with Art. Enjoying Montana as always. Said she'd made a friend, a woman at a real estate agency in Clarkville." Stevens's words tumbled out quickly. He continued on, "Nora Spivey, she said. Nothing else. Hey, wait, here's something. She said she'd been getting strange phone calls lately from some scammers asking for her auto insurance policy number, something about an accident, implying she'd been in a hit and run or something. She said she knew nothing about that. I told her to ignore that shit and just block the phone number. I had to walk her through the blocking procedure. She's kind of a Luddite."

"Okay. Let me know what you find out at her apartment. Meanwhile, I'll work this end."

"Man, you've got to find her. This is totally insane."

After reassuring Stevens and hanging up, Brian reflected on his comment about the car accident calls. He remembered a story in the Chicago Tribune a few days earlier involving insurance fraud, a gang of people purposely causing traffic accidents where the victim was made out to have triggered the collision and was then blackmailed. Probably unrelated, he thought. He returned to his own cabin and turned in. As he drifted into sleep, he made a mental to-do list for the next day. He'd be up early and would check in with Sands. There were people in the nearby town of Clarkville he needed to see, and he'd interview the ranch staff as well.

Chapter 7
(Day 3)

Darcy McKay and Becky Stanton sat at a table in the coffee shop in the Strand Student Union. Each chair had a stylized letter "M" cut into the wooden back. The floor was thick gray carpet, which kept the noise level down. It was a comfortable place to talk or study.

Darcy glanced out the window. Beyond the full parking lot, sawtooth mountains with snow fields up high dominated the view. She noted with appreciation how different this place was from her previous home in Chicago. Her uncle and only living relative, Brian McKay, still lived there. They were as close as twins, though he was sixteen years older. They'd both survived some dicey circumstances in the past two years. When it came to keeping cool in stressful situations, her uncle was the OG.

She and Brian communicated by phone message pretty often. Yesterday, he'd texted, said he was on his way to the Arthur Sands ranch in the Crazy Mountains. She remembered the place, a huge bison ranch. Not that far from Bozeman. She hoped to have the opportunity to see her uncle soon.

Darcy and Becky would be starting the graduate program in Earth Sciences at MSU in a couple of weeks. They planned to share an apartment…if they could find one. Their backgrounds growing up were totally different: Darcy a city girl and only child orphaned while in high school, while Becky'd been the middle child of five in a close-knit Montana cattle ranching family. But they'd become as close as sisters during the dinosaur fossil dig they'd been on together two years earlier. They'd shared a tent and developed their friendship. Darcy had a skim latte in front of her and Becky had an oversized black coffee. They were taking a break from their apartment hunting safari in Bozeman.

"Rents are crazy," Becky said. "Up twenty percent in the last year, I heard."

"Yeah, they're charging two thousand a month for a one bedroom. This town is growing so fast. Housing's not keeping up with demand," Darcy replied. "Lot of rentals going to vacation people."

Becky sighed. "Yeah, it's turning it into another Aspen or something. Anyway, let's hit those other two places this afternoon."

As Darcy was about to respond, a tall lanky young man wearing rimless glasses approached their table. His tan face cracked into a grin as he said, "Hey, great to see you two again."

Darcy flashed back to the dinosaur dig at Bone Mountain. The guy was the field supervisor, Will French. He'd watched over the work of the student volunteers, including Darcy and Becky.

"Hi," Darcy said. "Uh, like to join us?"

He grabbed a chair. "Wow, how cool. Are you guys in school here?"

"We're both getting ready to start the MS in Earth Sci," Becky said.

"Cool. I'm a TA for Geo 521," Will said.

"Dinosaur Paleontology. I'm taking it," Darcy said. She knew Becky would also be in the class and that she thought of Will as a big brother. But Darcy suspected he might have a crush on Becky.

Will frowned as he addressed them. "I was so worried about you that time. That gunshot and…"

"Well, it all worked out," Darcy said. "Anyway, we're looking for an apartment. Would you happen to know of a cheap two-bedroom around here?"

"You could stay at my place while you're looking. It's only a couple blocks away, over on Sixth. My roommate bailed, so I've got a spare bedroom."

Darcy and Becky exchanged a wry glance. "We'll keep it in mind," Darcy said.

Becky: "We've got a monthly contract on a tiny apartment at Grant Chamberlain through the end of the month. Then, we're on our own." She was referring to University-sponsored housing for graduate students, not their preferred option. "Anyway, thanks."

Chapter 8

amilton Massey, former Chief Financial Officer of Belcoe Incorporated of Chicago, dropped his rear end onto his bunk at the East Moline Correctional Center in East Moline, Illinois. The facility was classified as a minimum security prison, meaning it housed mostly white collar criminals who'd committed financial crimes such as fraud or embezzlement. The inmates were not considered violent and thus not posing a danger to society. Nevertheless, it was still prison, with inmates fenced in (albeit a low fence not topped with concertina wire) and watched over by guards. Personal freedom and privacy were both in short supply. Inmates wore a uniform of long-sleeve khaki shirt and pants and black work boots whenever outside their cells. The food was institutional, not unlike hospital fare. For a fastidious former high living man like Massey, it was a lukewarm version of hell. He wished he could sleep all the time. But he was now facing another nightmarish day.

He slumped forward on the cot and began to sob. Tears ran down his face and dripped onto the concrete floor at his feet. This continued for a few minutes. It was a pitiful display of grief, something unthinkable in the man's previous life as a powerful and autocratic corporate executive. But now he was known as inmate M79862, nothing more than a white-collar criminal paying for his conviction on seven counts of financial fraud. He'd been found guilty in a federal jury trial of falsification of financial reports to the public, insider trading and abetting the sale of weaponry to hostile nations in violation of the Arms Export Control Act. His sentence ran for five years, with eligibility for parole after three. He'd done just under a year of soft time.

Massey was known to the other inmates and to the guards as a sorry specimen worthy of little respect. He alternated among agonized self-flagellation, braggadocio about past glory and seething resentment. To anyone who would listen, he'd bloviate about his past success, with a staff of dozens of financial professionals hustling to fulfill his every edict. He'd tell anyone who would listen about how the Wall Street analysts hung on his every word on company earnings and prospects for the surging stock price. Bragged about how he'd implemented innovative financial reporting techniques designed to maximize the stock share value, standard accounting principles be damned. How he'd been named CFO of the year by *Financial Officer* magazine. He regarded himself as a supreme winner. But he was self-aware enough to know that the attitude and aggressiveness rewarded in business could get you killed in prison. He quickly learned the rules, among which were: never take someone's seat in the TV room or ask a stranger what landed him in prison. Unlike, many of the inmates, he shunned the racks of free weights and workout machines. His only exercise was walking the outdoor track for an hour every day. Commercial jets would fly over, many setting out from or gliding in for landing at Chicago's O'Hare airport, some 160 miles to the east. The sight of those planes gnawed at Massey. The freedom of movement that most people took for granted was something he would never again undervalue.

Though security was light for a prison, there were virtually no escape attempts. If a prisoner were caught attempting escape, an additional seven years would automatically be tacked onto his sentence. Massey hoped to be out way before the end of his own sentence. He had a high-profile lawyer in Chicago working on his case. He'd become quite a student of the gubernatorial clemency process in Illinois.

Massey did not mention to anyone else how his professional life had collapsed when a former FBI agent named Brian McKay had been called in by the company's board to investigate the murder of an accountant in Massey's department. The Chicago Police had come up empty in their investigation. McKay and his young niece, Darcy, had uncovered much of the financial wrongdoing in the course of their probing into the killing. The murder victim happened to have been Darcy's boyfriend. The McKays had seen their lives turned inside out while bringing down Massey and other corrupt executives at Belcoe.

Massey vowed revenge on both McKays. This vow was internalized, not spoken to anyone else. But his vengefulness burned white-hot in his gut, threatening to consume him. He'd decided to take action against them even as he rotted in prison. All his known assets had been confiscated after he'd been convicted, and he'd gone into bankruptcy. To the outside world, he was nearly penniless, could barely afford the more desirable snacks at the prison commissary. But he had millions stashed in several hidden bank accounts in the

Cayman Islands. He loved the Caymans: no income tax, no capital gains tax, no property tax. Maybe he'd move there.

And, financial innovator that he was, Massey had invented a technique for transferring funds internationally without visibility to American authorities, including the IRS. He was poised to transfer funds in, money needed to carry out some plans for retribution as well as investments in lucrative, albeit illegal activities.

Massey had ambitious plans: through outside contacts, he was investing currently with the expectation of long-term profits. A murder had been sanctioned at a luxury resort under development in Montana, eliminating an owner and opening the door for Massey to take over. A kidnapping had been arranged, the aim being extorting a windfall from a wealthy Chicago businessman named Arthur Sands, whom Massey happened to envy and thus hate for his success. The third act would be an audacious theft of a unique artifact for Massey's personal use and eventual sale at a significant profit. The final project would be bringing about the gruesome deaths of Brian and Darcy McKay.

Massey had a smuggled cell phone, which he used to communicate surreptitiously with people on the outside whom he was using to carry out his dark plans. There was a pair of thuggish brothers in Montana and a guy in Chicago who might be helpful. So far, the plans were unfolding as he'd hoped.

Though the East Moline Correctional Center lacked the high walls topped with concertina wire found at higher security penal institutions, it was still a miserable place to spend time. A total contrast to his former rambling North Shore estate on ten lush acres. Massey now resided in a barracks, sleeping fitfully on a thin and lumpy mattress. The showers were open, with no privacy whatsoever. His fellow residents were a demoralizing collection of grifters, swindlers and con artists, many of them corporate refugees like himself.

His reverie was interrupted by a mocking voice outside his cell. "Hey bigshot, want to buy a Snickers bar? I'll sell you one for, let's see…how about a blowjob?"

Chapter 9

Brian helped himself to coffee in the cabin's kitchen. He'd just finished a phone conversation with Arthur Sands and was eager to get to work. He'd promised to check in later.

He Googled Nora Spivey in Clarkville and found her real estate business on Main Street. He decided to stop there unannounced and see what she might know about Barbara Hardy's situation. Chewing on an energy bar, he drove down to the town in the valley far below Sands's mountain retreat. He located Spivey's business, "Montana Untamed," downtown on Main Street, tucked in between an independent hardware store and an art gallery. The buildings appeared to date back to the early 20th century. He lingered at the gallery's front window. Inside were framed paintings and prints featuring whimsical scenes of animals and people in paradoxical situations. The largest was an acrylic painting of a gigantic trout fishing for tiny people swimming in a river. Another print showed a black bear rowing a boat toward a cabin on shore where a couple of cubs stood, waving. A third depiction featured a bear riding atop a Yellowstone cutthroat trout. The images were imaginative and skillfully fashioned. He made a mental note of the artist's name, Winslow Elwood, and moved on to the real estate office.

As Brian entered, a short plump woman with light brown hair cut in bangs approached with a smile. She said, "Help you find your own personal bunker?"

He was a bit taken aback but kept his expression blank. "Hi. I'm Brian McKay." He extended his right hand.

She shook hands and said, "Nora Spivey. Sorry for the 'bunker.' I can tell you're flummoxed. I specialize in properties allowing people to retreat to personal doomsday prepper ground. You still look puzzled."

He shrugged. "I think I get the gist."

"You'd be surprised," she continued. "Doctors, lawyers, politicians, high-tech gurus, contractors, everyone's runnin' scared."

"Of what?"

"Civil unrest in the big cities. The police have lost control. Plus, the threat of nuclear war, pandemics gone wild, revolt of the minorities, yada, yada, yada. Montana's a safe haven, they believe. Living off the grid in some cabin in the mountains has gotten to be mucho popular, at least as a part-time or emergency option. Who am I to say different?" She smiled again.

"Huh. Say, I'm a friend of Barbara Hardy's. I understand you know her, too. That right?"

The agent's expression was neutral. "Yeah, I do. Why?"

"She's disappeared. Her husband's hired me to find her."

Spivey whistled. "So that's why she didn't show up for lunch yesterday. Jesus Christ, that's a shocker. You a private eye?"

"Yes."

"But the gal's never mentioned any complaints. Ya never know, though…"

"Well, as you probably know, her ex-husband is pretty well off and—"

"You're thinking snatched for ransom, like in the movies?"

"Don't know at this point, but it's a possibility. Maybe she wasn't really so happy, just bolted on her own. What do you think?"

"Possible, but not likely. We did talk about this bunker mentality thing last time we got together. She said Art's ranch is a sort of bunker, though a big-ass luxurious one. I wouldn't mind hangin' at a place like that."

"Did Barbara seem interested in the kinds of properties you sell, at all?"

"Now you mention it, she did ask a few questions last time, like what do they cost, how comfortable would an off-grid cabin be, how safe would one be from break-ins, the usual stuff prospects ask, ya know."

"Huh. Why do you suppose she was asking?"

"She's a painter, you know, and maybe she wanted a studio. I dunno."

"What kind of painting?"

"She's been doing landscapes. Said she wanted to try a new direction, sort of like the stuff next door." She nodded to her left in the direction of the Winslow Elwood gallery. "Matter of fact, Barb's been in there a few times, chatting up ol' Win. I got the impression they hit it off. He's the kind of guy'd make a hell of a mentor for a beginning artist. And he likes the ladies. That's a fact."

"You know him very well?"

She hesitated for an extra beat. "Not really. I used to, kind of…"

Brian let that one lie. "You do much business in the Crazies?"

"Matter of fact, they're my specialty."

"Can you show me what's available up there?"

"Well, if you're trying to help Barb, I guess I could. Multiple listings are public information of course, but this'll save ya some time." Spivey sat down at her desk and motioned Brian to a visitor's chair. She opened her laptop and began moving fingers on the trackpad and clicking keys. "Right now, I've got twenty-three properties ranging from seventy-eight thousand to eight-point-seven million. I'd think a single woman wanting a getaway place might be in the market for a hmm…300k to 500k property. But then, if her ex was in on the deal, the range could go a helluva lot higher." She stared at the screen and operated the trackpad and keys. Brian had the impression she was comfortable now, in her element. And she seemed to be willing to help her friend. He calculated the commissions on twenty-three sales at six percent on an average sales price of say, eight hundred thousand. More than a million dollars.

Finally, Spivey stopped clicking and leaned back in her chair. The front of her blouse pulled tight across her ample breasts, outlining her nipples. Brian guessed this was not an unintended effect. She eyed him impassively. He waited her out.

Finally, she said, "Well sir, wanna see what I got?"

"Uh, sure."

She stood up and patted the seat of her desk chair. "Sit and have a look." He dropped into the chair, noticing the seat was still warm. He looked at the screen, while she stood at his shoulder. He scrolled through descriptions of mountain properties, one after another. He concentrated on the ones with a building, rather than just bare land. There were nine places with a cabin or house. All of them were on unpaved roads, far from the nearest town. Nothing jumped out at him. In any case, Barbara Hardy had not purchased any real property. He stood up.

"Could you print me the details of those nine properties with buildings on them?"

"Sure, no prob."

Brian stood and Norah sat down again. After the printer stopped, she gathered the pages and handed them to him.

"Thanks. By the way, where do you live?" he said.

She hesitated, then said, "In town."

"Are you, uh, on your own?"

"Yup, happily divorced."

"I'm being nosy, but is your ex-husband in the area?"

"Matter of fact, I sold him a good sized prepper spot off the Shields River Road coupla years ago. Sweet setting. Couple hundred acres, mostly trees. If you wanted to hide, say, a counterfeiting operation, that'd be the place."

"Prepper?"

"Yeah, ya know, he's one of those folks who think some big catastrophic disaster is right around the corner. So they make preparations, like stockpiling food, guns, ammo, whatever. They figure they're gonna need to hunker down for an indefinite time and they don't want to be caught with their pants down, so to speak."

"Oh. What does your ex do for a living?"

"He's a small-scale logger. Portable sawmill, custom cut boards, beams, poles, whatever people need for their projects. Plus he does firewood. Got one a them giant tree feller-grabber machines. Sells to contractors and carpenters. And a few of my own customers who need to fix up their places, build storage facilities above and below ground, etcetera."

Brian had no idea what a feller-grabber machine was. He obtained the ex-husband's name and address and set up a new contact in his phone: Seth Delmer.

Chapter 10

Darcy listened as Doctor Dave Bakeno spoke to his seminar students grouped around the conference room table. Each participant had a beverage, a phone and a laptop close at hand. Darcy's chai in a foam cup emitted a vapor of steam, nice and hot. The course in Dinosaur Paleontology was one of five she was taking in this, the first semester of her Master of Science in Earth Science at MSU. The subject matter was fascinating, but other thoughts kept intruding. Had Becky returned to the apartment they'd just rented to meet the landlord and make the damage deposit as they'd discussed? Becky was seated at the table with her, but had arrived late, so the two of them had not yet had a chance to talk. What about Will French, the teaching assistant she and Becky recently visited with in the student union cafe? He seemed interested in both her and Becky. Maybe just a friendly guy? He was kind of attractive in a bookish way. Since he was not in the room, and he'd said he was a TA for the course, she guessed his role was probably grading papers and tests.

Darcy glanced at her MacBook screen. An email had just come in from Brian. He said he was on the Barbara Hardy disappearance case he'd mentioned in an earlier text. Said he'd just left a meeting with a real estate woman in Clarkville.

Darcy remembered that Barbara Hardy was the ex-wife of Arthur Sands, the Chicago billionaire with a huge ranch in the Crazy Mountains. She flashed back to two summers ago when she'd been on the Bone Mountain *T. rex* dig in the Crazies with a group from the University of Illinois. Seemed so long ago…

"Darcy, what are your thoughts on the issue of fluvial erosion of shallow internments of Mesozoic sauropods in the Hell Creek area?" Doctor Bakeno's mellow baritone intruded on her reverie.

"I've been thinking about that, and I believe that the effects of fluvial erosion have been minimal," she said. "Mainly because of the semi-arid climate and the inelasticity of the sedimentary formations that dominate." Darcy had always been fast on her feet when it came to classroom discussion. And she really cared about this particular subject. Within seconds, she was once again fully engaged in the conversation.

After class, Darcy and Becky went to their apartment and changed clothes for an afternoon away from academia.

Chapter 11

Darcy and Becky arrived at the Timberline Creek trailhead in the Crazies a little after noon. They took their mountain bikes off the rack on the rear of Becky's pickup and pumped fifty pounds of air into the tires. They checked the chains, making sure they were cleaned and lubricated. The bikes were new, recently purchased at an outdoor store in Bozeman. The sun shone brightly ahead of them as they began peddling up the steep trail toward the jagged mountain skyline. They wore tee shirts and gym shorts, exposing their tanned and muscular legs to the sun. Darcy, the stronger of the two, led the way, standing over the pedals, working hard in a low gear. It felt good to push herself, like back when she played varsity softball at the University of Illinois.

A quarter mile up the trail, two men stood by the side of the path in an open meadow area. The shorter one, rangy and with a tanned bald head gleaming in the sun, mopped his brow. "Thought I heard voices down below," he said.

The other man, his elongated and narrow shape suggesting a tube of toothpaste, cocked an ear in that direction. The ear was the size of a dessert plate.

"Maybe I was mistaken. With ears like yours, ya should have hearing like an owl." He paused. "Or an elephant." He snickered.

The taller man, Doctor Phil Banham, smiled. He was used to Jimmy Brownleaf's gentle jibes. The two men hiked in the mountains together when the doctor managed time off from his busy schedule at the Clarkville health clinic. Jimmy's schedule was less encumbered. He hadn't worked fulltime in years. He managed to get by with disability benefits and occasional part-time jobs. They'd met when Jimmy became a patient of Banham's and the two had quickly formed an unlikely friendship based largely on their mutual love of exploring the wilderness surrounding the town. Both men were single, with Jimmy a widower and the doctor between girlfriends.

Darcy and Becky churned the pedals as they ascended the trail, navigating switchbacks and loose stones. Their breath shortened and sweat began to seep through their tee shirts. Concentrating on the terrain just ahead, the two young women did not have the luxury of admiring the spectacular alpine scenery. That would have to wait until they took a break, which would be any minute now. As they broke out of a hairpin turn, Darcy suddenly heard voices ahead. Then, in a small meadow where the trail leveled off, she spotted a couple of men standing still, silently regarding the two cyclists. She eased up on the pedals and coasted to a stop a few feet from them.

"You look mighty familiar," said the shorter man wearing a tattered tank top." He smiled at Darcy. She noticed a large gap between his yellowed front teeth. His bald head was brown as molasses from exposure to the sun. His lean arms were covered in tattoos from wrist to shoulder. The vibe was homeless but friendly.

Darcy looked at him blankly. She knew she'd seen him before, but she couldn't place him.

The tattooed man said, "Jimmy Brownleaf. And this here's Doc Banham. We were at that 606 Ranch last year when the fire broke out."

She realized that these men were the ones who'd reported the huge arson fire at the 606 Ranch a year ago when she and Brian had been there. Without that intercession, the whole place might have been destroyed, and the lives of her uncle and herself might have been in jeopardy as well. She and Brian had been introduced to the two by the local sheriff. She smiled in recognition. "Jimmy, good to see you again. You too, Doc."

"Hey," said Doctor Banham. His eyes were shy, only occasionally making contact. "It's been what, a year since you and Brian were out here?"

"Yes, but I live in Bozeman now, student at MSU. We, uh, just found an apartment, thank God."

"Great. What are you studying? Wait, let me guess. Paleontology?"

"Yep. MS in Earth Science, actually. Meet my roommate, Becky."

After introductions and Darcy's commenting on Brian's current case involving the disappearance of Barbara Hardy, Jimmy assumed a serious expression. "Something I should tell ya. Slightly unusual thing by a cabin over in the Elk Creek drainage." He gestured to the south with his chin. "I was up on a trail near there yesterday and, well it's hard to describe." He mopped sweat from his brow with a limp bandana.

"The cabin's up around 8,000 feet, off the trail on one of those checkerboard inholdings," Owned by a local logger who lives alone, kind of a hermit. Got some acreage, leases some more, logs the forest. Anyway, coulda sworn I heard a guy yelling, something about the graybar hotel, which means jail." He shrugged. "Probably no big deal."

Darcy was familiar with the area from two summers ago when she'd been held prisoner in a cabin that must have been somewhere in the area of the one Banham had spoken about. Or could it be the *same* cabin? In any case, it didn't seem relevant.

They chatted for a few minutes and parted ways, the men heading down toward the trailhead.

Becky said, "So tell me about those guys."

Darcy explained what she knew about the doctor and Jimmy from a year ago, and then they continued their ride up the rocky trail, steadily gaining elevation.

As they neared rocky Timberline Pass, the head and shoulders of a large mountain goat appeared from behind a pale gray triangular rock about a hundred feet above them. The shaggy white animal regarded them silently with shiny black eyes for a few seconds and then dissolved into the rocks like a diaphanous ghost. Darcy knew she'd seen the creature, her first sighting of the species, and yet the experience didn't seem real. She wondered if the incident described by Jimmy, the sound of a man's voice yelling about the graybar hotel, coming from near a remote cabin nearby, had been any more substantial.

Chapter 12

The phone on Arthur Sands's desk rang. Caller ID showed "unknown caller."

"Sands," he said.

After a long pause, a rustling sound, as if the caller had accidentally brushed against his phone. But nothing was said.

"Who is this?" Sands demanded.

Finally, the person on the other end spoke in a whiny voice that reminded Sands of the actor Bruce Dern. "Listen to me carefully, Mr. Sands. If you want to see your ex-wife again with all her natural parts attached, you'll do exactly what I tell you. Got that?"

Sands felt like his guts had been scooped out. "Who is this?"

"The two million you are gonna pay us will be in untraceable hundreds. I'll give you the details in a bit. No sheriffs. No washed-up FBI agents. No bullshit. You'll have until this time tomorrow to deliver the cash. If you don't follow my orders, Barbara Hardy is history."

"How do I know you have her?"

"Hang on, man." There was a delay of about thirty seconds, during which time Sands held onto the phone so hard, the case began to bend.

Finally, a very faint woman's voice, a choking whisper: "Art, it's me. This guy kidnapped me. I'm—"

The phone call was abruptly terminated. Sands held the phone to his ear for a long moment before setting it on his desk. It had definitely been Barbara's voice just before the abrupt hang-up. He assumed her captor had cut the call off to stop her from saying anything that might reveal information as to her whereabouts. He tried to determine whether he'd ever heard the male caller's voice before. The guy sounded like someone born and raised in the area, his way of speaking kind of like his ranch manager Ray Chaffee's. But it wasn't Ray or anyone he knew. Interesting that she'd said, "this guy," as if there were only one person involved. But the man on the phone had said, "You are going to pay *us*," suggesting more than one person.

He decided to sit there at his desk and wait for the details of the ransom demand. The guy had implied he'd call back. But what if he didn't? *Jesus.* As he thought further, he decided they'd call, all right. They wanted the cash. To him, two million was not much money. But of course, he didn't have it in hand. He'd need to talk with his main banker in Chicago and arrange for a transfer from liquid funds to a local bank, where he could pick it up. He hoped the kidnapper would realize you can't just pull that much cash out of the air. It would be a stretch to have it in hand by this time the next day, but he was pretty sure he could get it done. He started calling to arrange for the required bank transfer. He'd have to persuade the local bank not to contact the sheriff or any other authorities—his large account balances would probably do the trick.

After talking with his bankers and receiving assurance that he could pick up the cash before the close of business in Clarkville, he called Brian McKay. Sands considered himself a man of action. But he'd need help dealing with the asshole who'd grabbed Barbara. And McKay, with his FBI background and proven intelligence and grit, should be able to provide it. Once there was the detailed ransom demand, they'd need to move fast. He'd do whatever it took to get Barbara back, no question.

Chapter 13

As Brian stepped from Nora Spivey's office onto the sidewalk outside, his cell phone sounded off, the ringtone the beginning of Bob Seger's "Katmandu."

Sands sounded agitated, his voice an octave higher than normal. He spat out his words like bullets from a machine gun. "Brian, I need your help. Now. I just received a call from some goddamn bozo who's got Barbara. He put her on the phone for a second. She sounded awful. Guy says he wants two million dollars. That's not a problem but I'm gonna need to get you involved."

Brian knew that he had to be calm and professional, had to reassure Sands. "I'll do whatever I can," he said. "Stay right there with your phone. I'm in town, so it'll take a while. I'll get there as fast as I can."

"Make it faster," Sands said.

Just over an hour later, Brian skidded the pickup he'd borrowed from Sands to a stop at the huge log building housing his client's office. Sands stood on the porch near the entry door, nervously shifting his weight from one foot to the other. Opaque sunglasses hid his eyes. He gripped his phone and frowned as if he'd swallowed a bite of rotten fish. "C'mon in," he said.

Inside, they sat on opposite sides of Sands's desk.

Sands said, "I've arranged for the cash. I want you to help me deliver it."

"Look, Art, you should call the sheriff. He's competent and he should be able to deploy some deputies to conduct the transaction."

"Nope. I want you on it alone. No discussion."

Brian knew it would be a waste of time to argue with the excitable billionaire. "Tell me exactly what the caller said."

"He said that if I want her back all in one piece, I'd pay two million in untraceable hundreds. That I should not involve the sheriffs or any, quote, 'washed up FBI agents.' Then he put her on the phone and all she said was, 'Art it's me. This guy kidnapped me.' Then the call ended."

Brian thought, but didn't say, washed-up, eh? I should feel insulted. But how would these guys know about Brian being there and his background? He said, "No details as to where and when the ransom is to be dropped off?"

"No, not yet. I'm waiting for another call."

"All right, I'll stay with you."

Sands slumped into his chair, seemingly exhausted. Just then, his phone rang. "Unknown caller" again. He accepted the call and put the phone on speaker.

The same whiny male voice he'd heard on the earlier call said, "Okay, dude, here's the deal. Put the cash in a duffle bag. Two million plus one hundred thousand, all in hundreds. No marks, no dyes, none a that shit. Deliver it to the Altman lumber yard parking lot in Clarkville, behind the dumpster, at exactly midnight tonight. Just set the duffle on the ground and drive away. Do not tell anyone else about this. I will call you later to tell you where to pick up the woman. You fuck with me in any way, she's dead. Got it?"

"I've got it. If you harm her, I will—" *Click*. The call was ended.

"That son of a bitch. Something about that voice. Familiar, but not really," Sands said. Notice how he added on another hundred thousand. Plus, he said this time tomorrow in the first call, and now it's midnight tonight. Probably figures if I don't have the cash by then, I won't have it at all."

"*Can* you have the cash ready by then?"

Sands glanced at his watch. "Yes. I've got to follow up with the banks." He glanced at his Rolex. "Hang loose and then we'll work out a strategy. Okay?"

"Sure. But in the meantime, I've got some ideas. While you're working on the cash, I'd like to have a look inside the employee cabins. Do you have a list of all the staff and their assigned living quarters?"

"Yeah, lemme find it here." He opened a file cabinet and riffled through some hanging folders, extracting one with a tab labeled "Personnel." He extracted a sheet of paper and handed it to Brian.

There were ten people listed, along with their job titles and assigned cabin numbers, two through ten. Brian knew that cabin number one was Barbara Hardy's. Judging from the first names, a couple of them were females, the rest males. Brian recognized the names Ray Chaffee, the ranch manager whom he'd met a couple of years ago, and Josie Wilshire, the woman who'd picked him up at the airport and driven him to the ranch the evening before. The others were not familiar. Titles included veterinary technician, mechanic, office manager/bookkeeper and several ranch hands. Interesting that there was no longer a security manager listed. The previous one, Tom Norton, had died two years earlier during the violent events at the nearby Bone Mountain dinosaur dig.

"Could I have the keys to the cabins? I don't want to invade anybody's privacy. I'll knock first, of course. If they're around, I'll talk with them. But if they're not home, I'll take a quick look inside."

Sands hesitated. "I guess that'll be all right. Just go easy, okay? I have a hard enough time hiring people." He opened a desk drawer and rooted inside it. "Here they are," he said, holding up a keyring with a leather fob in the shape of a bison. There were about a dozen steel keys, all the same size. They looked like regular house keys for Schlage locksets. "The cabins are lined up just past Barbara's. The single folks are generally here full-time. Saves on commuting. Plus, with the off the charts housing market around here... anyway, the married folks, like Ray, have houses in town and only stay here when job demands make it necessary, like during calving in the spring."

Brian accepted the keys and stood. "I'll get on it. Call if you need me."

The employee cabins were spread out along the road west of the headquarters building, starting just past Barbara Hardy's place. They were all constructed of logs and had metal roofs. There was a number next to the door of each, but no other identifying information. He walked to the door of cabin number two. The structure was about twice the size of the guest unit he had slept in the night before. According to his list, it should belong to Ray Chaffee. He rapped on the door. No answer. He inserted the key in the lock and entered. The layout was similar to Barbara's place, but much messier.

After ensuring the place was empty and after a quick look around, he went on to the next cabin.

Same result with each of the smaller cabins three through nine: nobody around and nothing notable inside. And then he got to the last cabin, number ten. The employee list indicated the occupant as Gustav Delmer, a ranch hand. A dark Ram pickup with oversized all-terrain tires sat next to the structure. Brian approached the cabin and knocked on the door. He could hear someone moving around inside.

"Anyone home?" Brian shouted.

After a few seconds, a male voice came from behind the door. "Yeah, who's there?"

"Brian McKay. Mr. Sands asked me to stop by."

After another minute, the door opened and a man with a wild red beard filled the doorway. He blinked sleepy eyes and said, "What's this about?"

"Mr. Sands's ex has gone missing. Barbara Hardy. I'm looking into it, trying to find out if anyone here knows anything that might be helpful. Mind if I come in and ask a few questions?"

"Sure. I mean, I got nothin' to hide." He thumbed his dirty ball cap up an inch on his forehead and nodded. "Gus Delmer." He backed off to allow Brian room to enter the cabin.

Brian took in the sloppy interior. Basically, one room. Clothing on the floor. Beer cans and fast food detritus on every flat surface. "Any ideas as to where Ms. Hardy might have gone?"

"Shit, no. Never even met the woman. Those folks are a little outa my league." He nodded in the direction of the Sands house and Barbara's cabin. "I'm just a ranch hand. I do what Ray tells me to do. I'm off today, catchin' up on my sleep." He rubbed his eyes with scarred fists.

Brian recognized the man's last name, having heard it that morning from the real estate woman, Nora Spivey. "Any relation to a guy named Seth Delmer?"

"Yeah, he's my brother."

"I hear he has a place in the Crazies. That right?"

"Yep. Some acreage up there."

"What's he do?"

"He's got a woodlot. Mills lumber, sells firewood."

"Been up to his place lately?"

"Not for a month or so. I'm so busy here and he pretty much handles all that stuff himself."

"Okay. Thanks. I may need to talk to you again," Brian said.

As he was leaving Gus Delmer's cabin, his phone rang. Sands: "Brian, get back here. We've got to talk about tonight."

Chapter 14

Seth Delmer exited his cabin and boarded his pickup. He drove up a rutted two-track into a copse of Douglas firs. Along the way were hundreds of stumps from trees large and small, the result of logging he'd done over the past year. He'd leveraged his property to the hilt to buy the logging and sawmill equipment. And he couldn't have swung the purchase without the loan from the man now in prison in Illinois. The guy was a former bigshot executive in Chicago, but he'd been convicted of a bunch of white-collar crimes. He was serving a five-year sentence. The guy said he had a shitload of money. Seth guessed he'd hid it from the authorities in offshore accounts or something before they nabbed him. According to Seth's Internet research, they'd levied fines on the guy to make restitution to investors he'd cheated. He'd forfeited all his known assets to the government. But the loan money to Seth was real. A valuable backer for sure, but a real pain in the ass to deal with. They only communicated via texts and terse phone calls. The prisoner had bribed guards to provide him with a cell phone.

The first thing he'd done for the guy in prison was haunting him. He'd taken another man's life for a fifty thousand dollar fee. Disposed of the body in a place he hoped would never be found. But the images of the actual killing would not go away. He knew he'd live with them for the rest of his life. Nobody else knew about the hit, not even Gus. Nothing he could do about it now but move on, try to keep the dark memories at bay. Good thing he had plenty of work to keep him busy.

Payback on Seth's investment in the logging and sawmill operation was off to a promising start, as more and more people were moving to the mountains of southwestern Montana. They'd see a plastic image on TV of a lifestyle that never existed and never would. Rich guys from both coasts and overseas snatching up big ranches for ungodly sums. Just the other day, he'd read in the local newspaper, some media baron from New Zealand had bought a nearby ranch of more than 300,000 acres for hundreds of millions of dollars. Seth figured he might as well cash in as much as he could. Trouble was, he worked alone. The shortage of reliable workers these days meant he *had* to. His brother Gus preferred working on that Sands place, though he'd pitch in helping Seth on the weekends sometimes. Anyway, outside employees had a tendency to blab in the bars. Gus had a girlfriend who seemed to think Seth was a bad influence.

Seth tried to make an honest living. Contractors needed dimensional lumber and specialty materials like purposely distressed-looking beams for new construction. Rough pine planks were in great demand, and the home improvement stores were perpetually short of inventory. Another of his sources of income was selling cut and split firewood to people throughout the surrounding area.

Vacation homes were springing up everywhere, even here in the backwaters of the Crazy Mountains. There was already talk of a local ranch hosting helicopter tours of the

Crazies for well-heeled hunters and backcountry skiers. Though Seth was no environmentalist, he wondered whether any of this could be considered wise land use. More important, would he eventually be forced out and doomed to a life living in a town? He shivered at the prospect. He'd never felt comfortable having neighbors in close proximity. And he generally tried to keep away from people except when he could make a buck off them.

He missed Nora. They'd been married for eight years and then had just fallen out of love. Well, if he were honest about it, she'd gotten over him and he'd been unable to win her back. Funny thing, though: they remained friends. And in a way, business associates. Her real estate business was thriving, and she referred people needing wood products to Seth, while he told his customers about her real estate shop. Sort of a mutual backscratching. Sometimes, he wished it were more.

After driving about a half mile on the two-track, he got out of the truck. He stretched his arms over his head and looked around. He was proud of his operation. He'd managed to get a good deal a few months before on a 35-ton John Deere feller-buncher from a guy who'd decided to hang it up and move to Florida. The hulking machine stood ten feet tall and just as wide, sitting atop a pair of bulldozer-style metal tracks twelve feet long. The beast was capable of traveling on steep and muddy slopes and could harvest trees up to two feet in diameter. It could gather or "bunch" several good-sized trees simultaneously in its two pairs of mammoth grasping front arms. He walked over to the machine and patted it fondly on the nearest track. "Damn fine," he said. He turned to admire his other major piece of logging equipment, the venerable dual arch grapple skidder, a mammoth log-moving machine with chained tires nearly as big around as Seth's six-foot height.

His phone rang. A familiar number. His brother Gus. "What's up?"

"This dude Brian McKay just left my cabin. He's snoopin' around, tryin' to find the Hardy broad. I played dumb, didn't tell him shit."

"Good. Ready for tonight?"

"I guess so. Gotta catch a few zees first."

"Okay, as long as you meet me at eleven and bring the stuff we discussed."

"No problem, bro. I'll be there, cocked and locked, ready to rock."

Chapter 15

Brian entered Sands's office and found him pacing about like a barefoot man on an ice floe. Sands spoke first. "Okay, here's the deal. I'll pick up the cash at the bank in a little while. You'll go with me. You armed?"

"Yes. I brought my personal handgun on the plane."

"I didn't think you could do that, even on a private jet."

"According to the law, the weapon has to be unloaded, in a locked hard case and stowed with the luggage. TSA supposedly makes random checks on general aviation flights, but I've not experienced it. Anyway, I complied. Didn't want to take a chance on being delayed."

"Well, I hope you don't need to use it. Come on. Let's get moving. We can discuss logistics later."

They boarded a black Suburban and Sands drove toward Clarkville, keeping at five miles an hour over the speed limit once they hit the paved highway.

At first, Sands was silent, gripping the steering wheel tightly and sighing. Then he spoke in a tight voice, as if struggling to breathe. "Those sons of bitches better not… If they harm a hair on her, I'll… You be ready to shoot those bastards if they—"

"Art, worrying's not going to do us any good. Try to stay calm and—"

"How the fuck am I supposed to stay calm? You'd be out of your god-damned mind too, if it was *your* ex got caught up in this fucked-up situation!"

Brian kept silent, knowing nothing he could say would mollify the man. No more conversation until they arrived at the First Intermountain Bank in Clarkville. Sands careened into the small parking lot adjoining the bank and skidded into a space marked EMPOYEES ONLY.

"Wait here. I'll be back in a minute." He strode swiftly into the two-story Greek Revival building.

Brian reflected on this client he was reluctantly assisting. Sands was solipsistic and imperious. Overly sure of himself, unable to empathize with the rest of the world, Brian thought. He knew the man had grown up lower middle class in a tough Chicago neighborhood, put himself through college and failed in several entrepreneurial ventures. Finally, in his late thirties, he'd achieved monumental success in real estate and manufacturing businesses he'd started in the city and expanded into nationwide enterprises. Brian also knew Sands to be a workaholic, even at the ranch. He apparently had few close friends. Barbara Hardy remained a big part of his life. Her abduction seemed to be affecting his normally shrewd judgement.

To Brian, Barbara seemed amazingly dissimilar from her ex-husband. A thoughtful and capable woman of few words, but a little melancholic. Brian remembered when he'd first met her two years before at the Sands ranch. She'd struck him as having a good relationship with Sands as well as with her son, Scott Stevens. But she'd been obviously a bit of a drinker. He wondered why she and Sands had divorced, and what sort of assets she'd ended up with in the aftermath. Anyway,

Brian knew he'd receive ample pay from this endeavor—Sands was no piker.

Suddenly, the bank's door burst open and disgorged two men, Sands and a uniformed bank guard. The guard carried a bulging black duffle bag sporting the Nike logo. Sands stayed glued to his elbow. As he walked toward the Suburban, the guard scanned the parking lot as if prepared for sniper fire. He made it patently obvious that he was toting a load of something valuable. Cringing inwardly, Brian got out of the Suburban and opened the rear passenger side door. The guard approached and set the duffle on the floor.

As Sands got to the driver's side door, the guard opened it for him and offered a salute. Ignoring him, Sands jumped in, slammed the door shut, keyed the big engine to life. He K-turned the SUV around and sped out to the street.

"Okay," Sands said. "Here's the plan."

Chapter 16

On the rapid drive back to the ranch, Sands told Brian he wanted him to accompany him to the lumber yard in town well before the appointed hour. They'd arrive around eleven and stay hidden in the dark away from the dumpster. They'd scout the area on foot, watching for all ways in and out of the parking lot. When the kidnapper arrived, Sands would drop the cash behind the dumpster as had been specified. Brian, hiding in the shadows, would cover him with his pistol. If Barbara was not immediately turned over to them, Sands, would demand they do so and would back the demand up with a gun. Brian would be ready to shoot if necessary.

Brian took all this in, then shook his head. "No."

"No? What the hell do you mean, no? I just laid out a perfectly reasonable plan."

"Look, Art. We're not wild west lawmen in some movie. But I've had a little experience with this sort of thing in my career with the FBI. This guy, or possibly more than one guy, want the money. Nothing else matters. They get the dough, they'll leave with it. They'll release Barbara somewhere else. They've probably blindfolded her and have nothing to gain by not releasing her. If she's not with them and we kill them, how will we find her?"

"Well, that's a point. But still, I hate to let the bastards get away."

"Ninety-seven percent of kidnaps for ransom end with the victim returned safely. But if people go with their gut instinct, their anger, bad things can happen. Their loved ones are put at extra risk."

"Good speech. Sounds like something right out of the FBI manual. But this is my flesh and blood. Chances are, we're dealing with some lowlife scum with no excess supply of brains."

"Could be. Anyway, tonight may not be as simple as what was said on the phone. Quite often, kidnappers change the terms at the last minute, demanding more money, or telling the family member to move on to another location for further instructions," Brian said.

"Yeah, I know. We're gonna have to be flexible, alert, ready for anything." He sighed. "I'm so damned jumpy now, I can't wait until we move on this thing."

Brian's stomach growled noisily. "Me, too. Funny, but I suddenly realized I haven't had anything to eat since breakfast." He glanced at his watch. Just after 4:00 P.M.

"I'll call the kitchen, have them fix you something. You're right, an army travels on its stomach. But me, I'm too damned nervous to eat. I'd feel better if you did, though."

He directed Brian to the ranch's well-stocked dining hall. There, after a short wait, he was served a ham sandwich and fries by the cook. After he'd eaten and was checking his phone for messages, it suddenly rang. Sands.

"Brian, I forgot to tell you. They demanded another hundred k in that last phone call. When's this shit gonna stop?"

"Do you have it?"

"I do. I had the bank provide a little extra and I've got cash reserves in a safe to make up the difference. But this had better damn well be the last zigzag in the road. Jesus. Hang loose I'll see you in a bit."

At 9:45 P.M., Brian met with Sands again in his office. Sands told Brian he had the two million one already, along with a loaded Glock 19 pistol. Brian had his Sig, hoping he wouldn't need it and that Sands would not be thinking he needed his own weapon.

They climbed into the Suburban, Sands at the wheel, and headed into the black night.

Chapter 17

They arrived at the Altman lumber yard on the outskirts of Clarkville just after eleven P.M. The business was situated up a narrow driveway, not far from the highway. Sands rolled the Suburban up the drive and braked to a stop in the back of the lot, about a hundred feet from the large green dumpster. A pair of floodlights on tall poles illuminated the lot. A door to the office part of the building was nearby. Dim lights shown in the office windows. There was no sign of anyone around the facility. Complete silence except for the murmuring wind and the occasional vehicle passing by on the highway.

"Stay put," Brian said. "Let's wait until 11:30. Then, we'll look around. If it seems okay, you can drop off the cash."

Sands just grunted by way of reply.

After waiting in the vehicle, followed by a short tour of the surroundings, Sands grabbed the duffle bag and toted it over to the dumpster. The bag was firm and full and weighed about forty-five pounds. He walked around to the rear of the container. A few scraps of trash littered the ground next to the steel bin. A dense wood of junipers and cottonwoods flanked the property, impenetrable until Sands switched on his powerful flashlight and pointed it into the trees. A faint path about five feet wide appeared, perhaps carved out by the passage of all-terrain vehicles over the years on the rolling ground. He waited for about five minutes, standing motionless in the shadows next to the dumpster. The sound of a motor came very faintly from the direction of the trees. A growling four-stroke engine, drawing closer, ever so gradually. In another couple of minutes, the noise came very near, a powerful all-terrain vehicle almost upon him. He moved to the adjoining side of the dumpster, next to Brian, keeping to the shadows.

A dark-colored four-wheel utility vehicle with a small cargo bed suddenly broke out of the trees and emerged into the dim light. Two men occupied the bench seat. The bed behind them appeared to be empty. A man of average size jumped down from the passenger seat and walked in a simian crouch to the dumpster. He appeared to be wearing a dark mask. Spotting the duffle bag, he reached down to grasp the handle.

Leaning out from the corner of the Dumpster, Sands yelled, "Okay, there's the money. Where's Barbara?"

The man with the duffle scrambled to the waiting ATV, hefted the bag into the back and jumped aboard. As the driver turned the short vehicle around, Sands fired his gun in their direction. He missed badly, the bullet shearing limbs off the nearby trees. The vehicle's engine roared as it accelerated into the trees. The engine noise receded rapidly and died away.

"Stop shooting!" Brian yelled. I'm gonna take a look." He ran a few yards into the trees and stopped. Chasing after the vehicle on foot and in the dark would be futile. The duffle bag containing two point one million dollars was long gone. And they had no idea where Barbara Hardy might be. He hoped to God they hadn't pushed the kidnappers into killing her. He felt defeated. He couldn't imagine how hopeless Sands must feel.

As the two men returned to the Suburban and opened the doors, the ululation of a siren approached from the highway. A dark Geyser County sheriff's SUV careened to a stop behind the Suburban, blocking it from exiting.

"Fuck!" Sands screamed in frustration. He tossed his handgun on the floor behind the driver's seat.

Brian stepped away from the vehicle, hands held high above his head as Sheriff Jim Reid and a tall, broad-shouldered deputy approached on foot. Sands reluctantly followed suit. The sheriff held a large black flashlight the size of a small baseball bat, illuminating Brian and Sands like a honkytonk on a Saturday night. The deputy pointed a service revolver at them. He looked familiar, but Brian couldn't remember his name.

Reid blinked. He lowered the flashlight so it pointed at the ground. "Brian McKay. Haven't seen you in what, a year? Can't say I'm happy to see ya now. What's going on?"

"Art's ex was kidnapped. We were delivering ransom money over there." Brian nodded toward the dumpster behind him. "They grabbed the cash and took off on a four-wheeler through the trees."

Reid's expression clouded. The previous summer, Reid had been involved with the Montana part of the investigation dubbed "Dirty Money" by the media. A jet piloted by a criminal crashed in the nearby Absaroka mountains. Brian wondered whether Reid might think of him as the madman from Chicago. Best case, he'd consider Brian a guy who'd helped get rid of a big-time lawbreaker who'd caused plenty of harm in Geyser County. Brian hoped for Reid's forbearance, but realized he and Sands were likely in serious disfavor for freelancing on the sheriff's turf.

"Jesus Christ," Reid said. "you could've called me." He shook his head. "The missing woman is Barbara Hardy, right?"

Sands spoke up. "Damn right. I'm just doing whatever's necessary to get her back. Not that we've done much so far except maybe lose a couple million bucks." He waved that off. "But I don't care about that. Let's get these guys."

"What was the small arms shot we heard just now?" the deputy asked.

Sands looked sheepish. "Guess I got impatient. Didn't hit anything, though."

Reid: "Jim, let's have a look. You guys wait right here."

The two lawmen walked around the dumpster, prowled for a few minutes, then returned.

"Nothing interesting. Ground's too dry for useful footprints.," Reid said. "But a four-wheeler recently moved through the trees, judging from the tracks."

"Where does that path go?" Brian said.

"Eventually comes out on 89, about a mile from here," Reid replied. We'll take a look, but those guys are probably long gone. C'mon, follow me and we'll stop there before heading to the department. I'm gonna need statements from you guys." Without further comment, Reid and his deputy got in their truck and moved swiftly back to the road. Sands and Brian followed as directed.

They stopped at a small turnout along highway 89.

"Wait here," Reid said. He left Brian, Sands and the deputy, whose name tag read "Vaught," standing at the edge of the trees. Reid disappeared into the trees, his flashlight bobbing up and down as he walked the narrow track. A few minutes later, he returned.

"Tire tracks in there, look like a pretty common type, eleven inches wide, rear tire, same as the ones back at the lumberyard. Probably from the guys you saw," Reid said. "That and a Hershey bar wrapper." He put the candy wrapper in a plastic bag and pocketed it. "I'll send someone out to investigate the tracks in the daylight. Let's go to my office. Like I said, I'll need a statement. And I've gotta talk with the state police about this kidnapping situation."

Without comment, Brian strode into the woods. He was careful to avoid the fresh knobby tire marks embedded in the moist soil. He pulled out his phone and took a couple of flash-assisted pictures of the tracks. Brian thought, but didn't say, that he would call Bill Thorsten, his FBI friend in Bozeman. He knew that the bureau did not normally get involved with abduction of adults within a state.—the normal role was to "consult" with local authorities. He figured Reid would resent the FBI getting involved at all.

As they drove into downtown Clarkville, following the sheriff's truck on the empty road, Brian wondered what had prompted Reid to suddenly show up at the lumber yard. Had an alarm been triggered? Had Reid received a call from somebody about suspicious activity? Or could it have been simply a patrol that happened to end up there at the same time as the ransom drop-off?

Chapter 18

(Day 4)

Sands parked in the lot outside the City-County complex. The dashboard clock showed 1:12 A.M. as the two men headed into the building. The deputy who'd been at the lumber yard, Vaught, appeared in the lobby as they approached the building, let them in and locked the thick glass door behind them.

"C'mon this way," Vaught said.

The three men filed into Sheriff Reid's office and pulled up chairs across his desk.

"Guys, this'll be a verbal statement," Reid said. "I'll record it and have somebody type it up in the morning. Later this morning, that is." He rubbed his eyes. "Mr. Sands, why don't you start from the beginning. When and how did you learn of the kidnapping? What communications with the kidnappers? What have you done and said?"

Sands fidgeted. "Look, Sheriff. Time's wasting while we sit here. Barbara's been missing now for more than 48 hours. We've gotta get moving."

"Hold on. First things first. You've got your phone on and charged, I take it," Reid replied.

"Yes, but—"

"Then you'll be waiting to hear from the kidnappers. They'll want to let Ms. Hardy go so they no longer have to hide her. Anyway, do you have any clue as to her whereabouts at this point in time?"

Sands shrugged. "No. Maybe we oughta contact the FBI."

Reid grimaced. "This is not their case. I *will* contact the state crime investigators. They have lots of resources. In the meantime, Mr. Sands, I'm gonna need your statement."

Sands related how he learned his ex was missing, his calling Brian in Chicago, Brian rushing to the ranch, the phone calls from a man who said he had Barbara, her frantic voice on the phone and the delivery of the ransom money at the lumber yard. He described the ATV and the man who ran to pick up the duffle bag of ransom money, though it was too dark to see much detail. "You know the rest," he concluded. Brian followed with his own statement, not adding much beyond what Sands had said.

Reid switched off the tape recorder and yawned. "My department's got some good people. But, y'know, Geyser county covers more than 2,800 square miles. That's damn near the size of Delaware. We've only got eight deputies and one detective. I'll get them up to speed and on the case ASAP. You guys let me know if you hear anything more."

"I'm curious," Brian said. "How did you know we were at the lumber yard?"

"Motion detector set off a silent alarm. They've had some thefts of wood siding materials. Specialty stuff, sells for a lot these days. The owner's been raising hell." He sighed. "Now, I need to call the state DCI, so if you'll excuse me…"

"Wait a second," Brian said. "What type of tires made those tracks?"

Reid hesitated. "Well, they looked like Duro, based on the tread pattern. Standard on the Polaris Ranger and some others in that class. Nominally nine inches wide in front and eleven in back, but actual width on the ground is less. Very common size around here. We've got casts and will look for distinguishing characteristics."

"Thanks. We'll get out of your hair."

In the parking lot, Sands said, "Y'know, I'm pretty exhausted, so, if you don't mind driving..." The billionaire looked dejected, as if he held scant hope for ever seeing Barbara again. Brian couldn't blame him—her recovery would be less probable now with a couple of days gone. And with the ransom in hand, the kidnappers' main priority would be eliminating any incriminating evidence.

Brian got behind the wheel with Sands riding shotgun. As they rolled through Clarkville, he called Bill Thorsten in Bozeman. He got his voice mail and left a message. Brian gunned the big Suburban onto the deserted two-lane highway and up the valley west of the Crazy Mountains. He gazed groggily out the windshield as miles of rangeland flew by. Occasionally, a whitetail deer appeared in the headlights as it made its way across the highway. Fortunately, he avoided hitting any of the animals. They arrived at the Sands ranch around 3:00 A.M.

Chapter 19

At ranch headquarters, the two men parted ways without further discussion. Brian went to his cabin, shucked off his clothes and got under the covers. He immediately dropped into a dreamless sleep.

Seemingly minutes later, his phone chimed, indicating a text. He awoke abruptly, cursing himself for not silencing the phone before turning in. The message was from his sometimes girlfriend in Chicago, Michelle Emerson. It read: *Brian, haven't heard from U, I'm checking in to see if UR still alive. M.*

The phone showed 5:47 A.M. He groaned. Michelle was an early bird, and it was an hour later in Chicago. They'd been drifting apart and hardly ever saw each other anymore. Their work schedules made it hard to find time and, to be honest, Brian was losing interest. He guessed Michelle felt the same way. He'd get back to her later. He rubbed the sleep from his eyes and got out of bed to use the bathroom. Then he returned to the cozy bed and tried to get back to sleep. No dice. A little before eight, he got up for good and trudged into the shower. As he rinsed off, his phone rang. Bill Thorsten, returning Brian's earlier call.

"You sounded keyed up in that message this morning, buddy." Thorsten said.

"I was, and here's why: We delivered the ransom in Clarkville last night and the two guys who showed up for it took off on an ATV. No sign of Barbara."

"Whoa."

"Yes. She's been gone two days, now."

"Shit. Law enforcement involved?"

"Sheriff's department. Reid says he's gonna call in the Montana DCI. Thought I'd give you a heads-up as well. I'm at the Sands place."

"Glad you called. Of course, I won't be officially involved unless SLC gives me the order. But maybe I can be helpful off the record. Anyway, the state guys are good. What's your plan?"

"I'll be sticking here for the time being. There are a couple of things I want to check out around this place. I've got a hunch that this might be an insider. Remember that attempted kidnapping at the Lassiter ranch near Choteau?"

"Sure. Big national story, with such a hotshot celebrity involved."

Danny Lassiter was then the host of a nationally televised late-night talk show. He divided his time between New York City and a 3,000-acre ranch in western Montana. He was there on vacation with his wife and two-year-old son three years earlier when an attempt was made by a ranch hand at kidnapping the boy. The hand tried to enlist the help of the child's live-in nanny. The idea was, the nanny would take care of the kid at a hidden location while they awaited the multi-million-dollar ransom payment. They'd split the loot. Fortunately, the scheme fell through when the nanny went to the sheriff instead. The would-be perp was currently serving a ten-year term in the Montana State Prison at Deer Lodge.

"This Sands situation would lend itself to that kind of scheme," Brian said. "There's a bunch of long-time employees, some carried over from the previous owner and some hired by Sands. No doubt, they all know the guy is worth a mint. There was no bodyguard protection for Barbara, which strikes me as kinda loosey-goosey. Plenty of places near the ranch to hide her while they wait for the ransom. No nanny necessary."

"You might be on track with that thought. Let me know if you want to bounce any ideas off me."

"Deal."

Chapter 20

Brian wanted to take another look at the employee cabins. He went by each one without stopping or knocking on any doors. He was curious about vehicles. There were a couple of Subaru wagons, some pickups and SUVs, but no all-terrain vehicles like the one used to pick up the ransom money. He worked his way to the end of the row of buildings and stopped at number ten, the one assigned to Gus Delmer. He knocked, waited and knocked again. No answer. He went around the cabin and looked in the side and back windows. No sign of the occupant. Same messy interior as his previous visit. Tire tracks alongside looked like they fit the pickup Brian had seen there last time. He saw no one outside any of the cabins. He guessed everyone was away at work.

He walked back to the big building housing Arthur Sands's office and went straight in. Sands was on the phone and motioned for Brian to have a seat. The billionaire's eyes were dark and glazed like the flat black eyes of a child's doll.

"Okay, got it. But keep me posted, dammit. Anything at all. Talk to you later." He set the phone on his desk and slumped back in his chair.

"Montana DCI. They've got nothing, so far. They've talked to Reid and the ranch staff. They've been out looking for evidence and possible witnesses all around the lumber yard. Said they've talked with a couple possibles. But so far, no solid leads. That's it, so far."

"What do you know about ownership of ATVs by your ranch staff?"

"Not much. If they've got 'em, they don't bring 'em to work. We have our own fleet of ranch four-wheelers. I think I see where you're going with that. Good thought. See Ray. He'll fill you in. Probably in the east barn now."

"Thanks." Brian got up and headed outside.

He found Ray Chaffee in the large red wooden outbuilding about fifty yards from headquarters, a huge barn with a white-trimmed cupola centered on the gray metal roof. The hinged doors on the end of the building were wide open. Inside, Chaffee was loading bags of animal nutrients into the bed of a utility vehicle. A row of five similar vehicles had been backed in parallel to each other, along the wall to the left. He noticed three were dark green Polaris models and two orange Kubotas. Each of them had a bench seat and a small cargo bed in back. Same configuration as the small vehicle Brian and Sands had seen racing away with the ransom money.

Hey, Brian, heard ya were here," Chaffee said. "Good to see ya." He offered a faint smile and an extended hand.

"Yeah, same here, Ray," Brian said as he shook hands with the ranch manager. "You probably know I'm trying to find Barbara Hardy."

Chafee pushed his hat brim up an inch on his wide forehead with a thumb. "Yeah. Hell of a thing. I'd help for sure, if I knew how."

"Maybe you can. There are two guys involved, that we know of. Mr. Sands and I delivered ransom money to the Altman lumber yard last night, back by the dumpsters next to the woods there. These guys showed up on an ATV, snatched the bag of cash and roared off into the trees. Long gone by the time we and the sheriff got on their trail. Dark-colored machine, two men seated side by side, small cargo bed in the back, which is how they carried off the duffel bag of cash. Here's a picture of the vehicle's tire tracks."

Brian pulled up a photo he'd taken the night before and handed his phone to Chaffee.

"Well, they look familiar. Rear tire print. Kinda like these tires here."

Brian took a knee and examined the rear tire of the machine in front of him. The tread seemed like a match for his picture, very knobby and off-road oriented. The raised letters on the sidewall of the tire read, 'Duro 26 x 11-12.'

"How common is this tire?" he asked.

"It's as common as any in the area. Good, tough, not terribly expensive. Matter of fact, we use 'em on our fleet here when tires need replacing. Of course, there's a bunch of other brands out there, like Carlisle and Maxxis."

"I see some scrape marks on the front fender of this machine. What do you suppose that's from?"

"Hmm. Happens pretty often. Rubbing against brush and whatnot. All these machines 've got 'em. We don't worry too much about cosmetics, just working capability."

"Any chance an employee might've borrowed one of these after hours?"

"Nah. We've got two levels of security. First, this building's padlocked at night. And second, the main gate's locked with a six-digit code."

Brian noticed a key in the ignition of the machine next to him. "Are the keys usually left in the machines?"

"Sure, saves time."

"Who has a key to this building, besides you?"

Chaffee frowned. "Well, there's Josie and, let's see, Gus has one, 'cuz he takes care of equipment maintenance and such."

Brian considered this: Josie, the woman who'd picked up Brian at the airport, and Gus Delmer, whose brother was a 'prepper' with a woodlot.

"They both at work today?"

"Yep."

"I know there are other gates besides the main entrance." Brian said. Are they always locked?"

Chaffee hesitated. "Well, not always. See, we've gotta move animals and supplies around, and we try to avoid the main gate, especially when Mr. Sands is here."

"So an employee with access to this building could take one of these four-wheelers out at night and, as long as they got it back in before daylight, nobody'd be the wiser, correct?"

"I guess so, but that's a stretch."

"By the way, have any employees missed work in the last few days?"

"Nope. They've all been here." Chaffee's face reddened. "Nothing unusual with any of 'em. And I can tell ya for a fact: none of them's involved in Ms. Hardy's going missing. We don't hire criminals here."

This was the first time Brian had seen Chaffee anything but cordial. But the defensiveness he'd just displayed seemed perfectly warranted. Brian guessed that, if he were in Chafee's shoes, he'd resent the implications of the questions he'd asked.

"Well, I've gotta get these supplements out to pasture," Chaffee said. He climbed aboard the Ranger and drove outside, where he waited for Brian to follow him out of the building.

Discouraged, Brian pocketed his phone and left the barn. He heard the sound of Chaffee's motor receding, sounding much like the machine at the lumber yard.

Chapter 21

(Day 5)

The Delmer brothers unloaded the all-terrain vehicle out of the truck bed and rolled it down the steel ramps to the ground. They'd arrived back at Seth's cabin in the early hours and were dead tired. Pitch blackness surrounded them, the only illumination a soft glow from a lamp inside the cabin.

"I'm so fuckin' tired. Gotta catch some Zs," Gus said.

"All right." Seth sighed. "You can use the extra bed. I'm beat, too. But tomorrow, we've got a few things to take care of. I don't wanna be looking over my shoulder from now on."

Mid-morning, half rested and still worried, Gus Delmer phoned the Sands ranch and told his girlfriend Josie Wilshire, he was sick with the flu and would not be in for work that day. She said she'd tell Ray. He and Josie had been high school classmates and friends. They had dated for a short while and then drifted apart. Recently, after going to work for Sands, they'd reunited as a couple.

Gus grabbed a jack and tire iron and got to work changing the tires on the Polaris Ranger. Seth had purchased a set of four used Carlisle tires from a guy in Big Timber, forty miles away, for cash, no paperwork. The plan was to take the Duro tires that had been on the vehicle when they picked up the ransom money to a tire recycling bin, where they'd disappear in the mix, also with no paperwork generated. Seth had insisted all the extra driving was worth it. They couldn't afford to leave traces of their involvement in the kidnapping. Gus planned to head to the recycler after a lunch break.

An employee at the Sands place had mentioned to Gus the day before that Brian McKay, the guy from Chicago, had been checking the ranch fleet of Rangers and Kubotas in the equipment barn yesterday. He said it looked like McKay was examining the machines and spent quite a bit of time in there with Ray Chaffee. Lotta good that would do. Fuck 'em anyway.

Despite the successful kidnapping and payment of the ransom, they were in a fix. The duffle bag full of money sat on the floor of Seth's cabin. They'd counted the money twice and got the same total both times: two million one hundred thousand dollars in hundreds, just as Seth had demanded in his phone call to Arthur Sands. After a careful search, no dye packs or hidden transmitters had surfaced. Seth glanced out the window. The sun was dropping below the serrated Bridger mountains across the Shields valley to the west.

They sat across from each other at the small kitchen table. Gus seemed distraught, like he might break down or just take off running. Seth had seen the signs before. His younger brother was a little soft when the rubber hit the road. He'd damned well better get focused.

"I don't know. They figure it out, we spend the rest of our lives in Deer Lodge," Gus said.

"C'mon, man. We've gotta stick with the plan," Seth said. We get rid of the woman tonight. Tomorrow on, we both go about our business, just like always. We don't act the least bit suspicious. It all blows over, and we're golden."

Seth rubbed his eyes. His face was flushed. He'd had a few swigs from his always-present bottle, but, despite the bravado in his words, the whiskey had done nothing to calm his tattered nerves. "We've got enough problems as it is now. We can't start freelancing."

"There's a shitload of investigators nosing around," Gus said. The sheriff we can handle. But this McKay dickhead is babysitting Sands. And now a coupla guys from the state police are on the case, which concerns me."

"Yeah, that's all true. My ex tells me McKay was in town askin' her questions. So, we just hafta be cool," Seth said.

"Just a matter of time 'til they show up here."

"Which is why we get rid of her ASAP." Seth nodded his head toward the room in back. They'd left their hostage trussed up, blindfolded and with cotton balls taped in her ears. The foam ear plugs kept falling out, so they'd improved the hearing blockage. They were pretty sure she hadn't heard their voices clearly enough to recognize them later.

They sat arguing and watching satellite TV for the next several hours. One of the arguments pertained to divvying up the money. Should they deposit Massey's share in the bank account in Bozeman as he'd specified? Or should they stiff him and risk the consequences? The man was a criminal and he no doubt had connections. The balance in the bank account in Bozeman could easily be checked online. Seth was for carrying out their end as agreed with the jailed executive. Gus's opinion was that they were the ones risking their necks on this kidnapping caper, so why should the guy sitting on his flabby ass in prison profit from *their* work? Sure, the man had given them the idea and detailed instructions on how to carry it out. But hell, they could have come up with the whole thing themselves.

The deciding factor was that Seth owed Massey a half million dollars for the secured equipment loans. He insisted they play ball with the white-collar criminal, at least for now. Maybe he'd pay off the loan with the ransom money. Gus reluctantly agreed.

Gus kept his half million share along with Josie's one hundred thousand cut in a small blue backpack. Seth took his five hundred thousand outside, drove to the place he thought of as a secret graveyard, and buried it in a metal box next to a tree.

Just after midnight, Seth pushed his Ram crew cab diesel-powered pickup north on highway 89. He kept the truck at a steady 68 miles per hour, a hair under the speed limit. Gus rode shotgun, silent, a frown creasing his bearded face.

Barbara Hardy lay on the floor in the back of the cab, behind the front seats. With the rear seat folded up, there was a flat floor space about four feet wide and three feet front to back. The blindfold over her eyes and cloth gag covering her mouth were uncomfortable as could be. The stuff clogging her ears made it hard to distinguish anything the two men said. Her wrists and ankles were bound with rope. Everything was tight and irritating. The skin in the bound areas had been rubbed raw. But her nose was free, and she could breathe almost like normal now. She began doing her deep breathing exercises, which helped take her mind off her predicament. That evening, they'd taken the gag out of her mouth and put a bag containing a fast food burger and fries in the room she'd inhabited for the last two days. That and a couple of energy bars represented her total diet while held captive. They'd re-gagged her before loading her into the vehicle. Anyway, she wasn't hungry, and she'd had a bathroom visit before they'd tossed her in the back of the truck cab.

By then, the voices of the two men who'd held her hostage for two days were somewhat familiar to her, even with the crumby ear plugs. One had a whiny voice and he occasionally slurred his words, probably as a result of drinking the whiskey she could smell on him. The other one had a smoother, younger-sounding voice. She'd heard them arguing in the front room of the cabin before the truck ride but couldn't make out the words, just the tone of agitation. She'd not seen either's face, which she took as a good sign. Maybe she'd survive this ordeal after all.

She had heard fragments of a recent conversation between the two, when they were close by. She gathered that Art had paid them a ransom of more than two million dollars. She felt a little undervalued; a couple million wouldn't be much money to Art. She managed a smile at what his reaction would be if she confronted him about her monetary value. She hadn't slept much the last two nights and, amid the relentless drone of the engine and the regular reverberation of tires over expansion strips on the road, she eventually dozed off.

Just before three in the morning, the black pickup eased into the outskirts of the city of Great Falls. With 60,000 residents, the town was Montana's third largest in population, behind Billings and Missoula. The downtown streets were deserted, and traffic was almost nonexistent at that hour. Seth pulled into the parking lot of a chain crafts and sewing store. There were no other vehicles. He got out and went to the rear door on his side of the truck. He opened the door wide. The dome lights remained off, so darkness enveloped the vehicle.

"Okay, sister, this is your stop," he said. He grabbed the rope between Barbara Hardy's wrists and pulled. Once her feet had cleared the doorway, he let go and she crashed to the pavement. He quickly got behind the wheel and accelerated out of the lot, headed back toward the highway.

Barbara had awakened when the truck stopped. Her head was clear, and she'd been prepared for a struggle when the door next to her head had been yanked open. Then, suddenly, she'd been deposited on the rough paved surface, still trussed like a luau pig and unable to see or cry out. Her head had hit the ground hard, resulting in a dull pain in the back of her neck. Probably whiplash, similar to an injury she'd sustained in Chicago a few years ago, when a careless driver rolled his car into hers at low speed while she was stopped at a toll booth, feeding coins into the machine.

She rolled onto her side and attempted to loosen her bonds without success. By the lack of ambient light or sounds, she figured it was dark and empty where she lay. Must be nighttime. The only noise she could discern through her clogged ears was the faint sound of an occasional vehicle on a road, apparently a distance away. She was still wearing the clothes she'd had on when she'd been abducted, jeans, long-sleeve tee shirt and running shoes. She could smell the sour odor of her body. She felt dirty and helpless. The temperature seemed to be around 55 degrees and there was a slight wind. She was a little cold, but it wasn't bad. She knew her situation could have been a lot worse.

She felt the liquid from tears soaking the blindfold over her eyes. After being stoic for these two agonizing days and nights, the floodgates had burst. She thought of her son, Scott. He'd be tormented by worry, probably unable to function in his role teaching college students paleontology at the University of Illinois in Chicago. As she often did, she wondered whether Scott would ever settle down and get married. Would she ever have the immense joy she'd seen in so many women of cherishing grandchildren.

She wondered whether she was in a spot where someone would find her. And if so, would it be a Good Samaritan or some rotten specimen like the two who'd held her captive. Nothing was certain. But she held out hope; she had no other choice. She settled in to wait.

Chapter 22

"Holy guacamole!" A woman's voice, close. Barbara Hardy tried to speak through the gag still muffling her mouth, but it came out as a groan.

Half an hour later, she was in the emergency room at the Great Falls Hospital on 15th Avenue South. She'd been treated for dehydration and assorted bruises and lacerations on her face, wrists, hands and ankles. For her sore neck, they'd given her painkillers. They'd told her she'd recover fully in time, but had to stay with them, hooked to an IV, for the rest of the day and likely overnight. She demanded access to a phone. A friendly nurse lent her his. She called Art Sands to let him know that she was alright and where she was. He'd been uncharacteristically emotional, nearly breaking down after an agitated expression of relief. He'd said he'd be there soon. In fact, he arrived two hours later, having been driven by Josie Wilshire, at warp speed up U.S. 89.

Scott Noble Stevens received the call from his mom in his office at the University of Illinois. Overcome with relief at the news of her returning to safety, the noted professor of paleontology felt like a young boy again as he and Barbara Hardy conversed. They were both crying before the conversation ended.

"Look, I'll drop everything and fly out," he said.

"There's no need. I'm fine now, and you've got classes to teach. Let's get together in the fall. I'll come there."

They agreed that she'd see her son in Chicago in a couple of months. As they hung up, they were both glad they'd talked, but were quite happy to return to their individual lives.

Art Sands's call to Brian later that morning was short and to the point. He related the recovery of his ex in Great Falls and said he, Barbara and Josie would be back later that day. "Brian, you've been a significant help to me. But there's still work for you. I want you to find the two assholes who took her, and I want them to face certain justice."

"You mean by turning them over to the authorities, right?"

Silence on the other end for a second. Then, "Well, yeah, of course. Let's meet at my office tomorrow. I'll call you late morning. Meanwhile, the cabin is yours. In fact, you're welcome to stay indefinitely."

Brian grabbed his phone and called James St. Claire.

James opened with, "Yowzah.'"

"Good to hear you rocking the professional image, Special Agent St. Claire."

"What the hell you doin'? Thought maybe you up and died."

"I'm still at the Sands place. He's my new best client."

"Good kind to have, loaded as he is."

"You got that right. Anyway, Barbara Hardy is back."

"Oh yeah? How bad?"

"Pretty damn good, considering she was gone three days. She wasn't assaulted or seriously injured. I delivered the ransom money, couple million."

"And you subdued the dudes, am I right?"

"No, they got away. They dumped her on the ground last night up in Great Falls, and a Good Samaritan took her to the hospital."

"What about our pal out of Bozeman? Thorsten, he get involved?"

"Nope. Woulda though, if it had dragged on much longer."

"So, when you comin' back?"

"Don't know. Sands wants me to find the kidnappers."

"Could be an indefinite gig, then."

"Maybe. But I need to get back to Chicago soon. Gotta take care of some client business, pay the rent, maybe see Michelle. But I'll be spending a lot of time here this fall. Pay's good. There may be an independent business opportunity for me. And Darcy's living just down the road."

"Oh yeah. How's that master's program goin'?"

They chatted about Darcy's courses, her roommate, the new apartment on campus and how she seemed to be flat out killing it. Brian said he'd be seeing Darcy the next day and James said to give her his best. He said he might come out that way for a few days' R & R some time, maybe drive the black beast (his Ford pickup) out, but Brian was doubtful. He'd love to see his former protégé but figured it would be back in Chicago. He knew the young agent would be reluctant to leave the city for a trip out west—not unless the Bureau sent him. Plus, his new wife was a city girl as well.

"What's happening there? J. Edgar surviving?" Brian said. He was referring to the supercilious paper-shuffling Special Agent in Charge of the office, a man for whom neither James nor he had much respect.

"Sonuvabitch is like a cockroach. Nothing seems to knock him out. Gives me the jimjams, knowing he calls the shots for a thousand employees."

After the call with James, Brian picked up his Kindle and resumed reading the latest Thomas Perry novel. Though the story was a page-turner, his mind kept wandering. He planned on meeting Darcy the next day at her apartment after his session with Sands. The two of them and Becky were on for lunch at an Italian place in Bozeman called the Ironsmith.

Later that morning, Sands phoned him, and they set a meet in the billionaire's office. Brian got there first and eyed the desk as he entered. He spotted a piece of paper with what appeared to be some kind of typed agreement. Unable to resist, he read it upside down from the visitor's side of the desk. He'd developed that particular skill as a financial crimes investigator for the FBI. He guessed that Sands wanted to give him a preview before their get-together. The document specified that Brian would conduct investigative work for Sands for a period of one year, in any circumstance and at any location specified, at an hourly rate of two hundred. He would operate as an independent contractor, rather than an employee. All contracted activities would be legal and confidential. The work would commence that day. Either party could terminate the agreement without cause at any time.

As Brian eased into a visitor's chair, Sands entered the room and sat behind his desk. There were bags under his eyes and his complexion was sallow. Like Brian, he hadn't had much sleep the last few days.

"Thanks, Brian," Sands said. "You've done well. Barbara seems okay, according to her and the release document from the hospital up in Great Falls. But I'm still worried about her. And I'm supremely pissed off. I want you to be my investigator. Finding the kidnappers is first priority."

"I'm interested, but it's gonna be only a part-time gig. And I can't commit to a year. You retain me on a specific task basis, and I'll bill you hours and expenses. But how are you gonna keep Barbara safe? And yourself, for that matter? I'm no bodyguard."

"Got that covered. I've identified a man in Chicago. Ex-Navy Seal. I've gotta know if I can trust him completely. In fact, I'd like you to interview him, give me your impressions."

"Okay, but, just so you understand my situation: I have other clients. I still live in Chicago, though I like to spend more time out here. In fact, I've gotta go home tomorrow. I can work on the kidnapping soon and with all my attention. But I need a little breathing room."

"All right. You've got it. But I'm anxious. Very anxious."

Chapter 23

The black Audi A8 sedan eased into the visitors parking lot of the East Moline Correctional Center in northwestern Illinois near the Mississippi River. Walter "Scooter" Berman, a man of below average height and possessing a pear-shaped body, levered himself out of the car and slowly made his way to the door leading to the visitors intake area. A scattered assembly of people, mostly women, sat in uncomfortable-looking vinyl-seated chairs staring into space. To Berman, it looked like a departure gate waiting area for a delayed flight at any American airport. He stepped up to a check-in opening shielded by bulletproof glass in the far wall. As he slid his required photo identification through the narrow slot at the bottom of the glass, he spoke into the mic, "Mr. Berman, attorney, here to see Hamilton Massey."

The man behind the glass, sepia-skinned and apparently of South Asian descent, was thin as a scarecrow. The gatekeeper eyed Berman impassively, then studied the Illinois driver's license as if it were an ancient scroll in some unknowable foreign language. After several minutes, he picked it up between two fingers and carried it to a copy machine. Another couple of minutes elapsed as he copied the item, carefully removed the reproduced image from the machine and set it on his small desk. Berman fidgeted but kept his cool. An old hand, he'd been through this routine dozens of times. And as a well-known and outrageously egotistical defense attorney, he knew that time was money…*his* money, to the tune of a thousand dollars an hour. Finally, his license was returned, along with a visitor's pass on a lanyard, which he looped around his pudgy neck. He was instructed to sit and wait to be called.

As Berman waited, he checked his phone for messages and then sat back and considered the situation. First, there was no telling who'd previously sat in the orange chair he now occupied. He'd selected the seemingly least filthy one, but still, he'd strip off his suit and toss it in the dry-cleaning bag as soon as he got home. That unpleasantness covered, he moved on to the client and his sorry situation. No doubt, A. Hamilton Massey deserved his imprisonment. The man was a typical high-level financial cheat. He made up his own rules and referred to them as "innovative best practices." When caught, he'd tried to shift the blame onto his staff. He'd been convicted of several felonies by the state, including insider trading and falsification of financial information of a publicly traded company. In prison, he'd done nothing but whine, to anyone who'd listen. And yet, Berman, as an inveterate professional, would do his best to extricate Massey from his miserable situation. Certain powerful people wanted Massey freed…as long as he provided the required up front quid pro quo, which was considerable. Berman's job now was to facilitate (i.e. grease the skids for) the transaction. After a twenty-minute wait, the lawyer was summoned by a uniformed guard with a foghorn voice. He rose to venture further into the belly of the system.

The guard had Berman surrender his phone and pocket contents into a plastic basket, everything to be returned later, of course. The guard also went over a few of the rules. You will sit with the inmate at an assigned table. The visit will not be monitored or recorded, since this had been pre-arranged as a confidential attorney-client visit. No contraband allowed. The visit will continue, at a maximum, until the end of visiting hours, which meant a couple of hours. But Berman figured the meeting would be far shorter, since the issues at hand were simple.

The lawyer was guided down a seemingly endless hallway, through a couple of locked metal doors, each unlocked by the guard with a keycard. Finally, he was ushered into a meeting room and then to a square wooden table anchored to the tile floor. He sat in one of the two empty chairs, both also bolted to the floor. The guard left the room after telling Berman to wait for the prisoner. A few minutes later, another guard escorted Massey into the room and beckoned for him to sit. Berman was shocked at how gaunt and pale Massey looked. He'd met the man once before, at his arraignment. The former executive appeared to have aged five years and dropped thirty pounds since his incarceration a year earlier.

After Massey was seated, the guard addressed Berman. "I'll be outside. If you need anything, knock on that door and I'll be here in a flash." He exited the room, leaving them alone.

Berman spoke first. "My role is facilitator. As my client, your interests are foremost. At the same time, you want something very precious, your freedom. No surprise there. With good conduct, you could be out of here in one to two years."

"Not acceptable, and you know it." Massey's steely tone belied his shopworn appearance. "I am prepared to financially augment the uh, facilitation process."

"Good. Then we understand each other. You have the capability to complete wire transfers?"

"I will, when I need to."

"Are you prepared for IRS scrutiny of such transfers?"

Massey's expression brightened. "As you know, I have a sophisticated knowledge of such matters. Let's just say I have devised a unique methodology for executing international and domestic wire transfers leaving not a trace of a trail for governmental snoopers."

"That's good. Maybe you can market it to others at some point."

Massey just shook his head.

"All right. You will transfer three million U.S. to a certain bank account. Once that's done, I will submit your petition for clemency to the Illinois Prison Review Board. Normally, the board has two to three months to review a petition for recommendation to the Governor. Yours will be expedited. It will be with the Governor's Director of Administrative Affairs as soon as it's submitted. The Governor should approve the pardon right after the Director recommends it to him."

"This is an absolute pardon with no conditions, right?"

"Correct."

"Done."

Berman was surprised but he didn't show it. Usually, they tried to bargain. Though he still considered Massey a weasel, his impression of the guy had just improved a tad. "Keep in mind, the key to success here is the facilitation fee."

"Got it. What assurance do I have that, once the fee is paid, all of that clemency stuff will happen?"

"You have my word. And you will have your own documentation of your transfer of funds. If we were not to deliver, you could raise holy hell and perhaps smear the Governor enough to hurt him in next year's election. He would not like to see that. Your uh, contribution will enhance his campaign. It will be paid to an account controlled by his super PAC. Everyone benefits, you see?"

"Yes. Give me the account information and I will make the transfer."

Berman recited a bank name and an account number. "Can you remember that?"

"I've committed it to memory. The transfer will occur tomorrow. When will my release take place?"

"It'll happen within days. No longer than a week." Berman stood up. "I'll be in touch. And I'll make sure the process runs smoothly."

Massey nodded.

Berman knocked on the door through which he'd entered the room. A few minutes later, the guard escorted him back to the checkpoint, where he collected his possessions from the clerk who'd retained them. In his car, he made a call to a Springfield, Illinois number.

Edward "Fast Eddie" Nolan, the Governor's chief fixer, picked up immediately. "We got a deal?"

"Yes," Berman said.

Nolan said, "Look, the Governor would like you to meet with me in person to finalize the uh, arrangements. Tomorrow at eleven A.M., my office. Okay?"

"Okey-dokey," Berman said. He hung up and guided the Audi out of the prison lot, resigned to spending three hours on the highway for the trip to his suburban Chicago home.

Chapter 24
(Day 6)

Scooter Berman guided the big Audi down I-55 south toward Springfield, the Illinois state capitol. He was racking up the miles on his fancy new ride, after the trip to East Moline the day before. But that was okay—he was in for a big payday when this project was settled. He'd left his home in the suburb of Highland Park at seven A.M. to allow enough time for his meeting at eleven with Eddie Nolan, whom he thought of as the Governor's toady-in-chief. The weather was cool for late August and the sky a perfect cobalt blue. He appreciated the dry and relatively empty road as he dipped into the throttle and gradually eased the big sedan up to a cruise-controlled seventy-five. Though that velocity exceeded the limit by five miles per hour, he was continuously passed. Green metal signs on the right side of the highway advised him of the towns he passed through: Pontiac, Bloomington, Lincoln. Finally, he exited at Springfield.

He followed Peoria Road into town and then 9th Street to the capitol complex. As a history buff, he knew that there was a really interesting national historic site for Abraham Lincoln's home near his destination, the state capitol building. But today, there would be no time for sight-seeing.

Nolan had promised to relay A. Hamilton Massey's request for clemency to the Governor of Illinois, Hollis D. Langdon III. Berman knew that Langdon came from a wealthy family that had made a fortune manufacturing hitch assemblies and other parts for railroad freight cars starting in the 1880s. He'd grown up just north of Chicago in old money Kenilworth, the wealthiest community in the midwestern United States. Langdon had attended an exclusive prep school in New York and earned a master's in political science at Yale. His top assistant, Nolan, on the other hand, was from lower middleclass Chicago stock. He'd worked his way through DePaul law and then landed in Springfield as an entry level legislative aid. Serendipity and a common interest in raw political power had brought the two men together. Riding Langdon's considerable coattails, Nolan was now a fixture in state politics in his own right. Langdon was currently serving his second four-year term and would be facing re-election in two years.

Berman parked in a lot at the domed capitol building and walked inside. In the lobby, there was strict security, including metal detectors, a patdown and briefcase search. Uniformed Illinois State Police officers were scattered around the common area, reflecting added security since a band of crazies plotted to kidnap the Governor of Michigan in the fall of 2020. The men and women of the security detail in the Illinois capitol were under strict orders to take no chances.

In the vast marble-floored lobby, Berman found a stairway and ascended to the second floor. The steps were wide but not very high, making them awkward to negotiate. Not an athletic man in the best of circumstances, he nearly stumbled a couple of times on the way up. At the top, he walked into an entryway leading to a large sunlit marble plaza beneath the capitol rotunda. He asked a waiting state trooper for directions to Nolan's office. The cop made him show ID and called to confirm that Berman was on the appointments list. Passing that test, the lawyer was free to proceed to the end of the hallway, where he endured yet another metal detector screening. Eventually, he arrived at Nolan's office, located next to the Governor's, reflecting the close relationship between the two men. Three flagpoles stood incongruously in the hall outside the Governor's suite: U.S.A., Illinois and one Berman could not identify.

He stopped at the administrative assistant's station just outside the gubernatorial domain. A woman with straight gray hair looked up from her keyboard. "Help you?"

"Walter Berman here to see Ed Nolan. I have an—"

A nasal voice came from behind the woman: "It's okay, Rose. Let the man in."

"Good to see you, Eddie. You look... prosperous," Berman said. He'd noted the substantial belly straining at the waistband of Nolan's suit pants.

Nolan frowned. "Well, you don't exactly look poor. C'mon, Scooter."

Berman followed Nolan into his office, a space big enough to qualify as a two-bedroom apartment in Chicago. Marble everywhere, including a wood-burning fireplace. An interior door was open, revealing a spacious bathroom. Berman took a seat across from Nolan, now enthroned behind his aircraft carrier desk.

"Let's get business out of the way," Nolan said. I spoke with Holl about this thing yesterday. He's on board. Of course, discretion is essential. Expeditious submission of the uh, consideration will be expected."

"Fine with us on all counts. A wire transfer will be forthcoming as soon as we have appropriate assurances that the paperwork has been finalized. Tomorrow okay?"

Nolan sighed. "You know, the pressure on the Governor is immense. I mean, he runs every four years. He has to fund-raise every friggin' day and most nights, from here on out. This deal we're talkin' about, it's a necessity for him. Nothin' wrong with it. Your client, he's nonviolent, no threat to society."

"I know all that. I've got no problem sleeping. Let's just move ahead. Are we good?"

"Listen, you've been around. Nothing's gonna be in writing. Our verbal agreement will have to suffice."

"Naturally. But would it be possible to have the Governor provide assurance to me personally?"

"I'm afraid that won't be possible. You see, he's—"

The door to Nolan's office suddenly opened, and a tall lean man with fine facial features entered. The smile on his lean face seemed genuine, but Berman knew it to be well-practiced and not necessarily sincere. Coatless, the Governor wore a pale blue dress shirt with faint white stripes and French cuffs fastened by oval brushed gold cufflinks.

"Holl Langdon," he said as he extended a hand with long tapered fingers, like those of a concert pianist. "Eddie tells me you're an old friend." Langdon's eyes were blue and bright like chips of stained glass catching the light.

"Walter Berman. Yeah, he and I go back a ways in Chicago."

"Great. How may I help?"

"I understand you and Eddie have discussed the matter involving my client residing in East Moline."

"We have, and I am in agreement that we must do something to alleviate the uh, injustice to your client."

"And he, coincidentally, desires to support your efforts in a perfectly legal manner so that good government may continue unabated in this state." Berman congratulated himself on delivering the line with a poker face. He waited for a rejoinder.

Langdon clapped his hands like a child delighted by an unanticipated Christmas gift. "Good!" he cried. "I like doing business with a man who likes doing business. We'll get the required action done as soon as the benefaction reaches the committee. Is that fine by you?"

Berman nodded. He knew "the committee" was the super PAC organized by close supporters of the Governor's next re-election campaign. Technically, the PAC was independent of the campaign, but, in fact, it would spend millions advocating for the Governor's re-election. The law provided that the advocacy expenditures could not be made directly to or coordinated with the campaign. Nevertheless, the PAC would advertise heavily on TV in favor of the Governor and against his opponent, not unlike hundreds of other such PACs linked to politicians running for office.

Langdon dropped into the visitor's chair next to Berman and crossed an ankle over a knee. "Now that that's out of the way, who's gonna have the better b-ball season this fall, the Illini or DePaul?" he said.

Berman noticed that the Governor wore ultra-thin pink socks with tiny clocks woven into the silk fabric. Langdon noticed him noticing. "I've always been a sock man. Dunno why. Maybe a little touch of style."

Berman paused for a beat. Then, "To answer your question, I say DePaul. No contest."

The Governor stood and beamed down at Berman. "I believe you are correct, Mr. Berman. Anyway, good to meet you. Keep in touch with Eddie." The bright smile emerged again and then he rushed from the room as if his trousers had instantly caught fire.

Nolan handed Berman a slip of paper with the name of the super PAC's Springfield bank and an account number. Nolan promised that Berman's ten percent facilitation fee would be delivered to him in cash at his Chicago office within twenty-four hours, once the funds hit the PAC account. They chatted for a few more minutes. Nolan stole a glance at his watch and Berman took the hint. As he stood, he said, "I'll see our mutual friend again tomorrow morning. I'll instruct him to initiate the transfer."

"Excellent. The clemency paperwork on our end will follow right after credit to the account. I'll watch for it. Hey, let's do dinner in the city. I'll be up there early next month."

They shook hands and Berman descended to the immense lobby. He found his way out, being only slightly delayed by security checks, He felt the eyes of an armed state trooper on him as he reached the exit doors.

Chapter 25

Brian went to his lunch date with Darcy and her roommate Becky in Bozeman despite his new assignment to find the kidnappers. That could wait. He wanted to see Darcy before heading back to Chicago. Without speaking further with Arthur Sands, he drove his loaner pickup down the ranch access road to 89 and then to I-90, heading west to the burgeoning "micropolitan" area of Bozeman. He mused at the changes he'd recently read about the university burg. From a quiet college town of 20,000 around the year 2000, the population had swelled to more than 55,000. The growth had strained resources such as affordable housing. As Darcy had told him, apartments near campus for under two thousand dollars monthly were like goldfish knees.

He thought too of where he'd been, where he might be headed. Right now felt like a moment of transition. White male, middleclass, making a decent living, he knew he was privileged. He could continue on the current arc, working for a few clients, making excellent money, maybe being useful. He had no doubt he could extend the current gig with Arthur Sands into something like a job. He was confident he could find the men who'd abducted Barbara Hardy. After all, the crime was simple enough. But simple enough that local law enforcement might beat him to it.

After that task, however it might end, he could return to Chicago and carry on his investigations business. His relationship with Michelle could possibly be rekindled, but it had become like a recalcitrant campfire doused by intermittent rain. He wondered whether he wanted to expend the effort. With each day of no communication between them, the prospect of rejuvenating the relationship became more of a longshot.

A Lexus SUV cut Brian off and raced through a yellow traffic light on Main Street, snapping him out of his reverie. Reminded him of the north side of Chicago. What was happening to Montana? He made a left, heading up Highland. Another reminder of the rapid growth in the Bozeman area: the medical complex north of downtown reaching its arms out like an octopus, expanding in all directions. New medical specialty buildings surrounded the hospital, including a cluster of orthopedic sports medicine establishments, all recently built and flashy looking. Sports docs thrived here, with so many people skiing, climbing mountains and biking—a knee surgeon's paradise. He eased the pickup onto Kagy and west toward the MSU campus.

The restaurant was almost full. Brian told the greeter he was with the McKay party and was pointed toward a booth along the outside wall. He spotted Darcy's blond head and ponytail tossing as she conversed with a young woman seated across from her. The other gal looked familiar. Boisterous competing conversations created a din. Everyone in the place raised their voices to be heard. He switched off the ringer on his phone. Just then, Darcy turned her head and spotted him. She leapt to her feet and closed in for a bearhug. Seeing them so unabashedly affectionate, Becky knew they were tightknit as twins.

Darcy introduced Brian to Becky, who he vaguely remembered from the dinosaur dig two years before. They ordered lunch and began trading information: Brian described the kidnapping and rescue of Barbara Hardy. The two young women filled him in on the beginning of classes and their new apartment.

"So, you gonna stick around at that ranch?" Darcy asked.

"Yeah, I'm staying in that cabin there. Kinda growing on me, feels almost like home. Sands has hired me to find the guys that kidnapped Barbara. Pay's good. Though I'm leaving tomorrow for home. Gotta catch up on a few things, then I'm back out here."

"How's Michelle?"

Brian felt color rising to his face. He shrugged. "We haven't been in touch for a while."

"Whoa. Have you seen that banker lady in Clarkville since you came out?"

"Not yet. But I plan to."

Darcy grinned and faced Becky. "Carol Jensen. She's a serious babe. And Brian is smitten."

The conversation was put on hold while they ate like cart horses. Each had a plateful of pasta and a glass of white wine. Cannolis for dessert. It felt like a celebration.

After lunch, they walked five blocks to the new furnished apartment on the MSU campus. The redbrick three-story building looked perhaps three years old to Brian. It appeared to be in good repair. He noted with approval the solid-core front door with a sturdy lock. Darcy pulled a keycard from a jeans pocket and let them in. They took the stairs to the second floor, to an interior door labeled 2A. This time, Darcy used a brass key to unlock. Brian and Becky followed her in.

The apartment was modern but a bit sterile to Brian's eyes. A large living room, with IKEA furniture. Modern abstract art prints with black frames hung on the off-white walls. A combined kitchen-dining area came next. A mysterious machine made of stainless steel held a prominent place on the kitchen countertop. Brian noticed a hopper of coffee beans on top, an array of knobs and dials on the front and a set of tubes leading to a metal pitcher and a pair of white coffee cups. Becky noticed him studying the contraption. "Espresso machine," she said. We got it on sale. Less than a half month's rent. And worth every penny when you're into coffee."

Brian was taken aback. Less than a half month's rent? Jesus, these gals must really appreciate their caffeine.

A short hall led to two bedrooms in the back. They moved in that direction.

"Don't look at my bedroom," Darcy said. "It's a disaster area."

He had a quick look, anyway. Darcy's room was actually a lot neater than Brian's first apartment bedroom had been. She managed to maintain a semblance of order despite the pressures inherent in graduate studies. He felt proud, thinking that she had an innate organizational inclination, kind of like himself.

After the tour, Brian hugged both young women and headed out.

Chapter 26

Russell Eagle Feather got up from his desk in the William Old Horn Dinosaur Museum and walked slowly around the large exhibit space. A glass-walled fossil bone preparation lab occupied one wall. He walked into the lab and looked at the countertops covered with fossilized bone dust, hand tools, specialized electronic equipment and some dark fossil bones. No one had worked in the lab for months. There had been a burst of activity at the beginning two years ago, but once the complete *T. rex* skeleton had been installed, there'd been a lull. He hoped another major fossil find would come to the museum soon.

He continued on to the Plexiglas display cases lined up on another wall. Each case contained dinosaur bones, along with photographs and illustrations of what the living animal might have looked like, all carefully captioned. Lots of educational information about the museum's star *T. rex* attraction, *Hornosaurus Ancienus*, along with the bone samples from other perennial crowd favorites that lived in the area within the Morrison formation of the late Jurassic, 65 million years ago: *Allosaurus, Diplodocus* and *Stegosaurus*.

He finished his walk, strolling by the stage used for public lectures and then to the center of the exhibit space, where the world's largest and most complete dinosaur skeleton of the *T. rex* family, *Hornosaurus Ancienus,* stood. The dinosaur was named after Eagle Feather's deceased uncle, a Crow Indian named William Old Horn. The older man had originally discovered the bones nearby in the Crazy Mountains, before being murdered by would-be thieves. The monstrous skeleton stretched nearly forty-five feet long and fourteen feet high at the hips. The peaked bronze metal ceiling with two skylights soared above the fossil structure.

Eagle Feather had been the Executive Director of the museum since its creation almost two years before, funded by Chicago-based billionaire businessman, Arthur Sands. The museum sat on a 20-acre piece of land in the northeast corner of the massive Sands ranch in the Crazy Mountains. A separate road ran from Highway 89 to the museum's gated entrance. Eagle Feather reported to a six-person Board of Directors. At first, the job was part-time, but had gradually evolved into a fulltime gig. His duties included administration of the facility, conducting education programs, including tours, fund-raising, marketing and supervision of the staff. He had recently obtained his Master of Arts in Native American Studies from Montana State University, much of the course work done on weekends and evenings.

Eagle Feather was a tall, broad-shouldered man in his mid-twenties. His skin was a deep tan color. He wore his raven-black hair rubber-banded into a ponytail. With his intense brown eyes and high cheekbones, many people thought he looked like a certain indigenous movie star whose light had burned brightly in several cable television dramas. He had on his usual garb, a snug black tee shirt, low-slung blue jeans and scuffed boots. A small feather-shaped silver earring hung from his left ear.

The first months in his position had flown by. Excitement reigned as the bones were prepped and the massive skeleton erected in the two-story main hall. The gargantuan skull, the museum's star attraction, was mounted separately inside a box made of Plexiglas and wood at floor level, its jagged-toothed mouth sizeable enough to contain a large man. A replica skull topped the huge dinosaur skeleton, far above the floor.

People had been hired at good wages, members of the Crow Tribe of Indians. Two tenured professors from MSU supervised the early bone prep and interpretive work: Dave Bakeno, paleontologist, and Anton Holt, Native American Studies instructor.

Public attendance was excellent at the beginning, but quickly tapered off, for a couple of reasons: first, the museum was located in a far corner of the remote Sands ranch in Montana's Crazy Mountains, an hour's drive from the nearest sizeable town. And second, the potential audience for such a museum was limited; once people in the area had seen the skeleton, that was it: *been there, done that*. The museum was a long way from the region's top tourist attraction, Yellowstone National Park. Mainly, they now got school field trips from around the region and tourists making the side trip while on vacation. Occasionally, faculty or students from MSU would stop by for research.

Eagle Feather was bored, but he had no plans to leave his job. He made a good salary with benefits, including health insurance. At the last Board of Directors meeting, he'd been given an excellent employee evaluation. He supervised the receptionist/clerk, along with a couple of women, local residents who worked part-time at janitorial and exhibit maintenance duties. There were also three guards: the day shift man, a night watchman who held the fort from five P.M. until 1:00 A.M. and a graveyard shift guard for the time from one until opening at 9:00 A.M.

The board members seemed quite pleased with his performance, but they agreed that the museum needed a new exhibit or at least a novel marketing program for the current one. If attendance didn't pick up soon and without additional fundraising, employees would have to be laid off. And perhaps the museum would only be open in the summer.

The board chair was a woman named Carol Jensen, a banker at the First Intermountain Bank of Clarkville. Eagle Feather knew that she was tight with the McKays from Chicago—Brian and Darcy. Board member and billionaire Arthur Sands, also a Chicagoan, had funded both the museum construction and the fossil bones prep work as well as the installation of *Hornosaurus Ancienus*. He insisted the museum operate at a break-even. The museum, a 501(c)(3) nonprofit, also received foundation grants and charitable contributions from the public, normally sufficient to cover operating expenses.

The board was rounded out by Doctor Phil Banham of Clarkville Healthcare; Henry White Swan, a Crow Indian historian and writer; Professor Holt, himself a Crow; and Winslow Elwood, a well-known artist from Clarkville. Eagle Feather knew he was fortunate to be dealing with a qualified and engaged board. And yet he remained unsatisfied with his work life. Not to mention his social life. He was a long way from the Crow Reservation, where most of his friends and family lived. His cabin, not far from the museum, was comfortable, but lonely.

In a phone call that morning, Arthur Sands had raised the question of security at the museum. In the wake of the kidnapping and recovery of his ex-wife, he pointed out that the exhibited dinosaur bones were potentially worth millions on the black market. A long discussion ensued about the burglar alarm system, locks, the need for upgraded fire sprinklers and smoke alarms. Sands had seemed mollified for the time-being.

At the most recent board meeting, Professor Bakeno made a brief presentation on next summer's planned fossil dig in the Hell Creek formation of northeastern Montana. The Montana State University Earth Sciences department would be operating the dig. Sands mentioned that he would be partially funding it, with the understanding that any significant fossil bones unearthed would be first displayed at the William Old Horn Museum. Bakeno enthusiastically endorsed this plan, and reminded the group that, normally, the Museum of the Rockies in Bozeman would get first dibs on any significant fossil finds unearthed under the auspices of MSU. Maybe the dig would yield some dramatic new dinosaur skeleton, something to shake things up.

Eagle Feather sat down at his desk, his only company the dinosaur bones on display. He tried to concentrate on the budget spreadsheet he'd been working on for the coming fiscal year, but his eyes drooped almost shut after a few minutes. Darcy McKay had texted him that morning to let him know she was now working on her master's at MSU, in Earth Science, concentrating on paleontology. She said she'd be participating in the next Hell Creek dig and hoped to see him sometime at the museum. He remembered her well from the Bone Mountain events two years prior: a cute young woman with blonde hair, blue eyes and boundless confidence. He was looking forward to seeing her again. He knew that the MSU campus was a two-hour drive from this place. As he thought about Darcy, he realized he'd *really* like to see her again.

Meanwhile, Russell Eagle Feather was hoping for something exciting to happen at the museum. In fact, that was about to occur, but he would not enjoy the experience.

Chapter 27

After his mid-day visit with Darcy and her roommate Becky, Brian returned to the Sands ranch and parked the loaner Ford pickup outside his cabin. He checked his phone and saw that Arthur Sands had called twice, the second time leaving a terse message: "See me ASAP."

Brian walked over to the ranch headquarters building and on to Sands's office. As he approached, he heard a phone conversation in progress. Sands's phone was on speaker. Brian stopped to listen outside the closed door.

A man's voice rasped from the speaker. "Yes, I'm ready. Locked and loaded."

"Have you met Brian McKay?"

"Nope. When you mentioned him though, I reached out to a guy who does. Bottom line, he seems capable. Law enforcement experience, of course. He did good on that Bone Mountain thing a couple years back. And that Belcoe corporate fraud last year. Yes, I'd say he's capable. Don't know about his suitability for your purposes, not having met him."

"Okay. Just so you know, I've engaged him as an investigator and have tasked him with finding the asshats who kidnapped my ex. Also, I want you to meet with him in

Chicago soon. He'll do a pro forma due diligence on your qualifications for the job here."

Silence for a couple of seconds. "Uh, you really think that's necessary?"

"Maybe not. You seem qualified. But I'm a careful person. Why do you ask? Is there a problem?"

"Hell no. I'm with the program. Anything else?"

"As I mentioned, what happened here recently must never happen again. Or anything like it. Your first priority will be to put in place measures to preclude the possibility of such a cock-up. If all goes well with Brian, I'll want you to start ASAP. You'll have your hands full here, Chicago and elsewhere. Are we clear?"

"Crystal."

"Other questions?"

"You said, 'if all goes well.' This meeting with McKay. Am I interviewing for the job? I mean, is this a hurdle I have to make?"

"Well…you could say that. I've got every confidence in you, Andrew."

To Brian, it sounded as if the conversation was winding down. As he rapped on the door, he entered the room. Sands was setting his phone on the desk. He looked up with mild annoyance in his eyes.

"Brian, I was just speaking with Andrew Garcia."

That name sounded familiar to Brian. Some guy he'd read about years ago, he thought. "Couldn't help but hear you want me to screen him."

"Hmm. Well, you heard right. The sooner the better. I want a bodyguard and all-around security man for this place, to protect Barbara, of course. And perhaps a second guy for

Chicago and other locations. As you know, I have several residences and businesses in the U.S. and elsewhere. I need highly-skilled security."

I hope it's someone better than the previous guy, Brian thought. That man, a crooked ex-cop, had died two years earlier during the Bone Mountain dinosaur case. The security post had been vacant since then, much to Sands's regret.

Sands handed Brian a sheet of paper with a brief bio of Garcia and contact information. Brian glanced at it and noticed the man was a former Navy Seal and current security contractor. He lived on the north side of Chicago, not far from Brian's apartment.

"How did Garcia come to your attention?"

"Through a guy I know with the city. Vouches for his competence."

"Okay. I'm returning to Chicago tomorrow to take care of some business. I can meet Garcia in the next day or two."

"Good. You'll have to fly commercial though. I need the plane here for my next travels. Let's keep in touch."

Brian returned to his cabin to pack.

Chapter 28
(Day 7)

Prisoner A. Hamilton Massey was released from the East Moline Correctional Center in northwestern Illinois on a rainy Tuesday morning in late August. As part of the checkout process, they gave him back his street clothes, cash and the few other possessions he'd had on him when he'd been incarcerated eleven months before. He carefully counted the cash—all there and enough to get him to Chicago. When he asked what the circumstances of his release were, the administrative clerk told him, "Governor's pardon." Just as he'd expected and paid for. A guard with all the warmth of an icicle walked him to an open gate at a side entrance and told him to take off.

The Uber ride he'd ordered with the smuggled phone he'd used and destroyed was waiting. Massey boarded the white Prius and directed the driver to the Peninsula Hotel 160 miles away in Chicago. The ultra-luxury hotel was located on the "Magnificent Mile" of Michigan Avenue at Superior Street. He knew that commercial rent on the Mag Mile was third highest in the United states, behind only Fifth Avenue in New York and Rodeo Drive in Los Angeles. The room he'd reserved went for more than a thousand dollars a night.

Money was not a problem. He'd soon wire funds from one of his Cayman Islands bank accounts into a local bank to cover his anticipated expenses for the near-term. He planned on living high on the hog, much as he had in his former life as a profligate executive.

Still wearing his prison khakis, Massey checked into the Peninsula and changed into his pre-incarceration street clothes of wrinkled white shirt, suit pants and black Ferragamo oxfords. Because he'd lost more than thirty pounds on the dismal prison food, the clothing fit him like castoffs on a scarecrow. But it felt beyond wonderful to be clothed as a civilian again. Grimacing with disgust, he threw the prison khakis into the nearest wastebasket.

He called room service and ordered a bottle of Glenlivet single malt Scotch with a bucket of ice, along with an assortment of appetizers, including a shrimp cocktail. He quickly downed a couple of drinks. It was the first alcohol he'd had in more than a year, and it nearly knocked him on his ass. He remonstrated with himself—he needed to stay sharp as he planned his activities for the coming days. He had to contact the people he'd lined up to carry out certain tasks for him, mainly conducting a heist and leveling revenge on those who'd brought him down when Belcoe, Inc. and his own life had imploded.

He'd stay at the Peninsula for a few days. After that, he planned on renting an apartment in that posh neighborhood. There were so-called "corporate" apartments available on a month-to-month basis at exorbitant rents. Long-term, who knew? Perhaps he'd relocate to the Caymans, not just for the financial advantages, but to banish the miserable cold of Chicago winters to the rearview. But before that, he planned to set in motion additional actions in Montana. It would make sense to buy a secluded home out there to serve as a short-term base of operations.

Massey found an elevator and descended from his eighteenth-floor perch to street level, where he bought a sport shirt and jeans, underwear and socks in a shop near the hotel. He donned the new outfit in a dressing room but stayed with his pre-prison nine hundred dollar Ferragamos. He asked them to dispose of the clothing he'd worn into the place. Next, he obtained a credit card from a nearby bank branch. He gave them an edited work history and current income, which proved sufficient to pass the superficial financial screening. He did not mention his recent incarceration.

Next, Massey visited the Apple store on North Michigan Avenue, where he employed his new credit card to purchase the latest iPhone and MacBook Pro. He paid full price without any qualms. The helpful female salesperson also set up a phone and data account with Verizon for him. She seemed somewhat puzzled when he told her he had no old phone to trade in and he had no contact list to be transferred to the new phone. Next stop was a small and exclusive men's clothing store on Rush street, where he'd often shopped before his fall from grace. He was miffed that the salesman he'd patronized in the past did not recognize him. Nevertheless, he purchased a complete wardrobe, including a couple of bespoke suits and a smart fedora, all to be delivered to him at the hotel once tailoring on the suits was done.

The next morning, Massey called Seth Delmer in Montana. Delmer updated him on the covering of tracks on the Barbara Hardy kidnapping: deep cleaning of the cabin and truck used to house and transport the hostage: disposal of ATV tires etc. Massey said he expected deposit of his half of the ransom into a bank account in Bozeman by the end of the day as previously discussed. He even complemented them on the efficiency of their efforts on that operation.

"Okay, here's what's next," Massey said. "You are going to obtain a used but reliable commercial van capable of hauling an object that is approximately a six-foot cube. It will weigh about 700 pounds. It will be very fragile, so it must be encased in thick padding before it is transported from its current site. Obviously, you will need sturdy loading ramps. You will drive this cargo to a destination approximately 100 miles distant. Oh, and by the way, you will be misappropriating this object in the nighttime."

"Okay. What's our cut gonna be?"

"I am prepared to give the two of you a generous share of the proceeds for the uh, cargo. What would you say to a million dollars? Not too shabby for a night's labors."

"I don't suppose you'd tell me what this cargo is."

"That will come later."

"When is the job?"

"Soon. I'll get back to you in a day or two."

"I'll talk with my brother. If he's in, I am, too."

"That's satisfactory. I'll be in touch." Massey abruptly ended the call.

Chapter 29

Brian caught a Chicago-bound Delta flight out of Bozeman Yellowstone International Airport, departing at 11:30 AM. Sands was picking up the tab and had insisted that Brian fly first class, which was fine with him. He settled into his window seat and accepted a free drink from the flight attendant. He hadn't had a Bloody Mary in a long time and enjoyed it, though he knew the same drink fixed by a competent bartender would be much better. The flight was packed with tourists returning home from vacation in Yellowstone country. As they gained altitude and pointed east, he watched the snow-topped peaks thousands of feet below disappear behind cottony cumulus clouds. The first leg arrived on time in Minneapolis. Brian deplaned and wandered the concourse during his brief layover. He found a Caribou Coffee near the next departure gate and settled in at a small table with a large dark roast and his phone. He called Andrew Garcia to set up a meeting.

"Brian McKay here. Art Sands asked me to contact you to set up a meet."

The voice was as hard as the blade of a shovel. "Yeah?"

"How's tomorrow look for you?"

Long pause. Then: "What time?"

"How about ten A.M. at my office?"

"That's jake."

"I'm located at—"

"I know where you're at. See ya." A sharp click. Garcia had severed the connection.

What a rude bugger. But he'd keep an open mind, pending tomorrow's meeting.

The second leg of the journey departed twenty minutes late. Brian had another Bloody Mary on the way to Chicago. He considered his options, personal and business. He'd enjoyed the past few days in Montana, especially seeing Darcy in her new life as a grad student at Montana State. He regretted not visiting with Carol Jensen or her nephew this time out. Next trip, he'd set up a dinner date. Date? He liked her a lot but wondered whether it was because she reminded him of her late sister, Laura. They were both curly-haired blondes with blue eyes, nice figures, medium height, thirty-something. He guessed Carol was younger by about three years. She being a banker contrasted wildly with Laura's sheriff's deputy job. But she seemed just as tough and capable as her older sister had been. And the kiss they'd shared after the dinner at her house…nice.

The plane rolled to a stop at Delta arrival gate M11 in a far-flung reach of O'Hare's Terminal five. Nearly six P.M. Brian waited in the taxi queue outside the terminal with his carryon bag at his feet. The air felt heavy and moist after the dry mountain atmosphere of Montana. Finally, his turn came, and he boarded a yellow cab in the form of a Chevy Equinox. The dark-skinned male driver wore a turban on his head and a bored expression on his face.

"Where to, sir?" he said.

Brian gave him the address of his apartment in Lakeview. The driver pushed down the fare flag and pulled into the heavy stream of traffic heading out of O'Hare. They passed under the large blue sign over I-90 that read: WELCOME TO CHICAGO, with an accompanying picture of the skyline along Lake Michigan. Brian never tired of pictures of the city's lakefront or, better yet, in-person views of the real thing. The cab continued onto the Kennedy expressway and headed southeast into the city. Traffic was the normal heavy flow, moving at just below the speed limit. They took the Addison exit leading to Wrigley Field, home of the Chicago Cubs. Brian watched with approval as the cabbie easily navigated his way down Clark Street and then over to Brian's place in the 800 block of Aldine. He paid the fare in cash, including a good tip, and emerged from the cab at six-thirty-five.

He climbed the steps to his apartment on the first floor of the Victorian two-flat, his home for the last five years. He unlocked the door and entered, dropping the carryon just inside the entryway. The air was stale, unmoving. The place felt abandoned. He sat on the couch with his phone and ordered a thin crust pizza from Vito's. He was facing the flat-screen TV, but he didn't turn it on. He sat quietly, waiting for his supper to be delivered.

He remembered an evening in this room the year before, with his FBI friend James and his niece, Darcy. It had been during the Dirty Money case involving the corrupt Chicago corporation, Belcoe. The sound system had been tuned to a rock station on Sirius. The three of them discussed pop music briefly, with Brian showing off his knowledge of classic rock from its peak era, years before he'd been born. James had offered a characteristic trenchant remark about tinny lily-white tunes. On a more serious note, they'd talked about Belcoe's involvement in illegal trading with Syria. James then left for an evening at FBI headquarters and Brian and Darcy had shared a pizza at the nearby restaurant from which Brian had just ordered. He sighed. Happier times. He felt unmoored, with one foot in Chicago and one in Montana. A girlfriend in the city, Michelle Emerson, with whom he'd nearly lost touch. A woman in Montana, Carol Jensen, with whom he seemed to be gaining a friendship…or possibly something more.

The pizza arrived. He set it on the coffee table in front of the couch and began eating. As he drank from a longneck bottle of Goose Island ale, a text came in from Darcy.

"U in Chgo? See Carol? All good here. Classes cool. Got text from Russell EF, problems at museum. Let me know when you're coming back."

He replied, "Back home. D/N see Carol, maybe next time. Interesting about EF. Will be here a few days. Back out there soon Be safe. See ya."

He also exchanged texts with Michelle Emerson and James St. Clair. Michelle's words seemed distant, but then it was hard to read much into a text. They made no definite plans to see each other. James suggested they go to the Cubs game against the St. Louis Cardinals the next day, his treat. Brian happily accepted the invitation from his former protégé. He had a second beer, read a little of his current novel, the latest from John Sandford, and turned in before midnight.

Chapter 30

(Day 8)

At 9:15 the next morning, Brian walked to the rented garage around the corner from his apartment. The overhead door faced onto the alley, very urban turf. He was always alert when he entered that alley. Over the years, he'd been accosted by street people, had chased off public urinators and been threatened by an armed would-be robber while approaching his garage. This time, he arrived at the door and rolled it up without incident. His white Jeep Cherokee waited under a layer of dust. Though idle for many days, it fired up immediately, the six-cylinder engine throbbing smoothly. Out on the street, he accelerated to the corner. It felt good to be driving his own vehicle after pushing the big pickup truck around Montana. Though the Jeep was clumsy compared to the classic Porsche he'd traded in on it, the SUV was a more practical ride for Chicago. Blasting through the occasional snowstorm in four wheel drive was always a kick.

He drove down Clark and arrived at his River North office with plenty of time to park in the multi-tiered parking structure next door, climb the stairs to his second-floor space, make coffee and check mail and messages before the scheduled meeting with Andrew Garcia at ten.

Garcia was there on the dot, flinging the door open without knocking. A sinewy man, slightly under average height, he had a short, spiky crown of gelled dark hair, shaved to the skin around his ears. No facial hair. His clothing was casual, but his posture military rigid. Without being invited, he took a seat in a visitor's chair. He rolled his neck back and forth a couple of times as if it were uncomfortably stiff. He looked about thirty-five years old, He stared blankly at Brian but said nothing.

Brian waited him out, sipping from his coffee mug. After a minute of silence, he said, "Well, I take it you are Andy Garcia."

"I go by Andrew."

Brian stood and proffered his right hand for a shake. Garcia got to his feet and grasped Brian's hand in an attempted crushing grip. Brian took in the pale face with dark eyes like holes poked in a snowbank. The eyes were expressionless, watchful.

"Good to meet you," Brian said.

Garcia nodded.

"Before we get started, could you please show me a photo ID?" Brian said.

Garcia's face tightened like a clenched fist. "What?" When Brian didn't respond, Garcia slowly extracted a black nylon wallet from his right front pants pocket. He thumbed it open , slipped an Illinois driver's license out and tossed it on the desk. As he did so, a scrap of paper fluttered out like a white moth. A draft of air from the open window caught it and it came to rest near Brian's feet.

Brian picked up the slip of paper. It was a receipt from a dry cleaning establishment named Goldner's located on the north side. He quickly glanced at the back, which showed a telephone number in blue ink. He memorized the number and handed the receipt to Garcia. Neither man commented on the cleaning chit. Brian carefully examined the driver's license, which was current. He handed it back to Garcia.

"Where have you been working?" Brian asked.

"Here and there in Chicago. Some projects for the city"

"Contractor?"

"Yep."

"Got a CV?"

"I texted it to you before I got here."

Brian picked up his phone and found the message from ten minutes ago. A two-page Word doc attachment showed Garcia had spent seven years in the U.S. Navy after high school in Chicago, and that he'd been a Seal. Bachelor's in computer science from DePaul. The document indicated Garcia's recent work as a security consultant with the City of Chicago, ending late the previous year. Listed accomplishments included organizing a fresh security team at City Hall, recruiting the new Mayor's bodyguards and managing implementation of security improvements to the city's computer systems. There were bullet points outlining previous client work, all of it with local corporations. Whatever else this guy was, he apparently had connections at City Hall. Brian finished reading and looked up.

"There's a gap between your Navy service and the client work."

Garcia nodded. "Well, I had a number of consulting clients. The city's the largest and most recent."

"Okay. But according to your bio, that ended months ago. What's your current work?"

"I've been taking a little personal time, weighing opportunities and so forth."

"You have references I can check?"

"I don't get why you're screening me. I've got a perfect skill set for Sands. I'm a proven entity. I feel like we're wasting time here."

"Well, I've known Mr. Sands for a couple of years. He's paying me to check you out before he takes you on. You may not like it, but here we are."

"I'll text you three names. That it?"

"Any other information you'd like to provide? Any questions about the opportunity with Mr. Sands?"

"I know security inside out. Corporate, individual, commercial, residential, you name it. I'm a former Navy Seal. I'm trained in close quarters combat." He glared at Brian as if challenging him to comment. "Anything that may arise with Sands, his family or his businesses, I can handle."

"Good to know. I'll call those references. You'll no doubt hear from Sands before long, one way or the other."

Garcia got to his feet. "You got any other questions, text me, bro." He was out the door quickly, moving as fluidly as a cat. Brian listened as his feet padded down the stairway to street level.

Brian had not had a chance to discuss the kidnapping of Barbara Hardy and the need for implementing security measures to prevent such an event in the future. After a few minutes, his phone dinged: the text from Garcia with three names and phone numbers. Brian sighed. Then he started calling.

Chapter 31

The references were mixed. Corporations had become very cautious about discussing former employees or outside contractors. Worried about exposure from possible lawsuits, they'd become close-mouthed. Verifying only dates of employment and titles were the preferred response to a reference request these days. Sometimes, a company rep would answer additional questions. With the first two places Brian called, the person said that Garcia had worked as a consultant for specified periods of time and that he'd been a competent professional. Per company policy, they could provide nothing further.

On the third call, after a bit of gentle prodding, the woman on the phone, a mid-level HR person with the City of Chicago said, "The guy's probably a fan of Robert DeNiro movies."

"What do you mean?" Brian asked.

"You know that character, the cabbie in Taxi Driver?"

"Yeah."

"Well, this Garcia, he's kinda like that. Got a chip on his shoulder. Projects an attitude. 'You talking to me?'"

"Hmm. So, he pissed people off on the job?"

"Well…our policy is never to say anything negative in a reference check. Legal department, you know."

"Got it. You've been very helpful."

Brian went online and checked Garcia's military record through a specialty database. The dates and ranks jibed, but Garcia had exited the Seals abruptly. Still, the discharge had been "honorable." He did the usual search for a criminal record through another subscription database and found nothing. Search engines revealed several news stories mentioning Garcia, mainly his working as a security consultant for the city. Nothing noteworthy. He seemed to have no presence on social media.

Brian was dubious about Garcia as security man for Sands. Impressive credentials, but an abrasive personality. He was still curious about the guy. He made one more phone call, this one to his old friend Dick Cissel at the Chicago Police Department. Cissel was known as the Bird Man, or just plain Bird. Brian and Cissel had grown up together in the Wrigley Field neighborhood and had been dorm roommates in college. Though their respective career paths had diverged, they'd kept in touch over the years. Cissel had risen steadily through the ranks at the CPD and was now in charge of homicide investigations for the Loop area and the north side of the city. They'd last spoken during the Belcoe corruption case the previous year.

After some bantering, Brian got down to business. "You know an Andrew Garcia, security consultant for the city of Chicago?"

"I know of him from a friend with the city. Haven't met him, but I understand he's kind of a jackass. But they say he did okay on that city job, considering."

"What do you mean 'considering?'"

"Mayor hired him, apparently because he had some juice with the administration. You know how that works."

"Yeah, I do."

"Anyway, the guy latched onto a plum contract to re-organize City of Chicago security systems. Had new software developed by somebody in Washington D. C. and got it installed in the various departments. He's got some connection to the government, I heard. Some hush-hush agency, maybe? Got the city into a huge deal for upgrading cameras and recording devices. Millions in contracts awarded with the usual mix of competitive bidding, cronyism and nepotism. From what I hear, this Garcia stayed hands off, delegated everything to the mayor's staff. Didn't actually do a hell of a lot but made a bundle and abandoned ship before much of it got implemented. City's still sorting it out, with the help of—wait for it—another high-priced outside consultant."

"Reminds me of the definition of a consultant: someone who borrows your watch, tells you the time and then bills you for it."

Cissel grunted.

"So, basically, Mr. Garcia is competent, but hands off and a bit of a dick?" Brian said.

"That's about it. Sometimes guys like that make out okay. One in a long line of seagulls."

"Seagulls?"

"Yep. Guys who swoop in, dump shit all over everything and fly out again. Anyway, why are you interested in this particular bird?"

"My client, Art Sands, is considering the guy for bodyguarding and security for his businesses."

"Hell, why doesn't he just hire you for the job?"

"He's got me looking for the dirtbags that kidnapped his ex-wife. That's enough for now."

"Oh yeah, I read about that. She came back unharmed, the news reports said. But anybody who goes through what she did, they're gonna be scarred. So, how're you doing on it so far?"

"Well, let's just say I'm confident. The kidnappers were not very sophisticated. The assignment means spending some time in Montana, where the ex lives. Which is fine by me, since Darcy's in grad school in Bozeman now. And I kinda like being out there anyway."

"Sounds like a paid vacation. Tell Darcy I said hello."

Brian then Googled the phone number he'd seen on the back of Garcia's dry cleaning receipt. The area code turned out to be Arlington County, Virginia, just outside of Washington, D.C. He knew that Arlington contained the Pentagon and a slew of other federal government agencies. Interesting. There was no other information online about the phone number. One way to find out—he called the number. It rang ten times. He was about to give up when a rough male voice said, "Yeah?"

"Hello?"

"Who is this?"

"Garcia."

Long pause. Your voice has changed, Garcia. Why's that?"

"Got a cold,"

"Nice try, pal." CLICK.

Brian wondered whether the guy who'd just hung up on him had actually recognized the difference in voices or whether he'd employed voice recognition software. Either way, it seemed like a dead end, for now.

He glanced at the time on his phone. A little after eleven. He'd better get moving. He was supposed to meet James St. Clair outside Wrigley Field at noon. James had box seat tickets for the game against the Cardinals.

Brian walked the three blocks up Clark to the ballpark. He'd grown up in the Lakeview neighborhood, what the real estate folks now called "Wrigleyville." The old neighborhood had reflected the makeup of the ballclub back then—about a third White, a third Black and a third Latino. A significant contingent of gays now called the neighborhood home. A string of gay bars lined North Halsted. Some people now called the neighborhood "Boys Town." With rapid gentrification, the area near the ballpark was attaining a paler complexion and becoming more affluent. Still, dozens of ethnic restaurants lined the surrounding streets, offerings from Afghanistan to Zimbabwe. As he worked his way through the sidewalk-spanning crowd, he thought of the changes over the last few years. Rents and home lot prices had soared. Many of the old two-flats had been razed for multi-unit luxury condos fetching upward of a million bucks per unit. He figured he'd be kicked out of his own apartment eventually when it was acquired by a condo developer as a tear-down. But meanwhile, this was an afternoon to have some fun…with a little business mixed in.

James was waiting beneath the huge red and white marquee sign dominating the wall of the venerable ballpark at the corner of Clark and Addison. The sign read in script letters: WRIGLEY FIELD - HOME OF CHICAGO CUBS.

Below was a rectangular electronic panel reading, CUBS VS CARDINALS TODAY 12:20 P.M. A lifelong Cubs fan, Brian knew the sign had been erected in 1934, modified over the years and remained a nostalgic symbol of Chicago major league baseball.

Stocky, dark-skinned, in a crisp white shirt with open collar, FBI Special Agent James St. Clair looked like what he was, one of thousands of office workers playing hooky at the ballpark. A grin split his face below his dark shades when he recognized Brian. They closed the distance between them and grabbed hands, ending up in a quick man-hug. "Got-damn, looks like that mountain man lifestyle agrees with you," James said.

"And being a newlywed sure as hell suits you, buddy," Brian replied. James just smiled.

They found their seats in a reserved box section between home plate and first base. "Best seats I've ever had," James remarked.

"How'd you snag them?"

"Guy owes me. Season ticket holder. When he can't get away, I'm on his short list. Lucky for you, today's one of those days. And I've been working so many hours, they won't begrudge me taking the afternoon off."

They purchased Vienna Beef ballpark franks and Old Style beers from vendors roving the stands. The string bean beer man was nearly seven feet tall and looked a lot like former Chicago Bulls basketball great, Scotty Pippen. Brian reflected that many Chicago taverns had large Old Style signs out front with the beer's emblem above the words "COLD BEER," "CERVEZA FRIA," or "ZIMNY PIWO," depending on the neighborhood. Sadly, in recent years, the easy-drinking lager had been largely supplanted. Chicago's current best seller was a Mexican import, Modelo Especial. The real shocker was the current prices at the ballpark—a beer went for over ten bucks and a hot dog for six.

The game began. The Cubs went down quickly, three easy outs in the first inning. The Cardinals scored three on a walk, an error and a home run in the bottom of the first. Brian and James exchanged knowing glances. This was already shaping up as one of those hopeless games.

"Ya know, I thought about you couple days ago when I got an update about your old pals, the criminals of Belcoe Corporation."

"I wouldn't call them pals. But what's going on?"

"That corrupt son of a bitch Massey was pardoned by the governor and released from prison. We're keeping tabs on him."

"How do you suppose he managed the pardon."

"Rumor has it he made a donation to the guv's PAC. No way to verify that, since there's no reporting requirement. Dark money. Free speech according to some."

"What about the others indicted for insider trading? I've kinda tuned out Belcoe since last year."

"All four convicted. Sentencing a joke: a few months in minimum security."

"VP Operations, Gutman was one of them, right?"

"Yep. Along with Nancy Northfield, Investor Relations; Ray Hunter, Sales chief and your favorite, Liz Wheaton of HR. Oh, and Akbar was convicted on kidnapping and illegal firearms charges . He'll be in the Marion penitentiary for ten to twenty."

"What about the company's accounting staff?"

"Nobody was charged. The D.A. concentrated on the big fish. The bean-counters all played the 'I was following orders' card."

As Brian was about to reply, serendipity weighed in. He caught a glimpse of a former young Belcoe accountant and friend of his niece Darcy, Natalie Katz. She was returning to a reserved seat in the outfield lower deck to their right. She happened to look up and their eyes met. He waved. She waved back with curled fingers and then immediately concentrated on her phone.

At the seventh inning stretch, Brian checked his phone and was surprised to see a message from Natalie. He looked over to the seat where he'd seen her earlier in the game, but she was gone. The message read: "Hi. Seeing U reminded me how U helped me big time at that place I worked. Can I buy you coffee? Soon? Please."

The message made him wonder if something was wrong. He knew from Darcy that Natalie had lost her job abruptly when Belcoe went bankrupt in the wake of financial fraud and other crimes by its top executives. The company's stock had been delisted and the employees all terminated. Brian texted her back and suggested meeting the next morning at the Nook Café, nine A.M. She accepted by return text.

James noticed Brian's unease. "Something wrong?" he said.

"I just got a text from Natalie Katz. Remember her?"

"Yeah, young number cruncher, friend of Darcy's. That turd Massey harassed her, right?"

"Yep. She wants to meet with me. Hope it's nothing bad."

"Yeah, she deserves a break."

"More important, when're ya gonna buy the next round of dogs and beers?"

The Cubs' built up a lead in the middle innings and blew it in the ninth, losing nine to eight. They lingered in their seats, allowing some of the departing crowd to thin out. They sat in comfortable silence, people-watching. Finally, they left the ballpark and emerged into the late afternoon breeze coming in off Lake Michigan. The temperature had dropped about ten degrees.

The two friends found a sunny spot to stand and talk away from the ballpark. James said, "I'm curious about that Natalie. If it's Belcoe-related, let me know, will ya? It's still my case. Lotsa followup, pending charges, possible new ones."

"Those creeps should serve their full sentences and then some. But there'll be paroles and good behavior credits. You keeping out of trouble?" Brian was referring to James' penchant for occasional strained relations with the bureaucrats above him in the rigid hierarchy of the FBI Chicago Field Office.

"Doin' fine. Received an 'outstanding' evaluation last month. Getting good assignments. They halfta keep the minority agent stats up. But I'm nobody's fuckin' token. Anyway, all's dopesthetic."

"Good. By the way, when's J. Edgar going to retire?"

"Man's got another couple years. How that douchebag survives I'll never understand."

They shook hands and split up. Brian knew James would be on his way home to his lovely new wife. He was alone now with no plans for the evening. He got his phone out and clicked on Michelle Emerson's number.

Chapter 32
(Day 9)

The morning crowd at the Nook was light. Brian sat in a booth a little before nine, swigging coffee and reading the early edition of the Chicago Tribune on his phone. He seemed to have what James had once called, 'jello brain.' The fogginess no doubt resulted from too much alcohol and not enough sleep the night before. He and Michelle had been out to dinner, including a bottle of excellent pinot noir. Then they'd gone to her Lincoln Park apartment, had a drink and started to make love, but it ended at foreplay. They'd both felt less than enthusiastic. Finally, he'd gone home to his own place, frustrated and disappointed. The feeling had been one of summing up the relationship. Was it played out? Coming to a natural end? He wasn't sure. They hadn't made plans for another get-together. His emotions moved in his head like a swarm of puzzled bees.

He looked out the window at his left, taking in the rich street scene. Harried office workers quick-stepped past, late for work. A constant stream of yellow taxis flowed along Halsted. The occasional street denizen, like the stocky man now wobbling by in a black Abe Lincoln hat, blaring boombox on his shoulder. The rap beat from oversized speakers made the window glass shake as the guy paused and peered into the café. He nodded at Brian and sauntered on his way along the sidewalk, the thumping beat receding in his wake.

Natalie Katz appeared at seven minutes past the hour. The young dark-haired woman strode to the booth as Brian stood. They came together in a brief arms and shoulders hug.

Natalie said, "Thanks for making time. I know you've got plenty of other things to do." Her clothing was fashionable: tailored jeans, leather boots, slouchy blouse. But her manner seemed reticent.

"That's all right. I'm not on a schedule," Brian said. "What are you up to these days?"

"Well, I've got a new job with AXC Beverage. General accountant in charge of consolidations and special projects. They're in the Loop."

"How are you able to get away from this new job? I mean, you were at the Cubs game yesterday and now you're here. Don't you work regular office hours?"

"I work from home quite a bit. A lot of it at night. They don't care, as long as the work gets done. I go into the office when I need to meet with my staff or my boss. A lot of what I do is spreadsheet analysis."

"Wish I'd had that flexibility with the FBI. When I was on the job I was *at* the job."

"The pandemic had some effect. The company has fewer people onsite at any given time. We timeshare cubicles, which cuts office rent costs."

"Sounds good. But I know you didn't get me here to talk office efficiency."

"You're right." She sighed. "I've gotta let you know about something." She looked around for possible eavesdroppers.

Brian waited. Finally, she said, "I saw Massey yesterday. Shocked me. I'm like, isn't that guy in prison?"

"Should be. He drew a five-year sentence but got pardoned after only one. Sometimes, justice really *is* blind."

"I know, right?"

"When did you see him?"

"Around noon yesterday, I'm walking up the 600 block of north Michigan Avenue when I see this familiar-looking tall guy stepping along, all dressed up. Looked like he did last time I saw him in court: smug, self-absorbed. But skinnier."

"You think he saw you?"

"That's the thing. He might have. Actually, I think he *did* see me. He happened to look my way just as I spotted him. Creeped me out. Since then, I've felt like I've got a duck water-skiing in my stomach."

"Say he *did* see you, so what? The guy's got plenty of other things to worry about. There are civil charges against him and his fellow crooks still pending. The FBI is still investigating him and his pals. No doubt, he's got a high-priced lawyer on retainer. You're probably the farthest thing from his mind."

She looked doubtful. "He's the most vindictive person I've ever met. A twisted jerk. Vengeance would be a priority for him. I gave a deposition on the financial fraud he carried out. He knows that."

"But—"

"And it's not just me. He no doubt hates you. And Darcy. I mean, you guys helped put the scumbag behind bars as much as anybody did."

Brian knew she was right. Massey and others who'd abetted him would have reason to blame the McKays for their predicament. They'd blame anyone but themselves, he figured. "Well, I guess it makes sense to be alert. But hell, you're what, twenty-four years old? Educated, attractive, got a great job in one of the liveliest cities anywhere. Enjoy it while you can. Don't be looking over your shoulder. Life's short."

"Yes, Dad." Her face reddened "Sorry, that was snide. I know you're just trying to get me on my tracks. I wonder, could you look into this Massey uh, situation, maybe find out what he's doing? I want to stay as far away from him as possible. I can pay you."

Brian considered her request. "Okay, I'll check him out. I'll be in town for a day or two. But there's no need to compensate me. I'm curious about this dipstick, since Darcy and I both have an interest. I'll let you know what I find."

"Thanks." She stood. "Tell Darcy I said Hi."

After she'd gone, Brian summoned the veteran waiter, Harold, and ordered another mug of coffee.

Then he got online and googled Massey. There were stories about the governor's pardon, but not much else. No clue as to his whereabouts. Next, Brian pulled up a list of the top luxury hotels in Chicago. Not surprisingly, most of the hotels were on or within a couple of blocks of the Magnificent Mile on Michigan Avenue, north of the Chicago River. He decided to try to locate a whiff of Massey by judicious phone calls. Not much probability of success, but a minimal investment of time. He got the phone numbers for the Peninsula, St. Regis, Ritz Carlton and the Waldorf Astoria. His first call was to the Peninsula Hotel. Luck was with him.

"Hello, Mr. Pelton calling for a guest there, a Mr. Hamilton Massey," Brian said.

"One moment, please." A pause of a minute, then, "I am not able to connect you with Mr. Massey. Would you like to leave a message for him?"

"No, thanks. I'll try again later. By the way, what was his room number. I seem to have forgotten—"

"I'm sorry, Sir. We cannot divulge guests' room numbers."

"Thanks again." Click.

Brian was amazed that the person answering the Peninsula's phone would let on that a named individual was a guest. His hunch had paid off, though. He figured Massey would find one of the most luxurious and expensive hotels in the city as a temporary roosting spot. The guy no doubt had plenty of money squirreled away. James had mentioned that Massey's palatial North Shore house had been sold as partial payment of the fines he'd been assessed, after he'd entered prison a year earlier.

Chapter 33

After leaving Brian McKay's office, Garcia regretted being testy. But he had a short fuse, had always been that way. He flat out hated to be judged by people he considered his inferiors. Which was just about everyone else on Earth. He had to admit though, McKay had acted professional. The guy had respectable experience. He hoped he hadn't screwed up too bad with the ex-FBI agent.

The thing was, he wanted the gig with Arthur Sands to get himself in place to accomplish the mission he'd been assigned. He'd been given a lot of leeway. He could step over the line of legality without judgement or blame, they'd told him. On the other hand, if he were caught, they'd disavow knowing him.

And one other important condition, true of all undercover operations: he could not personally profit from any ill-gotten gains. So, he would not be in for a big payday unless he arranged it on the side. He had a couple of ideas in that regard. The agreed upon remuneration as an outside contractor (oral agreement, nothing in writing, of course) provided for a few thousand dollars and the possibility of a powerful position in D.C., nothing guaranteed. Because of his business success to date, he had enough assets to tide him over for a couple of years.

An additional challenge was that much of his work ahead would be in Montana, a place he'd never been and had no desire to visit. Unfamiliar territory. And he'd likely have to depend on amateurs, people he didn't know, in fact had not met. His own considerable expertise could easily be undermined by those amateurs fucking things up. He'd have to make the best of a tricky situation.

That afternoon, Garcia received a phone call from Arthur Sands. The man told him he would not be hired as security chief after all. Sands hadn't given a reason other than he didn't think Garcia was the right fit for the position. When pressed, he'd said it was a possible lack of chemistry, nobody's fault. He didn't say, but Garcia suspected that McKay had eighty-sixed him.

He felt ambivalent. The mission in Montana would have been much easier under cover of working for Sands. But he'd find a way.

The more Garcia thought about it, the angrier he got at McKay. He was not one to let a wrong go unpunished. He believed in the old maxim in Chicago politics: *Don't get mad. Get even.* But he didn't want to go overboard. After all, not getting the Sands job was only a minor inconvenience. So his response to McKay's actions would be proportional, nothing more or less.

He had gathered some intel on McKay before their recent meeting. Now, he took inventory of the levers he could use on the ex-agent. He knew where McKay's office was. Couldn't find a home address online. Knew that McKay had a niece in college at Montana State University and a lawyer girlfriend working for a big Loop law firm, Coleman Davenport. Sands said he had hired McKay to find the businessman's ex-wife's kidnappers. That meant McKay would be returning to Montana soon. He knew some people who could fill him in on any other vulnerabilities McKay might have. Garcia was a firm believer that information is power.

Garcia boarded his black Dodge Challenger and motored over to McKay's PI office on north Dearborn Street in the River North neighborhood. The big V-8 rumbled as he backed into a curbside parking space a couple of doors from the renovated brick building. With a partial view of the building's main entrance, he settled in to wait.

As he sat in his car, Garcia mulled over his deal with the government. He'd been told by his contact in D.C. to expect to be approached by a man named Hamilton Massey. The contact said they'd planted the seed by telling Massey that Garcia was capable and motivated to help the ex-con get revenge on McKay. Massey had been convicted of financial crimes, a former executive in Chicago who had filed for bankruptcy before going to prison a year earlier. As part of his sentence, he had paid fines and made partial restitution to stockholders who'd lost money due to his fraud. Apparently penniless, he'd been locked up.

Massey had recently been released and had somehow managed to purchase a lavish home in Montana, not far from Yellowstone National Park. The government was investigating Massey's personal finances. They'd learned he'd become involved with a potentially lucrative Montana real estate development called the Paradise Preserve. Massey had also been making inquiries about rare dinosaur fossil bones. Bottom line: Massey had obtained substantial funding, likely from international sources.

If approached by Massey, Garcia was to appear reluctant to work with him but to ultimately agree. If he had not heard from Massey in the next two weeks, Garcia was to contact Massey and do whatever was necessary to bring his illegal sources of funds to light. He should also help Massey carry out any nonviolent crime proposed by the former executive. Ideally, Garcia would find a way to entrap him.

Chapter 34

In his small office, Brian caught up with email, spoke with a couple of clients and handled paperwork related to a false claim for disability benefits by a completely able-bodied man. Routine, boring work, but it paid the bills. A sole proprietor, Brian handled his own clerical duties, with no need for an administrative assistant. Low overhead meant he'd been able to make a living on his own ever since leaving his job as a Special Agent with the FBI two years earlier. By late afternoon, he was caught up. There was nothing important claiming his attention. He packed his laptop into his nylon briefcase, clicked off the lights and locked the door behind himself.

Descending from the second floor to street level, Brian approached the entry door to the redbrick office building. As was his habit, he peered through the small glass panel, checking the surroundings outside before opening the door. This practice had saved his life three years earlier when an irate ex-husband of a client had waited outside with a .38 revolver, intent on putting a bullet in Brian's head. Brian had shoved the door open forcefully, hitting the would-be killer in the shoulder, causing him to drop his weapon on the floor. He kneed the man in the crotch, incapacitating him, and then held him while he called the cops. They cuffed the guy and took him away. Brian completed a police report and agreed to be a witness for a charge of breaking and entering and possession of an illegal firearm. Later, he testified in court against the guy, who'd been found guilty and sentenced to four years in the state prison system. With possible parole, the man might be out by now.

As he reached the sidewalk, Brian noticed a sleek black two-door car at the curb a few doors south. He recognized the make and model: Dodge Challenger, a retro-styled muscle car. He'd seen it earlier that afternoon as well, when he'd glanced out his office window before meeting with Andrew Garcia. The car's windows were deep-tinted, so the interior was not visible. He focused on the front license plate of the dark vehicle: standard Illinois issue, light background with two letters and five numbers. He committed them to memory. Then he left the building and made his way to the parking garage next door.

Rolling onto Wabash, Brian checked his mirrors. He kept watch as he drove north. At first, nothing caught his eye. Then, at Division Street, he spotted the fender of a low black car three vehicles behind him. He continued north, keeping to the speed limit of 35 miles per hour. The black car stayed a consistent few lengths behind. By the time he'd reached Belmont, traffic had lightened. The black car was only separated from his Jeep by one other vehicle, a diminutive blue Mazda Miata roadster. The Challenger was clearly visible now over the top of the Miata. The driver was a male with dark hair and sunglasses. Could it be Andrew Garcia? Yes, it could. No need to have the police run the license plate after all. Was Garcia that sloppy at tailing? Perhaps the guy wanted Brian to know he was being tailed, for the harassment factor.

Brian drove into the alley next to his apartment building. No other vehicle in sight. He manually opened his overhead garage door and drove in, scrutinizing his mirrors all the way. Nothing unusual. He finished parking, walked out and pulled the door closed. As he locked the door with the small key, he mused that he ought to get the landlord to install a remote control garage door operating system.

As he removed his hand from the door handle, a loud CRACK came from nearby. A split second later, a cloud of brick fragments and dust showered onto the ground next to his left foot. A bullet had drilled into the brick side wall of the garage building, around the corner, a few feet away. Brian dropped to the ground, going to a prone position. He swung his head back and forth, alert to any movement. A second gunshot sounded, followed by a CLANG as a round pierced a nearby garbage can. After a waiting a full minute, Brian cautiously low-crawled away from the direction of fire. He got to his feet and listened carefully but heard nothing other than the rapid thudding of his heart and the normal city sounds—traffic and distant voices. He peered around the corner of the alley into the long narrow space illuminated by a mercury vapor streetlight. Nothing out of place, all the way to the end of the alley at the intersecting street.

Brian was curious. He retrieved a flashlight from his vehicle in the garage and went back out to the alley and looked around at the redbrick walls and at the gritty concrete surface of the alley pavement. The wall showed a pockmark about shoulder height where the dull red was a brighter color. The divot was about an inch in diameter. Three galvanized steel garbage cans were lined up against the brick wall. On the ground near the middle can was a misshapen gray object. He picked it up and examined it under the flashlight beam. A spent bullet, turned into a random grey lump of lead by the brick it had struck. Must have bounced off the wall and landed on the ground.

He moved the garbage cans away from the brick wall. On the concrete alley surface a nearly intact bullet lay. There was a hole on one side of the leftmost trash can. He rotated the can and found a matching exit hole on the other side. The bullet must have gone through the can, which was full of garbage, slowing its velocity, but not deforming it. He pocketed both the smashed slug and its more intact counterpart. He walked to the street at the far end of the alley. Nobody around, nothing unusual along the brick walls or concrete alley surface. No ejected shell casings on the ground. The report of the weapon had sounded like a handgun. He knew that, if a revolver had been fired, there would be no shells, but that with an auto, they'd be ejected to the ground. In which case, the shooter would have to have picked them up. He guessed it had been a revolver. The two shots had been fired in the dark and the shooter fled quickly, probably not having the time to search for and retrieve shells.

Back in his apartment, Brian dialed 911 and reported the shooting incident. About twenty minutes later, a CPD patrol car with flashing blue lights but no siren double parked in front of his apartment building. He took them back to the alley and described what had occurred. The cops listened without interruption to his account of the shots fired. Brian handed over the two bullets, which the younger cop bagged and tagged as evidence.

"Shoulda left the slug on the ground," the older man said.

"Yeah, you're right."

They asked a few questions and had Brian complete a written police report. They thanked Brian and left, with a promise to follow up. But, as Brian knew, without any damage to persons or property and no leads other than the bullets, there might not be much of an investigation.

Brian grabbed some leftover Chinese and a beer from the fridge. There wasn't much else in there. The gunshots in the alley worried him. They might have been strays, some gangbangers letting off steam, maybe. But he'd made a number of enemies over the years. The most recent, he figured, was Andrew Garcia. But would a successful consultant, a former Seal, go around Chicago, shooting at people he didn't like? Probably not.

Garcia's military experience had ingrained in him the philosophy that you eat and pee when you have the chance. Moreover, you should be reasonably rested whenever possible. So he grabbed a Greek salad at a small cafe, then went to his nearby apartment. There, he sat and had a glass of water, alcohol being a no-no in his rigorously healthful diet. An inane "reality" show played on the large TV screen before him in his large living room, but he paid it no heed.

His cell phone rang. Unknown number. He picked up.

"Mr. Garcia, we haven't met, but—" The male speaker's voice was reedy, with a trace of an accent.

"Hey, pal, I don't have time for—"

"Garcia, if you would just shut the fuck up." Now, there was steel in the voice. "My name is Hamilton Massey. I am the former CFO of Belcoe Corporation. I believe we have a common interest."

"What makes you think so?" Garcia said. "If you're the Massey I'm remembering, you were convicted of financial fraud and sent to prison. Is that where you're calling from?" Garcia recalled the instruction to be reluctant with Massey. He knew how to play hard to get.

"I am no longer incarcerated. And the common interest is Brian McKay. He meddled in my professional life as I designed and implemented state of the art financial systems that maximized shareholder value."

"The way I understand it, he exposed massively fraudulent financial reporting and you were then charged and found guilty on numerous counts. That about right?"

"I was the victim of overzealous regulatory prosecution on technicalities."

"Right. So, what's our common interest?"

"McKay prevented you from being employed by Arthur Sands. You are no happier about that than I am about the matters I just mentioned."

Garcia was surprised that anyone knew about the Sands deal. "How do you know this?"

"I have sources close to Mr. Sands. More important, we need to talk in person."

"All right. When and where?"

"The bar at the Omni Hotel. 676 North Michigan Avenue. Nine P.M. this evening." Massey was careful to set the meeting at a place near to but not at his own hotel, the Peninsula. He didn't want Garcia to know where he was staying.

"How will I recognize you?" Garcia said.

"I am tall. Someone once said I resemble the actor Tim Robbins. I will be attired in a black suit and a hat."

"Swell. I'll be there."

Garcia terminated the call with a jab of his finger. Based on his vocabulary and diction, Massey sounded as if his IQ might exceed his shoe size. Worth finding out.

Garcia jumped off the couch and did his usual multiple sets of pushups, crunches, dumbbell curls and presses and ended with a deliberate set of tai chi movements.

Chapter 35

After eating, Brian took the El down to the Chicago Avenue station. From there, it was a three block walk to the Peninsula Hotel. He set up an observation post sitting on a bench in the small public park near the landmark Water Tower. The spot afforded him a good view of the main entrance of the Peninsula, which was brightly lit. The temperature remained in the seventies in the early evening. He stayed alert, generally keeping his eyes on the hotel and occasionally scanning his surroundings. Tourists filed by, snapping pictures of the landmark buildings, taking selfies, slurping ice cream cones and generally having a good time. He envied them.

Garcia drove the Challenger down Michigan Avenue to Huron Street and into the parking garage at the Omni Hotel a half hour before the agreed upon time for meeting Massey. Inside, he walked past the posh-looking hotel bar without breaking stride. He'd mastered the technique of surreptitiously observing a room without being obvious. There was no one in the bar except the bartender and a couple conversing quietly at a table near the door. The square tables each had place settings for four, except the ones in the back, that were bare, no doubt meant for drinking. He guessed that was where he'd meet Massey. He took up a post in the lobby, sitting in an upholstered chair with a copy of the alternative newspaper, the *Chicago Reader* in front of his face.

Brian had almost given up on spotting Massey. But then, at 8:43 P.M., he had emerged from the Peninsula Hotel entrance, looked both directions and set out on Michigan Avenue. Brian slipped into heavy pedestrian traffic behind the former CFO and followed him as he walked to another nearby hotel, the Omni on Superior, just off Michigan. Massey entered the building. Brian stayed back for a moment.

Around nine P.M. Garcia noticed a tall stork-like man in a black suit and gray hat that looked like a prop from the 1940s movie *The Maltese Falcon* entering the lobby and heading for the bar. Garcia waited a couple of minutes and then got up and went in. The tall guy had snagged a table in the far corner and sat facing the entrance.

Garcia walked straight to the table and took a seat. He stared into the man's face. The guy looked a little nervous. About fifty years old. Pale complexion, skinny and not especially healthy looking.

The guy spoke, "I am Hamilton Massey. I take it you are Mr. Garcia?"

"In the flesh."

"As I mentioned on the phone, we have some things to discuss. I'm going to order a drink. Would you care for one?"

"I guess we'd better order something so we can hang onto the table." Garcia glanced around to make sure they were out of earshot of anyone else.

Garcia flagged down the bartender. The man came over and they ordered: Glenlivet neat for Massey and a mineral water for Garcia. They did not speak until the drinks were delivered and the barman had retreated to his spot behind the bar.

Brian entered the Omni's lobby in his makeshift disguise: a Cubs cap and wraparound sunglasses. Not much camouflage, but it would have to do. He scanned the lobby. No sign of Massey. He approached the bar entrance and glanced in as he walked by. Two men sat at a table in the back. Talk about strange bedfellows—it looked like Massey and Andrew Garcia, engrossed in conversation. Brian hovered outside the bar, out of view of the two men. He could not hear what they were saying.

Garcia trained his dark eyes on Massey. The thousand yard stare. "Cut to the chase. What's this about?" Garcia said.

"I am a world-class financial innovator. As a result, I have certain resources—"

"If you're so damned innovative, how'd you end up at East Moline? For that matter, how the hell did you get out?"

Massey blinked. "The person who committed actual crimes was a Vice President, now deceased. The alleged financial irregularities, though minor technicalities, ensnared several of us. This was largely the result of McKay's investigation. In any case, the governor recently decided to pardon me and here I am."

"How much did that cost? Ah, never mind. Where do I come into this sad story?"

"I understand Arthur Sands meant to hire you for a position as security director. He tasked McKay with screening you before making an offer. McKay did so and Sands decided against hiring you."

"How do you know all this, anyway?"

"I have a contact, an employee at Sands's ranch in Montana. Sands has been staying there recently. My contact has installed listening devices in Sands's office, his living quarters, his vehicle and even the patio where he spends a fair amount of time, lolling about in indolence."

"So, you heard that McKay is why I didn't get the job?"

"That is correct. And like you, I am not favorably disposed toward Mr. Sands. He is a vulgar person with more wealth than he deserves. In fact, I have—"

"You've already done him some harm, I take it. Let me see, what could that be? I don't suppose you had anything to do with the kidnapping of his ex-wife?"

Massey raised an eyebrow. "Do not make assumptions, Mr. Garcia."

"Yeah, yeah. So, you hate McKay and Sands, right? You got a proposition?"

"In fact, I do. We can combine forces to, as they say, kill two birds with a single stone."

Massey laid out a plan whereby he would provide the financing and Garcia would carry out an operation on the Sands ranch. There would be assistance from a pair of brothers, one of whom worked there. They discussed tactics, timing and an action plan. Bottom line: a sizable sum of money would be realized on the theft of a certain rare item to be turned over to Massey. Garcia's compensation would be a million. Should he agree to it, Garcia would eliminate the McKays and be paid an additional two million.

Garcia, though wary, agreed in principle to Massey's plans. He wasn't sure about killing the McKays. He'd have to give it some thought. As for the theft, perhaps there might be the chance for personal profit despite the government's ill-gotten gains rule. "Okay, let's get it done."

"I expect McKay will be returning to Montana soon," Massey said. "He is charged with investigating the recent kidnapping of Barbara Hardy. He will also be serving temporarily as primary security operative for Sands. You will need to travel there and quietly set up the operations we discussed. You can stay on the property of one of the local contacts I mentioned. There is a guest cabin and surrounding acreage, a wood cutting lot of some sort. I will make the arrangements."

"All right. I'll surveil McKay while I put the elements in place. He won't know I'm around until it's too late. But what about you? What are you doing?"

"Don't worry. I'm accomplishing things that will enrich both of us."

Despite this agreement with Massey, Garcia planned on pursuing only his own personal interests, as circumstances dictated. Most important was the assignment from the shadow people in Washington. It would be tricky, but he'd handle it. He recalled the Navy Seals unofficial motto: "The only easy day was yesterday."

Chapter 36
(Day 10)

Arthur Sands and Barbara Hardy sat side by side in heavy Adirondack chairs on the stone-surfaced patio outside the large log house. A few miles to the east, the Crazy Mountains grazed the clouds at elevations exceeding 11,000 feet. Snow fields dotted the upper reaches of the jagged granite peaks. Barbara raised her binoculars and studied an alpine bowl near the top of Crazy Peak.

"I see mountain goats up there," she said, pointing at a spot near the summit of the mountain.

"Clean your glasses. Those are white rocks." her ex-husband said.

Their friendly banter continued for a few minutes. Then Sands said, "You know, I'm thinking of spending more time here, maybe make it my base. I can work remotely and travel whenever I need to for business."

"Wow. I've got to say I'm surprised. What brought that on?"

"I love it here. I still need to be in Chicago quite a bit, but I've been thinking of making this my main residence."

She hesitated, then smiled. "And you'll keep the Chicago place, right?"

"Of course. So, what do you think of my spending more time here?"

"Fine by me. I mean, you've been more than generous, letting me live here the last two years. The things that split us apart have become less important in my mind. I feel we've grown closer since we've been together here this time."

"Same with me. And as time zips by, I'm more conscious of quality of life. Money's no longer driving me like a slave master. Hell, I couldn't spend my net worth if I lived to be a hundred and ten." He shrugged. "What about you? This a place to call home forever?"

"Well, forever's a long time," she said. "I'm not sure. But I'm content here for now. And, let's just keep on like we have. We're fortunate, you know."

"Yes, I do know. A lot of people would kill to have lives like ours."

Barbara blanched at the word "kill." Her thoughts turned inward. Yes, people do a lot of nasty things. Her recent abduction was proof enough. Money and beautiful surroundings were no defense against evil. "Yes," she said. "I'm sure they would."

"Ah Jeez. I didn't mean—" Sands looked at her face closely. "How are you holding up? I know you went through hell with that kidnapping. Need any help, like a doc or anything?"

"Art, I'm happy, but I'm still scared. You don't know what it's like to be imprisoned and held for days by horrifying people who might kill you at any moment. Treated like an inhuman commodity. It scars your psyche. I hear noises sometimes when there's nothing there. See ghosts too, I guess. The other day, I looked out the window and thought I saw a man standing in the yard. It was a deer. I'm not so sure a shrink would put me more at ease. I'll feel better when we have an armed guard with us."

"I'm working on it."

"What happened with that Garcia guy?"

"Turns out his references didn't pan out. Brian checked them and was not impressed. That's despite the City of Chicago giving him a substantial consulting contract."

"So what's the alternative?"

"Well, Brian has agreed to step in temporarily, while he looks for the kidnappers."

"Good. When's he coming out?"

"Soon. He's occupied with some stuff in Chicago right now." Eager to change the subject, he said, "How's your painting coming?"

She noted his abrupt segue. "Pretty good. I'm getting better. I showed my latest oil to Winslow, and he was encouraging."

"He does the whimsical wildlife stuff, right?"

"Yes, but he's also a fine art painter. His work is highly nuanced."

"You've lost me there. But I do like what I've seen of his stuff."

"In any case, he's invited me to a workshop he's conducting in Clarkville next week. It's a two-day class: oil painting landscapes. I plan to go."

"What, stay in town?"

"Yes, at the old Masters Hotel."

"Right on. Sounds like an opportunity."

His slight frown did not match his cheery words. Barbara wondered whether he might be jealous, or worse, worried about her safety while away from him.

"You know, Carol Jensen mentioned Brian," she said. "I saw her in town yesterday. I think she's ah, interested in him. He had dinner with her and her nephew last time he was out. Maybe they'll—"

Sands's phone rang. Brian McKay. He picked up.

"Art, there're a couple of things I've gotta alert you about." He sounded wound up, not the usual calm demeanor. "One, Hamilton Massey is out of prison. The governor pardoned him under suspicious circumstances. Two, this Garcia guy has been tailing me, first to my office and then my apartment. Yesterday, I located Massey holed up at the Peninsula Hotel. I followed him last evening to the Omni on Michigan Avenue. Get this: he goes into the bar and meets with none other than our friend, Mr. Garcia. The two of them sat there conversing like co-conspirators for a half hour."

"Any idea what they talked about?"

"No. Couldn't hear them. I pumped the bartender later, but he said he hadn't heard a thing. But both of those guys are pissed off at me. And neither of them is a fan of you. My guess is that Massey is planning something dodgy and maybe Garcia's involved."

"Well, I appreciate the information. Let me know if you find out anything more. We'll be on alert." He glanced over at Barbara, who was studying the distant mountains through her binoculars.

"One other thing. When I come out, I'll check for hidden listening devices in your living quarters and anywhere else you spend time."

"Good idea."

"Right. I'll be in touch," Brian said.

Josie Wilshire removed her headset. She'd listened to the entire conversation between Sands and his ex-wife, as well as Sands's side of the phone call. She needed to fill in Gus.

Chapter 37

While Darcy was sliding her MacBook into her backpack in the seminar meeting room after class, the rest of the students filed out. She took her time, sensing the seminar leader, Professor Dave Bakeno, wanted to have a word.

"Darcy, your comments were well argued today."

"Thanks."

"There's a special project involving the William Old Horn Dinosaur Museum. Thought you might be well-suited for it, if you're interested."

"Uh, well, I'm kinda slammed right now, with coursework and all."

"This would be part of your classes, actually. You'd work on behalf of the museum in lieu of attending my seminar for the next two weeks. Full class credit, of course. And it entails fieldwork with very high potential for success. *Allosauruses* may be involved." He smiled. "And I've spoken with your professors for your other two classes. They're flexible, said they can email you the course material."

Darcy was intrigued. She'd been fascinated by the massive dinosaur skeleton at the museum since she'd played a key role in finding and preserving the bones two years earlier at Bone Mountain. The opportunity of prospecting for additional bones from the Jurassic period of the Mesozoic era in the *T. rex's* backyard would be hard to turn down. But she didn't want to appear too eager. "What kind of work?" She asked.

"Well, as you know, dinosaur bone distribution tends to be scattered within our region, but with concentrations of specimens in certain localized rock formations. There's a small quarry on the Sands ranch, about a quarter mile from the museum. It's actually a pilot project. If it appears productive, it'll be expanded into a full-scale dig. I helped excavate it and have already explored a bit myself. I've found several intact *Allosaurus* bones in close proximity to the surface. And intriguingly, they are from a number of different individuals. The potential is tremendous. This is all confidential, of course."

"But where do I come in? Do you want me to set up a dig by myself?"

"Not exactly. We'll coordinate with Russell Eagle Feather. I've gotten him started on preliminary location of specimens in a small grid-mapped area. He's already made progress."

"So, it's me and him?"

"Plus myself and Becky Stanton. The four of us will work together. Darcy, this is a fantastic opportunity."

"You've already spoken with Becky?"

"Oh, yes. She's very enthusiastic."

Darcy was a little put out that Bakeno had approached her roommate before herself. She wondered why. Was there something between them? "When would we start?"

"We'll drive over day after tomorrow. The three of us will join Russell onsite."

"I'm in."

That evening. Back in the apartment she shared with Becky, Darcy microwaved a pair of leftover pizza slices and opened a can of Bozone Amber beer. After a few minutes, Becky came in and flopped onto the couch next to Darcy.

"I hope you saved me some of that," Becky said.

Darcy rolled her eyes. "Of course. Whaddaya think I am, a pog?"

Becky disappeared into the kitchen and returned with a couple of pizza slices on a paper plate, along with a can of beer.

"So, did Dave talk with you?" Becky asked.

"Oh, so now it's Dave, not Professor Bakeno?"

"Well, he *is* one of my biggest fans."

"Apparently. Yes, he did finally get around to me," Darcy said. "Seriously, that dig sounds cool. *Allosauruses* all over the place, he says."

"Yep, I'm in need of some fieldwork. Y'know, it's been two years since we closed down that Bone Mountain gig."

"Tell me about it. I'm itching for some major fossil finds. Not that the coursework's been boring but…"

"What's this Russell guy like?"

"Well, I only met him the one time, at the grand opening of the Old Horn Museum. He seemed cool, laid back, kinda sardonic."

"So he's got an attitude?"

"You might say that. Can't blame him, being a Native American. I understand he's got a masters in Native Studies, with Holt as his mentor," Darcy said. "He's been in that E.D. job at the museum since it opened. I wonder how that's working out. Seems like it'd be pretty boring."

"I'd guess. So this temporary fieldwork gig will probably seem like heaven to him."

"Especially with two babes like us along."

Chapter 38

Andrew Garcia flew United to Bozeman, arriving mid-afternoon. He rented a gray Ford Bronco with four wheel drive, pulled up Google Maps on his phone and entered in the location Massey had given him at the Omni bar the previous night. He then drove from Gallatin Field east on I-90 to the small town of Clarkville. From there he headed north on Highway 89, passing through a tiny settlement, little more than a gas station and general store. He noticed a high mountain range to the east. The tops of the peaks were jagged and rocky, pocked with snow, surrounded by clouds. Must be the Crazy Mountains.

He'd grown up in Chicago and traveled quite a bit as a Seal, training at the naval base in Coronado, California and subsequently being deployed to various assignments in Europe and the Middle East. He'd become quite adept at hand-to-hand combat, routinely defeating larger men during the intense Seals training. His last military posting had been as part of a small special operations group fighting ISIS in Afghanistan. He'd killed several enemy combatants via long range rifle shots and one hapless dude with a knife. He felt no remorse. After all, it was either kill or be killed.

Shortly after he returned stateside, to the base at Coronado, he'd gone on a two week leave, home to Chicago.

His parents still lived in a bungalow on the city's near south side, Garcia's childhood home. Another Seal, a buddy from the Chicago area, flew home with him. After the trip, there ensued a flap over whether he'd violated Navy ethics regulations. Apparently, some other Seal, some cocksucking rat, had complained to a superior officer that Garcia had engaged in fraudulent behavior. An internal investigation then uncovered evidence that Garcia had arranged for the fellow that flew to Chicago with him to work as a paid laborer in Garcia's father's construction business while still on the Navy payroll. Garcia was reprimanded and told that his future with the Seals was limited. Though he wasn't fired from the service, the message from his Commander was clear: future promotions would be difficult. He immediately quit in anger. That had been five years ago. He'd landed on his feet and, through connections he'd made in the Seals, had attained a good living as a consultant. He'd lived well in a nice apartment building near Lake Michigan. Now, he was playing a different game. Fortuity and a key insider friend had intervened, and he now found himself a paid contractor to an alphabet agency in Washington D.C.

Other than his military stint, Garcia had always lived in the Midwest. He'd called Chicago home for all his civilian life. A city boy, he'd never had much interest in the American west. His impression now was that he hadn't missed much. The view from the car heading up Highway 89 was mostly pastures containing cows and hayfields to feed the cows. The mountains above looked…unwelcoming.

An hour and a half from Bozeman, he finally reached a gravel lane marked Shields River Road. As directed by the female Google voice, he hung a right and followed the road east. The route climbed steadily as Garcia cautiously steered the Bronco up the middle of the road. The surface held intermittent muddy bogs and puddles. He shifted into four wheel drive high range. There was no traffic, and there were deep ditches on both sides of the road that looked like they'd be hard to get out of, regardless of how capable the vehicle. Garcia had to remain anonymous. The last thing he needed would be to get stuck in a ditch or to be stopped by some local yokel sheriff's deputy. A small river appeared from time to time alongside the road and he crossed it twice on narrow bridges.

About half an hour from the paved highway, he reached an unmarked two track lane where Ms. Google told him to turn left. Doubtful, he stopped the vehicle and studied the map on his phone. After a few minutes of deliberation, he decided this must be it. Massey had described the destination as "off the grid." Garcia made the turn and continued to gain elevation as the rental bumped along through muddy ruts and over rocks and grass. He was damn glad he wasn't driving his sleek Challenger.

Finally, the Google voice chirped "You have reached your destination." The entrance to a faint lane with tire tracks on each side and high field grass in the middle was marked by a lone log fence post. No address number. He guided the Bronco slowly up the curving drive. In about thirty yards, a log structure came into view. Standing in front of the building was a stocky man in work clothes holding a rifle at port arms. The man's expression was blank. He cradled the rifle in his left arm and held up his right hand like a cop signaling traffic to stop. Garcia did so and got out of the vehicle.

The man with the rifle stood still and said, "Identify yourself."

Garcia raised his eyebrows. "Tough guy, huh?" Then he shrugged. "I'm the one sent by your boss, Mr. Massey. How about lowering your weapon? You must be one of the Delmers."

The guy lowered the butt of the gun to just above the ground with his left hand wrapped around the barrel. He stepped forward and offered his thick right hand. "Seth Delmer. Welcome, I guess."

"Andrew Garcia. Where's your brother?"

"Inside." Delmer turned his prominent chin toward the log building behind him.

Garcia glanced that way and noticed a face with a red beard at the window to the right of the door. The face disappeared. He'd been watched surreptitiously by these guys, probably since he'd rolled in. Redneck brothers, he thought. He flashed to the movie, *Deliverance*. "Well, hell. How about some of that western hospitality I've heard so much about?"

"C'mon," Delmer said. He pivoted on a bootheel and trod to the building.

By then, it was late afternoon. The sun had eased behind the tops of the mountains, and dusk was not far off. Inside the log building, Seth Delmer introduced his brother Gus, who simply nodded.

Seth got out a bottle of Canadian whiskey and poured generous shots into thick but not particularly clean glass tumblers for all three of them. They sat on simple wooden chairs at a handmade square wooden table in the front room and, for a minute or so, made awkward small talk about the recent unseasonably wet weather causing the dirt road to become gumbo. As the room gradually darkened, Seth got up and switched on a floor lamp.

"So, you're not off the grid, after all," Garcia said.

"I set up a solar panel and generator with pretty damn good battery storage." Seth said. Makes it a helluva lot more comfortable. Power shuts off later."

Garcia said, "Let's get down to business. What did Massey tell you guys?"

"He said you'd come here to help us rip off some stuff and to uh, neutralize this McKay guy and his niece, some college kid."

A discussion followed about the McKays. Garcia asked a lot of questions. The Delmers did not have answers to many of them. He got what he could from them, going over the ground twice, alert for inconsistencies or possible fudging of the truth. The brothers seemed greedy and sullen but appeared to be telling the truth. He figured they resented that some Chicago guy had been sent out to supervise them. In their place, he knew he'd be resentful as well.

After a second drink and the conversation petering out to an uncomfortable silence, Gus said, "I better get back to the Sands place."

"They don't know you're here?" Seth asked.

"Nah. Told Chaffee I hadda see the doc in town."

"Banham?"

"Yep. Strange dude. But he knows his shit. I hear he hikes all over hell and back with that old retard, what his name?"

"Jimmy Brownleaf," Seth said.

"I'm outta here," Gus said, as he made for the door.

Garcia rubbed his hands together and turned to Seth. "I hate to interrupt, but I'm tired as hell. So, where's my bunk?"

"Follow me," Seth said.

They left the log house and walked a path for a few yards into a copse of aspens. A new-looking log cabin stood in a small clearing. The building was about thirty by twenty feet, with a blue metal roof and galvanized steel chimney.

"Built 'er myself last fall," Seth said, with obvious pride. Though the log walls were uneven in texture, they were straight and true. Seth must be a decent rough carpenter, Garcia thought.

Seth opened the door and led the way inside. He thumbed a switch and a small table lamp came on.

Garcia was pleasantly surprised. There was a front room with basic but functional furniture, a dining/kitchen area with a propane camp stove. A cot flanked a wall in the back, with a thick blanket folded on top.

"I don't suppose there's a cell signal here," Garcia said.

"Verizon signal comes and goes," Seth said. "See ya in the morning."

Chapter 39

(Day 11)

Brian called James St. Claire mid-morning and asked, "Anything new on Massey?"

"Still holed up at the Peninsula. Dude doesn't get out much. We've staked him out and we've been monitoring him with Sensorvault. Not much to track so far."

"Sensor what?"

"Sensorvault. Law enforcement can get what's called a geofence warrant to look at all cell phones in a given area, such as a crime scene at a point in time. We've got a warrant for North Michigan Avenue and have homed in on Mr. Massey."

"Can't someone avoid getting tracked by turning off their GPS or location tracking?"

"Nope. The tracking takes place whenever a device is on."

"What if he tosses his phone and gets a burner?"

"Then we got a problem. Unless we can ID the burner or at least narrow them down and track where we think his is."

"Hmm. Well, in any case, as you probably know, he met with our pal Mr. Garcia last night in a bar."

"Yes, and our guys also saw you on the scene there at the Omni."

"Did they record any of the conversation?"

"No, unfortunately. Didn't have a shotgun mic with them. But one of them followed Garcia home and staked him out. This morning, he cabbed it to O'Hare and flew to Bozeman. I let Bill Thorsten know. And Massey went back to the Peninsula."

"Okay. I'm catching a flight to Montana in a little while."

"Hey, one other thing. Massey went to the Field Museum yesterday. Like any tourist, he joins a 45-minute group tour of the Sue the *T. rex* exhibit with a docent. But then he sticks around for another hour and a half, taking photos of the dinosaur and asking questions of the guard there. He asks all kinds of stuff, like the weight of the bones, the size of the skull, the market value of the various parts. That type of thing. The guard told our guy he'd never had anyone ask all those specific questions before."

"Strange. But then, Sue is one of the top attractions in the city."

"True that. Well, have a slappin' trip. Tell Thorsten I said hey. And give my best to Darcy."

On the way to the airport, Brian checked in with Darcy via text. She wrote that she and her friend Becky were joining Professor Bakeno and Russell Eagle Feather on some kind of pilot fossil dig at the Sands ranch the next day. The group would be occupying guest cabins on the ranch for a few days. That made Brian happy, since he'd have a chance to see his niece. But, at the same time, he felt a little apprehensive. With Garcia visiting the area and the kidnappers of Barbara Hardy still unidentified, he wanted to urge Darcy to be careful. But she would resent the implication that she couldn't take care of herself. He'd just try to keep an eye on her. And he was bringing his personal handgun, a Sig-Sauer P226 with him—unloaded and locked in the cargo hold, per federal regulations.

Brian rented a silver Ford F-150 pickup at Gallatin Field. The vehicle would be capable and so common as to be anonymous. He'd discarded the idea of asking Arthur Sands to send a vehicle to pick him up. In fact, he didn't even contact the billionaire to let him know he was on the way. He arrived at the Sands ranch around ten P.M., entered the required code into the keypad at the main gate and drove in. Sands had mentioned a camera at the gate, but he saw no sign of one. At any rate, nobody would likely be monitoring it. He drove to his cabin. He thought of it as "his," since Sands had told him he'd have use of it indefinitely. Brian took that to mean as long as he worked for Sands. Anyway, the presence of his shiny new vehicle outside the cabin would let the ranch staff know he'd come back. Brian knew the ranch was like a small village. People watched all activity, keeping track of any vehicle arriving or leaving. He figured that innate nosiness might be a good source of information as he searched for the two men who'd abducted Barbara Hardy.

In fact, before Brian had even unpacked his case, Gus Delmer was on the phone to his brother Seth, letting him know about the return of the guy they'd been discussing earlier that evening.

"I'll let Garcia know. This could play right into our hands."

After a good night's sleep, Brian had a bite to eat in the ranch dining room. Next, he checked in with Art Sands, who gave him the go-ahead to check for listening devices.

Brian toured the headquarters facilities, searching for electronic eavesdropping devices. He checked the usual places: power strips, light fixtures, computers, phones, under furniture, electrical outlets. He also used an RF detector to check for devices. He found no unusual Wi-Fi or cellular networks nor any unexplained Bluetooth devices. His physical search turned up tiny wafer-like bugs hidden in a couple of electric outlets in the office, one in a potted plant on the patio, one in the dash of Sands's SUV. He even found one under the bed in the master bedroom. Real basic stuff, battery powered, voice-activated. Capable of transmitting through the ranch's regular Wi-Fi network. But to where? At the end, he met with Sands and discussed his findings.

"The thing that pisses me off the most is the one under the bed. Those fucking creeps."

"I know, right? Thinking back to our various conversations though, there's probably not a lot of valuable intel out there for whomever planted the bugs."

"I'd guess that's right. Barbara and I talk often, of course, and that may have helped the kidnappers."

"They'd be the likely suspects."

"Whoever the hell *they* are."

"We'll find out."

"Leave them be or pull them out?"

Sands hesitated for a moment. "Yank them out. Let me have them."

Brian left the temperamental billionaire in his office and walked down to the employee cabins. His destination was

Gus Delmer's place. He hadn't been comfortable with the man when he'd talked with him last time. And Nora Spivey's information about his brother Seth had bothered him as well. He walked along the row of employee cabins to the one on the far end. His knock was met with silence. Not surprising, as the guy was likely at work. He called Ray Chafee.

The ranch manager answered right away. "Gus? He's on the haying crew in the north hayfield. Should be back here by 4:00 P. M. Here's his cell number."

Brian added Gus to the contacts list on his phone.

A call came in: Dick Cissel, Brian's old friend with the Chicago Police Department.

"Got some news for ya."

""I hope it's good."

"Actually, it is. That guy you manhandled in your vestibule, the one who tried to plug you about three years ago? Noah Fargo?"

"He's been denied parole?"

"Got parole last month. Served three of his five and was back on the street. But here's the good news: He didn't stay out for long."

"What'd he do?"

"A uniform stopped him speeding on Lakeshore Drive yesterday. The dumb shit's got a .38 revolver on the seat next to him. As the officer approaches the open driver's side window, the dickhead grabs for his gun. Our man, quick thinker that he is, pulls his own, raps Noah upside the head, knocks him out."

"So he's back in jail pending charges, such as assault on a police officer?"

"Even better. His gun, this 38, is a lot like the one you took away from him three years ago. Must be his weapon of choice. The detectives checked his sheet, of course. Then they tested this current gun against the intact bullet you turned in to the beat cops after that incident in your alley a couple days ago."

"I think I see where you're going with this."

"The forensics guy says the lands and grooves and the other individual markings make a match. No question. He's the mug that shot at you. We asked him what his beef is with you, why's he takin' potshots. He says you fucked him over three years ago and he's been dreaming about settling that score ever since."

"Doesn't surprise me. I kinda thought he'd hold a grudge. That day in court when I testified against him, he was looking daggers at me. After the jury found him guilty, he turned and mouthed, 'See ya around, motherfucker.'"

"Not one of your fans."

"Ah well, as Marcus Aurelius said, 'Tranquility comes when you stop caring about what *they* say or think or do. Only what *you* do.'"

"And as an old vocalist once sang, 'Doo-bee-doo-bee-doo.'"

Chapter 40

The four-person dinosaur bone crew assembled under the relentless Montana sun early in the morning. Darcy and Becky sported MSU tee shirts and shorts, while Doctor Dave Bakeno, head of paleontology at Montana State University, had on his current favorite tee shirt with the legend, "Paleontologists have harder bones," along with baggy cargo shorts. Russell Eagle Feather maintained his understated cool in his perennial uniform of tight black tee, black Levi's and scuffed boots. The three young people wore ball caps, while Bakeno's broad-brimmed Indiana Jones hat protected his middle-aged ears and neck. They'd all slathered up with sunscreen. The temperature was already in the upper seventies at eight A.M. and was forecast to hit ninety by late afternoon.

All four were in high spirits, eager to begin fieldwork, free of organizational constraints for a few days. They stood adjacent to the small dig site, an acre of disturbed ground circumscribed by a white rope on steel fence posts.

As group leader, Bakeno made introductory comments. "A couple of weeks ago, I toured this area on my own as a guest of the Sands ranch. Knowing of the potential for fossil discovery, I invited myself. Art and Barbara have been more than gracious hosts. As I walked this area, I noticed a bony protrusion in the soil, which turned out to be the tip of an *Allosaurus* femur. Next, I removed the thin top layer of overburden the old-fashioned way — with a Pulaski, hand rake, trowel and paint brush. No need to go heavy with a jackhammer or anything. I only did a couple of square meters. Obviously, there's more surface layer removal to do within our designated area. You guys will be working that." He paused to wipe his brow with a bandana.

"Anyway, I uncovered well-preserved specimens in this bonebed here from at least one other *Allosaurus* individual along with the partial femur. I removed a tooth and a remarkably intact tibia. The bones were less than a foot beneath the surface and the soil cover is relatively loose, considering how dry it is here. Wind erosion has been working on this ground for millions of years. You can see one or two additional bones from where we stand." He nodded over a shoulder. The three young people gazed into the disturbed gravely plot but could not discern any bones at first.

After a few seconds, Becky blurted, "I see something. Looks like a short bone from here."

Bakeno nodded. "Good observation, Becky. I've stored the first finds temporarily in a nearby warehouse that Mr. Sands has kindly provided. There's wood shelving inside, which is ideal. Whatever we remove here will go into storage in that building as well. I don't anticipate the need for plaster casting at this time. As you can see, I've marked a series of one-meter grids in our little pilot plot. This will obviously be expanded eventually. To start, we'll each work one of the squares. We'll be using hand tools. At this point, I don't think power tools will be necessary. I'll try not to look over your shoulders too much."

"Sure, Dave. We've heard that one before," Becky quipped. Darcy looked at her friend with mild surprise.

Bakeno addressed Darcy and Becky. "As veterans of the Bone Mountain dig, you two obviously know the ropes. Russell, you and I will work as partners to start out and then you'll carry on independently after a bit. Let's all keep in mind how vulnerable these bones are. One sloppy move with a chisel and priceless eons of history can crumble into dust." He paused for a beat. "Keep an eye out for bones of *Stegosaurus* and *Brachiosaurus*. Al ate 'em." He winked. "Let's grab our tool sets and get to it."

He picked up the foldable nylon tool organizer with his initials marked on the outside and spread it open on the ground. Inside, neatly arranged, were a collection of fossil removal tools: rock hammer, trowel, hand rake, chisels, toothbrush, paint brushes, dental scraper, screwdrivers, tape measure, flagged markers, plastic bags, magnifying glass and assorted other paraphernalia. Each of the others followed suit. The tool sets had been prepared at MSU and were used on university-sponsored digs. Darcy frowned at the crusted dirt on a couple of the chisels in her kit and started cleaning them off with a paint scraper.

Darcy began working her square and immediately hit upon a dark dagger of a tooth, about three inches long and intact. She managed to extract it from the rocky dirt with her fingers. "Holy shit!" she said. As the others looked at her find, she began brushing the tooth with her toothbrush and then shifted to a dental scaler to remove the accumulated dust of 150 million years. She found it amusing that she was using modern dental tools on the tooth of a creature that couldn't have cared less about dental hygiene.

"Way to go, Darce," Becky said.

"Nice work," Bakeno added. "Get some photos and coordinates and tag and bag that baby." They all had a specialized app on their phones that used pre-loaded Google maps and recorded location coordinates overlaying photographs. Cell service was sketchy, but satellites were accessible.

And so it went for the rest of the morning. Each worker found one or two *Allosaurus* fossils apiece. Russell Eagle Feather proudly held up a caudal vertebra he'd discovered as Dr. Bakeno looked on. The laconic Indian had been notably quiet until that moment, but the ensuing praise from the others seemed to help nudge him from his shell.

"We've got eight teeth so far," Bakeno said. "As you know, *Allosaurus* had 55 teeth in his skull."

"Exactly 55? Becky asked."

Bakeno's smile was avuncular. "Give or take. Like people, they occasionally had some knocked out."

Darcy was stoked that she'd see Brian that evening. He'd texted her that he planned to be at the Sands ranch for as long as it took to find the kidnappers of Barbara Hardy. They planned to have supper at Carol Jensen's house in Clarkville. She had invited them both to join her and her nephew, Jerry for what she'd described as a "Montana seafood feast." Since they were seven hundred miles from the Pacific Ocean, Darcy wondered about the "seafood" part.

The crew broke for lunch around noon and went back to work a little after one. Darcy had a great eye for distinguishing bone from surrounding soil and rock material.

The texture of a bone or tooth was different, more porous. By late afternoon, she'd found another vertebra, nearly intact, as well as four teeth and a rib bone. Bakeno opined that there would be at least two *Allosaurus* partial skeletons and bits of others. He said he was cautiously optimistic they might end up with a nearly complete skeleton. Darcy knew that degree of completion of fossil skeletons was measured in either number of bones or in mass. Either way, the most complete *Allosaurus* skeleton to date was a specimen known as "Big Al" at the Museum of the Rockies in Bozeman.

As they worked, Andrew Garcia observed them through a pair of Canon 10 x 30 image stabilized binoculars. The binocs were designed to compensate for any movement, so he had a nice steady view. He easily identified Darcy McKay from the pictures he'd studied in Chicago. The group was about a hundred fifty feet from where he sat on a log, his back braced against an aspen trunk. The branches and leaves of the mature tree kept his body in shadow, invisible to the four people laboring under the bright sun. He'd arrived an hour earlier, breaching the ranch's electric perimeter fence using his Seal training, and slipping into place silently.

His first priority had been to spy on Brian McKay. Stumbling upon Darcy at work on some kind of archeology project was blind luck...and a good omen. Locating both McKays in the same place was a lucky break. But, as he got more familiar with the McKays, he was becoming even more reluctant to carry out the million dollar contract on their lives. Garcia had only killed in the line of duty, in war. The McKays were not enemy combatants. In fact they seemed like useful people. And what was Massey? A waste of oxygen, for sure. But what about the money he'd promised? Garcia knew that, with regard to his government-tasked activities, he would not profit from any illegal activity. Not unless it were kept secret.

He would have to think about his choices. Decision time would be upon him soon. He silently got to his feet and, behind the cover of trees and rocks, made his way toward the headquarters building where Sands had his office. He'd wait there until dusk and then move in. Maybe Brian McKay and Sands would meet, and he could listen in surreptitiously. The map drawn by Josie Wilshire and given to him by Gus Delmer the night before was remarkably detailed and accurate.

Chapter 41

Brian and Darcy enjoyed the mountain scenery as they cruised along in his rental pickup truck on the way to Clarkville. Darcy was tired but happy after a day of searching for *Allosaurus* fossil bones under the relentless high altitude sunshine. The summer sun remained above the horizon, but the temperature was dropping. A breeze from the southwest made the aspen and cottonwood leaves flutter like butterfly wings as the truck descended on the unpaved mountain road. Shortly, they reached the paved two-lane highway leading to the small town along the Yellowstone River named after Merriweather Clark of the Lewis and Clark expedition. Decades-old trees shaded the residential streets. Brian drove to Carol Jensen's address on Ash Street, where the houses were set well back from the street, enabling good-sized front yards. He pulled to the curb in front of a two-story frame house. The lawn was neatly mowed and the building looked recently painted. A brass knocker adorned the front door, which opened before they'd reached it.

Carol Jensen smiled broadly. Brian remembered the striking emerald eyes, and yet he was slightly startled by their intensity. He returned her smile and grasped her proffered hand in a shake that lasted an extra beat. Darcy's impression:

as she'd told her friend Becky, Carol's a serious babe indeed. And Brian was definitely smitten.

They went inside. Jerry, Carol's nephew, stood fidgeting in the living room. The fifteen year old boy had a shock of reddish hair falling over his forehead, nearly obscuring his eyes. He came forward to shake hands with Brian and then blushed as Darcy grasped him in a hug. Jerry was the only child of Carol's older sister Laura, who'd been murdered two years earlier. Carol had taken him in, and they'd lived together in her house since then. Brian remembered that Jerry's assignments included maintenance and landscaping at the house, while obtaining school grades in line with college.

"Jerry, the place looks good. You've been on the job, for sure," Brian said.

"Thanks," Jerry said, studying the floor.

"What's new?" Brian said.

"I'm uh, running track at school," Jerry said.

"And he's doing great," Carol said. "Sets a personal record every time out. I'm so proud."

Jerry looked like he wanted to dissolve into the floor. But he rallied gamely. "David and me caught some lunkers in Mather Creek last Saturday," he said. "You wanna go out with us?"

"Well, I'm working on a project for Mr. Sands," Brian said. "When I get a break, I'll call you and we'll set something up. I'm looking forward to it."

"Um, okay," Jerry said. He left the room. They could hear his feet clumping upstairs, presumably to his own room.

Brian and Darcy accepted beers from Carol and the three adults chatted, standing in the kitchen as Carol worked on dinner.

"Tell me about this Montana seafood deal," Brian said.

"This is your lucky day," Carol said. "We're having fresh Rocky Mountain oysters."

Darcy's face fell. Brian shrugged. "Great," he managed. He knew that the "oysters" were, in fact, cattle testicles.

Carol let out a loud guffaw. "Gotcha," she said. "I was just pulling your leg. We're actually having fresh rainbow trout, courtesy of Jerry. Speaking of whom…Jerry come on down for supper," she yelled in the direction of the stairs to the second level.

The four of them took chairs at the dining room table. Carol looked at Brian and said, "Would you like to lead us in prayer?"

"Certainly. Rub a dub dub. Thanks for the grub. Yaaaay, God!" Darcy joined him on the last two words. It was an old McKay family favorite.

Carol laughed again, while Jerry stifled a smirk. "I wasn't expecting that," she said. "But hey, it works."

As they ate, the conversation turned to Darcy's Master's program studies, Jerry's exploits on the track, Carol's banking work and her volunteer post as board chair of the William Old Horn Dinosaur Museum on the Sands ranch. Brian briefly mentioned his current project, hunting for the kidnappers of Barbara Hardy. The mood turned somber. They avoided talk of the violent history at Bone mountain and the Sands ranch. Brian once again cautioned Darcy to be vigilant, and she agreed with little enthusiasm. Her uncle tended to worry too much, she thought.

"How's the dinosaur museum going, now that it's been open for a couple years?" Brian was thinking of Carol's role on the board of directors.

"It's successful, but there are concerns," Carol said. "Fundraising's strong, so money's not a problem. We employ several Crow Nation members, which is good. Russell's done a fine job as E. D. But we're not growing."

"Attendance is down?" Darcy said.

"Yeah. It's dropped off a cliff. Russell's got to be getting bored. We plan to develop some new programs: interactive education for school kids, lectures in regional towns, YouTube videos, better social media. It's tough though, with limited staff and volunteer board members with day jobs. The novelty of our *T. rex* has worn off. We need something new, something big."

"Like an *Allosaurus*?" Darcy said.

"A complete one would be good. Or a couple of them fighting. Something dramatic." Carol sighed. "But in the meantime, we hope to move on education projects for kids and sharing exhibits with other regional dinosaur museums. Jerry tells me there's tons of interest in dinosaurs among his classmates. Right?"

Jerry blushed. "Um, right. That *T. rex* is the GOAT. The kids like to look at that stuff, but y'know a field trip with like digging up the actual bones would be dope."

"Would most of your classmates be up for an all-day fossil bone dig?"

"Oh yeah. It would hit different. The dinosaurs got rizz."

Carol smiled. "We'll work on it. Russell's got some ideas, too."

Brian noticed the light in Carol's green eyes dimming occasionally. He guessed her pensiveness stemmed from her looking inward, back to the death of her sister, no doubt triggered by the presence of the McKays. He wondered if that would be the case every time they met. He hoped not.

"Russell's stoked about our pilot fossil dig," Darcy said.

"How's that going?" Carol asked.

"Excellent. We've been finding *Allosaurus* bones close to the surface, much easier to get out than the *T. rex* we worked on two summers ago. So far, we've uncovered part of a skull, neck and tail vertebra and teeth, some of which are still in the skull. Dr. Bakeno is hoping for an entire skeleton."

"How's Russell doing? I mean, he's never done that kind of work before, right?" Carol said.

"Great. He's learning fast," Darcy said. "When it comes to fossil bone excavation, he's a natural. Turns out, he's a paleontology bibliophagist."

"Is that curable?" Brian asked.

"It means, bookworm, smarty-pants," Darcy said. "He reads articles online about dinosaur digs, historical and current. He was telling us about this guy in North Dakota who found a huge *T. rex* on private land and paid the landowner ten thousand dollars for what he says he thought was title to the bones. The landowner says it was only for the right to dig. There are lawsuits back and forth. Meanwhile, the bones are in a warehouse on the ranch where they were found."

"I hope they have good locks on that warehouse," Brian said. Darcy nodded, thinking about the ranch warehouse where their current fossil finds were being stored.

Carol nodded. "I was reading that a single *T. rex* tooth sold to a collector in China last month for a hundred thousand dollars. And a *Rex* skull is expected to fetch fifteen to twenty million at auction soon. Everyone from tech bros to new natural history museums in the Middle East are after the bones. They're worth whatever someone with the cash is willing to pay."

"Yeah. This *T. rex* named Stan went for more than thirty million at Christie's in New York a couple years ago," Brian said.

"That was about the time we excavated ours at Bone Mountain," Darcy added. "The one on display in the William Old Horn museum. Jeez, not to seem alarmist, but I wonder how secure the museum is."

Carol spoke up. "We've got a digital alarm system, redundant fire sprinklers, around the clock watchmen on site. Plus fire and theft insurance for more than those inflated values we've been talking about. I think we're covered."

"That's good," Darcy said.

"One problem with this runaway market for dinosaur bones is that scientists are getting priced out by megabucks collectors. That's why philanthropists like Mr. Sands are so important…and appreciated," Carol said.

"What about selling replicas?" Brian asked. "I understand that's a thing."

"We're negotiating some sales. Mr. Sands has been very helpful. I hope to sign a contract next month with a theme park in California on behalf of the museum."

The dinner was delicious. Jerry retired to his room after desert, ostensibly to do his homework. After thanks and promises to reciprocate with a restaurant dinner, Brian and Darcy headed for the door. Darcy eased outside and down to the truck, leaving Brian to have a moment with Carol. They stood next to the table.

"This was fun. I'm really glad we could get together," Brian said.

"Me too. We should do it again soon."

Brian took a chance. He wrapped his arms around Carol and pulled her close. She tilted her head back and looked him in the eyes. Their faces came together in a kiss. The kiss went on for several seconds.

Finally, Carol said, "Wow."

"What I was thinking."

"Call me," she said.

"I will."

On the ride back to the Sands place, Darcy smiled and said, "I knew you'd make a move."

"What? You couldn't see anything from the truck."

"Didn't need to see. I knew."

Chapter 42

(Day 12)

Mid-morning. The tension was evident. Seth and Gus Delmer stood stiffly while the man from Chicago lolled on the couch in Seth's cabin. They'd had coffee and donuts for breakfast, with very little conversation.

Gus had driven over from the Sands ranch. He'd made a decision to quit his job. After all, with this gig, he'd soon have enough money to tell the world to piss up a rope. Why continue to work like a peon at a dead end job? But this Garcia dude—something was off. Seth had tried to reassure him, but he knew his older brother had his own doubts. Also, Josie had told Gus about the phone conversation between Art Sands and an unknown caller the other day. She'd guessed the caller was Brian McKay. Sounded like he was reporting on some conversation he'd overheard. Could it have something to do with Garcia?

"Okay, so we've got a plan to steal some bones. Doesn't sound like much to me," Seth said to Garcia.

"Our friend in Chicago would disagree," Garcia replied.

"Friend? We've never met this dude and never will," Gus said.

"So what? He's gonna pay us. Enough money that none of us will have to work again for a mighty long time," Garcia said.

The Delmer brothers' faces reflected pure skepticism. This was not lost on Garcia. But he didn't really care what they thought as long as they got the job done.

"I'm scouting the museum today," Garcia said. "Nobody around here has ever seen me. And I'll be lightly disguised."

"Ya might wanna go heavy on the disguise. The cameras there'll pick you up soon's ya enter the joint," Seth remarked. Gus nodded.

"Right. So, I'll gather the info we'll need to carry out the job," Garcia said. "If all looks copacetic, which I'm pretty sure it will, we'll be ready to rock tomorrow night."

"What about ol' Robert?" Seth asked

"Who?"

"The night watchman, Robert Wolf."

"We'll deal with him," Garcia said.

"What do ya mean, 'deal?'" Gus said. I hope you don't mean 'kill.' So far, I haven't crossed that line, and I don't want to now. I mean, I can't see the death penalty in my future."

"Don't worry," Garcia said. "He'll be temporarily out of the picture. Nobody's gonna get killed. And we'll be totally under the radar. The cameras will be disabled. The alarm system as well. Our faces and hands will be covered. We'll be in and out and away hours before they show up to open the museum."

"We'd better be," Gus said.

"Do either of you know Robert Wolf? Could he recognize you?"

"Nope," Gus said. Seth shook his head.

"When's our payoff?" Seth said.

Garcia was to be paid in cash by the buyer of the item. He said, "Don't worry. You'll be paid promptly. I mean, you guys got your share of the ransom money immediately—right?"

"Yeah, because we collected the cash and took out our cut. This is different," Seth said.

"Well, don't worry. You'll be paid right away this time as well," Garcia said.

The Delmers scowled, which Garcia noticed. They didn't trust him. Why should they? He knew he had to string them along at least until the job was done. And he didn't rule out their trying to double-cross him. Honor among thieves? *Bullshit*. "Okay, gents. We'll meet tonight to finalize plans," he said. "Meanwhile, line up the van and the other equipment I mentioned."

"Most of it's done already," Seth said, his face flushed with irritation.

"You got the van?"

"Hell yes. Bozeman airport long-term parking, coupla hours ago. Swapped plates with some other vehicle."

"This a high roof van?"

Seth frowned. "Of course. The dingus should roll right in."

Garcia gave a quick thumbs up, climbed into his rental and drove out of the cabin area, heading for the road. He was on his way to the William Old Horn Dinosaur Museum located on the Sands ranch with a separate public access road.

The man entering the William Old Horn Dinosaur Museum had long stringy gray hair, topped by a worn ballcap with the legend on the front: I DON'T KNOW HOW TO ACT MY AGE. I'VE NEVER BEEN THIS OLD BEFORE. Of average height and lean, he walked with a limp and looked a little unsteady on his legs. Dark tinted glasses hid his eyes. His oversized shirt and pants hung on him like a collapsed parachute. He made his way to the reception counter, cleared his throat and said, "Where would I find those *T. rex* bones?"

The receptionist, Alice Pretty Shield, blinked. She cast a quick glance over her shoulder at the huge dinosaur skeleton soaring twenty feet above the floor toward the skylights in the vaulted ceiling. Was this doofus for real? She smiled politely and said, "It's right there behind me."

The scruffy man said, "Oh, silly me. Thank you." He bowed slightly and ambled over toward the *T. rex* skeleton.

A few minutes later, a teacher from the White Sulphur Springs elementary school shepherded her noisy class of eighteen kids into the museum. A second woman brought up the rear of the throng, ensuring no stragglers wandered off. Alice Pretty Shield was fully occupied with answering questions about the dinosaur bones from the kids and observing their tour of the facility. This fortuitous development left the man with the novelty ballcap to explore on his own. Which he did—thoroughly.

The guard on duty during the day shift, Al Swan, kept an eye on everyone who entered the museum. His was a well-paying job with benefits and he took his duties seriously. He dismissed the scruffy white man as borderline indigent and harmless enough. The prospective trouble might come from the boisterous school kids, especially the males, he figured. His worries were confirmed when a blonde boy of about ten approached the three foot high Plexiglas wall designed to keep people feet back from the dinosaur skeleton. The boy climbed over the barrier, limber as a chimpanzee, and dropped down next to the splayed three-toed foot supporting the dinosaur's huge left rear leg. He pulled a jackknife from his jeans pocket and with the blade, endeavored to pry a fossil toe bone loose. The teacher and her assistant began to scream at the boy like banshees.

"Todd, get back here! Right now!"

Swan was on his feet instantly, raced over to the young miscreant and roared, "Stop that or I'll tase ya."

The boy swiftly pocketed his knife and whined, "I didn't do nothing."

"You didn't do *anything*," the teacher corrected in a stern voice.

"That's what I said," the boy replied.

While all this excitement was being sorted out, the indigent-looking man noted the location of all the cameras in the exhibit space: one inside the main entrance, another overhead, pointing down at the *T. rex* skeleton. One camera was aimed at the separately displayed skull in its glass enclosure, one overlooked the bone prep lab along the east wall, and another was mounted at the rear cargo entryway.

Next, he carefully studied the glass box enclosing the *T. rex* skull, noting dimensions of the case, the skull and the rectangular wooden surface below the skull. The box was constructed thusly: black steel pillars at the corners, steel roof on top, a glass panel on each side, from the roof down to the level of the wood platform beneath the skull. From the bottom of the skull platform to the floor were exterior wooden panels. At the beltline where glass met wood panels, a rectangular sign jutted out on one side of the enclosure describing the skull of the mighty alpha predator. He noticed the end of the case off the *T. rex* snout showed a thin seam. There were subtle piano-style hinges on the left side of the case at that end. As he'd learned from the architectural drawings, the skull case was designed to be opened by authorized personnel with a key.

He paced off the distance to the large cargo door at the far end of the exhibit floor. He estimated the height and width of the cargo door—about ten feet high and wide. A roll up door on a track was powered by an electric motor. There was a large crank attached to the door for manual operation.

To the right of the cargo door was a pedestrian door with both deadbolt and knob locks. To its right a metal panel was embedded in the wall. On the front of the panel was a white sign with red block letters: ELECTRICITY – CAUTION! This must be the electrical control panel for the building. There was a separate alarm system control panel to the right containing a digital display indicating ARMED in vivid green letters at the top. An alphanumerical digital keypad covered the bottom portion of the screen.

Several offices lined a wall in the northwest portion of the main floor. The office windows faced the interior of the building and were all blacked out by shades, so he could not tell whether any office staff were present.

He turned his attention to the perimeter windows. There were a couple of double hung, vinyl clad windows on the east and west walls near the building entrance. He walked over and inspected one, acting as if he were admiring the view outside. A decal indicated tempered glass. As he expected, there was a wireless alarm sensor on the right side, with a magnet attached to the glass and a reed switch on the window frame. When you close a laptop and the screen goes blank, that's the work of a reed switch. He knew that the magnet held the switch's metal contacts together when the window was closed, allowing electricity to flow through the circuit. When the window was opened the magnet and switch would be moved apart and current would stop flowing, triggering an alarm. Satisfied, the man headed for the front entrance. As he passed Alice Pretty Shield's post at the reception counter, he tipped his hat and smiled. She was busy dealing with the school group and did not notice the departing visitor.

Outside, he circled to the rear of the building. At the cargo entrance, he pulled his ball cap low over his forehead and eyed the single camera above the door through his sunglasses. Magnetic alarm sensors were positioned near the top of the door, one on each side, similar to those on the windows inside.

Everything depended on electricity. If the power were out, none of the alarms or cameras would be operable. But, would turning off the power trigger an alarm? Often, alarm systems would automatically send an alert to the security company via a landline if the power went out.

An electric meter stood on a steel post to the left of the rollup door. A large conduit pipe ran from the post through the wall and inside the building. Probably the main power. The trick would be to get inside, turn off the alarm system, open the electric control panel and cut the juice to the building.

He followed the gravel driveway away from the door. The smooth path split after a few yards. The left branch made a sharp left and continued to the public parking area out front of the museum. The right branch led to the tall and sturdy chain link fence at the northeast corner of the ranch. A wide green tubular steel gate was secured with a hefty chain and chromed padlock. The gate blocked access to a road leading southward. He consulted his map. The road went about a half mile to a crossroad that led to highway 89. He took some photos with his phone. Then he retraced his steps back to the parking area in front of the museum. He passed a sign on a steel post at the edge of the parking lot indicating the premises were protected by a security outfit in Bozeman.

Driving down the highway toward Clarkville, Garcia was optimistic. This project had an excellent chance of success. He needed to shop for a few supplies. He kept his disguise wig and ponderous clothing on, but substituted a nondescript cap for the novelty number, slipped on a pair of polarized aviators and continued into town.

At a gun shop along the highway, Garcia purchased a box of ammo for the Colt .38 revolver he'd been given by Seth Delmer. He checked the gun—loaded. He continued on to a hardware store. There, he bought a short-handled sledgehammer, a couple of high-intensity flashlights, a roll of duct tape, a long-handled crowbar and various other tools. All of this went into the cargo area in the rear of the vehicle.

Chapter 43

The dinosaur dig crew continued into their second day of work. Darcy was a little tired. After Brian had dropped her off the night before, she'd stayed up well after midnight in the cabin she shared with Becky Stanton reading a textbook on the morphology of Jurassic era sauropods. She knew that she was expected to keep up with her studies during the week spent on the dig. The midterm exams would be the same for her and Becky as they'd be for the students who'd remained on campus. Becky, not quite as ambitious, had sacked out around eleven P.M.

The dig work, while interesting, did not require Darcy's full concentration. She was careful though, not to slip into goblin mode, a term popular on campus meaning lazy, tuned out. She methodically scraped and brushed and scooped away soil and rocky material, uncovering mostly uninteresting stones and occasionally the sought-after fossil bone fragments. As she worked, her mood turned pensive. She was happy overall, right? Living and studying in exactly the right place. Her uncle Brian staying nearby, at least temporarily. Rooming with her close friend, Becky Stanton, both on-campus and even here at this remote ranch for a week. Something was missing, though. To put it bluntly, any kind of love life. Since the murder of her boyfriend, Matthew

Growney, in Chicago two years ago, she had not had a serious relationship. She'd dated a few guys off and on, nothing memorable. Nothing current.

Darcy glanced over at the two men. Professor Bakeno and Russell Eagle Feather seemed to be developing a friendship. They chatted about Crow culture throughout the morning. Eagle Feather admitted that he was not fluent in the Crow language. He spoke a little, he said, but nothing like the generation before. His uncle, William Old Horn, had taught classes in the Crow tongue at Little Big Horn College on the reservation. The old man said he was trying to preserve the tribe's oral traditions in the face of overwhelming white culture. Eagle Feather's face lit up when he talked about his people. He had a bit of an attitude about white history as it related to Indians. But he wasn't an activist.

The work proceeded in fits. The four workers shared a passion for dinosaur bones and communicated freely. Bakeno was clearly the authority figure. The other three deferred to him, but also asked unfiltered questions. The pile of tagged fossil bones had grown. Bakeno remarked that they had about half of a complete *Allosaurus* skeleton at that point, plus a smaller portion of a second individual and a piffling amount of a third. He remained hopeful they'd unearth a nearly complete set of bones.

Chapter 44

Gus Delmer heard the crunch of truck wheels on the gravel lane outside his cabin. His girlfriend, Josie, skidded her pickup to a halt outside the door. She jumped out, slamming the truck door. Before she reached the cabin, Gus emerged.

"You alone?" she asked.

He sighed. "Yeah, for a change."

They embraced. He began to slip a hand up the back of her shirt.

"Not now. We've gotta keep it together. When are ya leaving?" she said.

"Few minutes, soon's I finish packing up my shit."

"Uh, let's go inside," Josie said. There was nobody visible among the employee cabins, but that didn't mean they were alone, she well knew. The walls had ears, and everyone was a gossip. A remote ranch with a group of employees thrown into constant close contact. She dreamed of moving on. But the pay was good. For now.

Josie glanced around the dimly lit interior space and spoke softly, as if concerned someone might be eavesdropping. "How are you and Seth getting along with that Garcia dude?"

He grimaced. "We aren't. Guy's a total asshole. Tries to order us around. He's just a fuckin' ignorant out-of-stater. Thinks he knows everything."

"What's the plan?"

"He said he was scouting out the dinosaur museum today. Says we're gonna rob it, split the proceeds. Millions, he says. My opinion: we'll never see a penny unless we grab it. Him and that ghost boss of his in Chicago plan to get the dough, while me and Seth get the shaft."

"Where *is* Garcia?"

"At the moment, I don't know. We're supposed to meet up with him later at Seth's. The three of us 'll hit the museum tonight. Seth's got a van lined up for the stuff we're gonna rip off."

"What about alarms, guards, security?"

"Garcia says he's an expert. Set up security systems in Chicago. I checked that online, and it looks like he's telling the truth. He says the museum's a piece of cake. I sure as hell hope he's right."

"Where do you guys go after the heist?"

"Dunno. We're supposed to go someplace to unload the goods to the buyer. Some rich guy with a house nearby. I've got no idea where that is."

"What about that phantom guy in Chicago? He gonna be on the scene? He's trusting you guys with the loot?"

"Beats me. I'm more worried about *our* cut. Ya know, it's weird. Out of the blue, Garcia starts askin' us questions about Brian McKay. What's he doing for Sands? Is he armed? That kind of shit. But I don't mind. Something happens to McKay, that's good for me and Seth. And you, too."

"You're right. Maybe this Garcia is a useful idiot."

"He's no idiot. But I'd trust him about as far as I could fling him."

"Lotta outsiders at the ranch these days. Makes me kinda nervous," Josie said. "McKay's niece, what's-her-name, is here. working on diggin' up some dinosaur bones with three other folks from the university. There's a professor, plus Russell from the museum and some other girl. I hope they have sense enough to keep their heads down."

"I'm more worried about you and me," Gus said. "And Seth."

"But that other deal, you guys got the cash they promised." She was referring to the ransom money received from Arthur Sands related to the kidnapping of his ex-wife. The Delmers split a million dollars between them. The brothers had demanded and received from Sands an extra hundred k beyond the two million Massey had instructed them to ask for. They'd kept their own shares, deposited Massey's share and Gus had passed on the extra dough to Josie for her limited role in the abduction.

Gus looked at his phone. Five. "I've gotta get movin'." He'd been humming the Johnny Paycheck classic country song, "Take this Job and Shove it," as he threw his belongings into the bed of his pickup before she'd arrived.

He handed his short note of resignation to Josie, who was to drop it off with Ray Chafee, Gus's boss, the next morning. He felt free in a way, but his stomach was churning as he worried about tonight's planned heist. A lot could go wrong.

"I'll call ya when I'm clear," Gus said as he got into his pickup.

"Any idea when?"

"All depends. Let's hope for the best."

Chapter 45

(Day 13)

Robert Wolf arrived at the William Old Horn Museum a few minutes before his graveyard shift would begin at one A.M. He approached the front entrance and waited for the night guard, Joe Yellowtail, to come to the door and unlock it. Wolf eyed the parking lot over his shoulder as he waited: empty except for his old Chevy Impala and Yellowtail's Tacoma pickup. The security lights near the parking lot and the front entrance glowed. The night was cool and the wind nearly calm. With the new moon, the sky was black. The stars shown with candescent intensity.

A set of keys rattled from the other side of the door. Wolf pulled the door open and entered, carrying the bird cage he brought with him every night. A cloth covered the cage. The clicking sound of claws on a wooden perch came from inside.

"Sounds like Fred's restless this evening," Yellowtail said with a smile.

"Yep, can't wait to get to work."

Once Yellowtail had left and Wolf had punched in on the digital timeclock, he pulled the cover off the bird cage, revealing a large green and yellow parrot. The bird blinked a few times as its eyes grew accustomed to the light. Then he squawked once, as if clearing his throat.

"Bite me, Jack!" the parrot proclaimed.

"That's not very nice, Fred. Who's a good boy?"

"Gimme a peanut."

Wolf unfolded a newspaper atop the reception desk and set the bird cage on it. Then he pulled a bag of dry peanuts from his pocket and slipped one to the bird through the bars of the chromed metal cage. Fred grabbed the peanut in his sharp beak and chomped as steadily as a combine working a wheat field. Finished with this morsel, the bird eyed Wolf silently. Never once had Fred said thank you when given a treat. Oh well, you can't buy gratitude.

Wolf turned to his duties. Per his normal routine, he toured the exhibit space in a large square around the perimeter. Next, he made his way to the *T. rex* skeleton and then to the glass display case holding the skull. He knew the skull in the case was the real thing, ancient fossil bone mounted on two steel rods that disappeared through the waist-high horizontal oak surface flush with the interior glass walls of the case. Wolf also knew the skull high atop the dinosaur skeleton was a fake made of resin. The reason the real skull was located in its case at floor level was to make access easier for visiting research scientists.

Occasionally, some professor from a university would show up by appointment and the day shift guard, Joe Swan, would open up the case so the academic could study the skull. Swan would unlock the hinged side of the case, swing it open and roll out the wheeled oak-topped table above which the 600-pound skull was mounted. A black steel frame like a low scaffolding supported the oak surface beneath the skull. It was designed like a heavy duty furniture dolly, so one could move it out of and back into the case without popping a hernia. The rolling platform was about thirty inches high, forty-five inches wide and a little over six feet long. It was surrounded by thick wood paneling, so the rolling cart was not visible to the public. The bony skull reached more than three feet above the oak surface, so the top of it was nearly six feet from the floor. Swan had joked that he was as tall as a *T. rex*. The visiting academics were allowed to take pictures, make sketches and study the skull from all angles, but they weren't allowed to touch it (though some of them did). Swan had related all this information to Wolf one time, when they'd bumped into each other in town.

Though he was not expected to open the skull case, Wolf knew how to do it. He'd been instructed to do so only in the event of a fire. If he were able to roll the platform holding the skull out of the building safely, he should push it out the nearest door. His personal safety was paramount, of course.

All was in order on the exhibit floor. He continued on to the bone prep lab, where he opened the door with a key and entered. A quick scan of the long narrow space revealed that all seemed to be copacetic. Since the lab had not been used in weeks, his check was perfunctory. Then it was on to the staff offices and conference room. Russell Eagle Feather's office was neat and orderly, as always. The other staff office, the one used by Susie Pease, the part-time bookkeeper, was also unremarkable. The conference room, with its long table suitable for handling a gathering of twelve people, was likewise tidy. Wolf sighed. This job had become boring as hell. He longed for some excitement. Nevertheless, he knew he was fortunate to be paid very well for this part of rural

Montana. No heavy lifting either. So he continued on, determined not to screw up.

Fred the parrot shuffled back and forth on his perch, muttering to himself. An occasional profane word could be distinguished. Wolf sometimes had to apologize to people for Fred's crude language. "He listens all the time, picks things up. His previous owner was a pretty rough customer. If he swears at you, it's nothing personal," he'd tell people.

He checked both doors in the rear of the building along the north wall. The deadbolt on the steel pedestrian door was set. Likewise, the heavy roll up cargo door was shut tight and locked. He returned to the front of the building, sat at his chair behind the reception counter and retrieved from under the countertop his current book, *Fools Crow* by James Welch. He had covered about forty pages when his eyes drooped closed and his chin lowered to his chest. Soon, he was asleep in his chair. This was not an unusual occurrence for Wolf. He'd often nod off for a few minutes for what he called a catnap. He'd never neglected his duties, nor had he been caught asleep by anyone. Nevertheless, he knew he had to be careful.

Around two A.M. a noise suddenly awoke Robert Wolf. Sounded like a vehicle going by the museum, traveling slowly along the west wall. Maybe a light truck. Something was wrong.

Fred yelped, "What the fuck?"

Wolf immediately sprang from his chair. There was no reason for a vehicle to be outside the museum at that hour. He turned to the video monitor atop the reception desk and selected the image from the camera mounted on the roof on the west side of the building. Nothing unusual outside. He tried the camera over the cargo door in the back. The screen was black. No video feed. Weird. He grabbed his flashlight and walked back to the pedestrian door adjacent to the cargo dock at the north end. He placed an eye to the peephole. Completely black. Normally, he'd see the glow from the floodlight mounted above the doors. Had somebody obscured the peephole? Turned off the light? Covered up the camera?

"Who's there?" Wolf yelled.

No answer. Sounded like someone moving around.

He knew he should immediately call the sheriff's department on the landline at the reception desk. No need to risk his own neck. And yet, maybe there was some innocuous reason for the unusual incident. Maybe somebody was lost. Or it could be kids pranking him. He'd look good if he handled the problem himself. He decided to just have a quick look out the door.

Wolf entered in the ten-digit code on the alarm system keypad to the right of the electrical panel. The small screen indicated the alarm system had been switched from ARMED to DISARMED. He twisted the knob of the pedestrian door's deadbolt lock and then the doorknob. He opened the door a couple of inches and shined his flashlight into the night. A man wearing a black ski mask faced him with something in his gloved right hand. The man chopped down at Wolf's forearm with a hard object. The flashlight fell from the guard's hand and clattered to the ground.

"What the hell—" was all Wolf managed to say before he was struck on the head. He lost consciousness and slumped to the floor.

"Help me get this guy inside and under wraps," Garcia said.

Garcia knew this was a stroke of luck. The screen next to the door indicated DISARMED. The guard must have turned off the alarms before he opened the door to stick his head out. What a fool. With clean access to the museum, they could get to work without worrying about triggering a perimeter burglar alarm. Nonetheless, they'd need to be careful There could be additional alarms inside.

Garcia and Seth Delmer, both wearing black ski masks and latex gloves, dragged Wolf inside the building and gagged the man with a rag secured by duct tape. They cinched his wrists and ankles together with duct tape. When that was done, Garcia found a large supplies closet and dragged Wolf into it. Shutting the door, he turned to Seth and said, "Okay, let's get to it."

The parrot interjected, "Fuckadoodledoo!"

Garcia and Seth both flinched at the sound of the bird's voice.

"There's someone else in here," Seth said.

They began a search for the other person. Garcia spotted the bird cage with the colorful parrot sitting on the counter up front. The bird murmured fitfully.

"Here he is," Garcia said.

"Jumpin' Jesus on a pogo stick," Fred remarked.

Chapter 46

Gus sat in the driver's seat of the cargo van. He'd backed it up to the loading dock at the rear of the William Old Horn Dinosaur Museum. With his side window rolled down, he heard Garcia and Seth struggling with the guard. They'd disappeared inside through the pedestrian door. After a few minutes, the cargo door rolled up. Garcia and Seth came out on the dock and grabbed flashlights, crowbars and the sledgehammer from the back of the van.

"Hang tight," Garcia said to Gus, as he and Seth went back into the museum.

Gus pulled off his balaclava, lit a cigarette and settled in. He was glad that he was driving. With Garcia riding shotgun on the drive to the museum, Seth had to ride in the cavernous cargo area in the back, without benefit of a seat. He'd complained loudly several times that he was getting bounced around, slow the fuck down. Gus had just laughed. If Garcia had a sense of humor, he hid it well.

Garcia confronted the electrical box next to the alarm panel. At first, he thought the metal access door was locked. Then he figured out that, to open it, you simply ran your hand along the bottom. A slim lever slid left, freeing the door. Inside were neat rows of clearly labeled circuit breakers. There were breakers for the individual interior and exterior lights, for the exhibit space, the offices, prep lab and the cameras inside and out.

What if disabling the alarm system at night triggered an automatic notification to the security service? Fuck it. Garcia didn't want to waste time looking for an external communications connection. If the phone up front rang, he'd answer it and tell them everything was fine. He knew that cell signal was sketchy up here.

Garcia tripped the breakers for all the cameras, the lights over the doors and the interior lights in the exhibit space of the museum. Outside, darkness descended around the van parked at the rear of the building like a medieval shroud. He left the outside lights at the parking lot up front and the nearby front entrance on so that, in the unlikely event somebody happened to drive anywhere near the building facade, it would look normal.

Garcia and Seth approached the box containing the skull. The enclosure had walls of thick glass for the top two thirds and dark wooden panels for the lower part. A rectangular blurb sign for tourist consumption stuck out from one side of the box at waist level. The text started with the words, MORE THAN JUST A PRETTY FACE, and described the features of the rust-colored skull. Seth was drawn to the sign and began reading.

Garcia noticed this and barked, "We don't have time to act like fuckin' tourists."

Seth frowned and kept on reading.

Garcia studied the box, looking for a way to get into it. He had covertly obtained the architectural plans for the museum online. The firm in Bozeman had made an excellent drawing of the glass "skull box" when the museum was in the planning stage two years earlier. Garcia had found it online, a stroke of luck. A casual visitor to the museum would not know the skull was portable—it looked like a permanent and very solid installation. But there it was in the specs: "rolling platform on six-inch steel wheels. 70 inches long, 46 inches wide, thirty inches high. Skull will roll in/out of box face first through hinged opening off face of skull."

The question was how to open the door to the box. The wall facing east was supposed to provide access. The specs showed a lock in the lower right corner of that side of the box near the floor. Garcia got on hands and knees and studied the corner. At first, nothing. Then he noticed an almost imperceptible inset seam about four inches square on the panel, just above the floor. With his Swiss Army knife, he poked at the edge of the tiny seam. It moved a little. He pushed it with fingertips, and it popped open, revealing a keyhole.

Garcia figured the guard had a key. He sent Seth to the supplies closet to drag the man out. Seth shined the powerful LED flashlight beam directly into Wolf's face. He'd regained consciousness. His eyes looked defiant as the younger man bent over him.

"Where's the key to the skull box?"

The gag made it impossible for Wolf to enunciate. Nevertheless, the words he tried to speak were clear enough: "Uck oo."

Seth kicked at the man's feet to get his attention. "We can do this easy or hard. Your choice, pal."

"O da ell." Wolf knew the key to the skull case was hidden in Eagle Feather's office, under a potted ficus tree.

Seth kicked the man in the legs. Then he noticed a chain running between his belt and front pants pocket. He grabbed the chain and yanked on it. A ring of keys came out of the pocket. "Hullo. What's this, mate?" he said, with a terrible British accent. He detached the key ring from Wolf's belt. Then, "Back in storage for you." He grabbed the neck of the guard's collar and pulled him like a sack of potatoes into the closet. He unceremoniously slammed the door and returned to the skull box, sorting through the keys on the chain as he walked.

Garcia grabbed the keys and commanded, "Hold your light on this."

With Seth's flashlight trained on the keyhole, Garcia tried the keys one after the other. None of them fit. He slammed the keys to the floor.

Garcia went to the reception desk and rifled through the drawers underneath. There were no more keys to be had.

He was beginning to get concerned. They'd been inside the building for twenty minutes. He'd planned on being in and out in a half hour, tops.

"Well, I guess we go to plan B," he said. "Let's grab those tools."

Garcia and Seth set their flashlights on the floor, pointed toward the front wall of the box. Garcia inserted the hooked end of his crowbar into the small seam where the bottom of the glass met the wood panel. "Tap on the crowbar with that hammer," he instructed Seth.

Seth pounded tentatively. The seam opened a half inch.

"Hit it harder," Garcia ordered.

Seth did so, and the gap widened to an inch. They kept at it for a few more minutes, working their way along the seam. Shortly, there was a six inch gap as the wood panel pulled away from the glass above it. They pried the top of the panel out from the structure, working the top and sides. As the gap widened, the loose panel wobbled precariously. Garcia raised a boot above the panel and stomped down, breaking the side attachments and causing the barrier to crash to the floor. With a little more strategic prying and yanking, they managed to dislodge the piece entirely and tossed it behind them. They could see a set of black metal wheels on the floor inside the case. They'd been making a hell of a lot of noise. A half hour had elapsed since they'd entered the building. Garcia glanced nervously toward the front entrance. All was quiet.

Then the parrot exclaimed, "Que pasa, hombre?"

Seth jumped at the sound of the shrieked words.

"Never mind that shit. Let's get the glass," Garcia said.

They studied the glass panel for a moment.

"Looks like it comes out by lifting the bottom," Seth said. "See those rubber blocks on each side?"

The glass was framed by a black metal framework with black rubber blocks at the bottom to hold the glass panel in place. They grabbed the bottom of the glass and lifted. After raising it a couple of inches, the bottom of the glass was freed from the blocks. They were able to pull it out and then slide it down to the floor. They set it on the tile surface behind them. Now, the skull stared at them without any barrier blocking the view.

The two men gazed transfixed at the fossilized russet-colored skull. The ominous butcher's knife teeth curved inward. The face seemed to smile malignantly at them. The bony snout protruded aggressively. A framework of tubular black metal rods had been threaded through the skull, ending with four vertical supports bolted to the oak platform top below. Large metal hooks cradled the jaw and base of the skull.

"Enough standing around. Let's get this sucker out to the truck," Garcia said.

He grabbed the end of the wheeled platform and backed up, pulling it out of the case. The platform rolled easily, requiring not much more effort than rolling a cart full of lumber at Home Depot. The engineering must have been excellent, Garcia thought.

"What's the skull weigh, do ya suppose," Seth asked.

"Six hundred pounds. Help me get this thing out the door," Garcia said.

Garcia and Seth each took a side, steering the platform toward the rear of the museum. The front wheels pivoted like a grocery cart's. At the cargo door, they stopped, and Seth pulled the heavy-duty folding aluminum ramp from the van's floor. He unfolded the ramp and placed it so it bridged the gap between the van's cargo space and the loading dock. They carefully lined up the skull platform with the ramp and slowly pushed it forward and into the van's cargo area. A final push, and the massive dinosaur skull was inside its new temporary home. They strapped the rolling platform securely to metal cargo hooks on the sides of the van cargo floor. The straps were ratcheted quite tight, so the platform was solidly in place. Seth chocked the four wheels. Finally, they folded and loaded the ramp inside the van, on its side next to the skull cart.

"Let's get those tools and make sure we leave nothing behind," Garcia said. Seth stayed outside on the loading dock, breathing in the clean night air. He was dreading the next leg of the journey cooped up in the rear of the van.

Garcia went back inside the building and pulled down the wide overhead door. He exited through the pedestrian door, lugging the tools in both hands. He failed to lock the door, an oversight that would have consequences.

Seth squeezed into the cargo area at the rear of the truck. Garcia slammed the van's two swing doors shut. There was barely enough room for Seth between the bony *T. rex* skull and the van's rear doors. He braced himself for an uncomfortable ride. He knew Gus would waste no time getting them away from the museum.

"Okay, pal. We're outta here," Garcia said, as he took his seat next to Gus. "We'll go out the back way. Less traffic."

Gus put the van in gear and cautiously made his way toward the locked gate at the northeast corner of the Sands ranch. As they rolled along, the skull on its wheeled platform rocked a little, but the chocked wheels didn't budge an inch. At the gate, a heavy steel chain secured the barrier to a thick wooden fence post. Garcia got out and picked the chromed padlock with a set of burglar's tools. A few minutes later, the van was through the gate, idling in place while Garcia swung the barrier closed, replaced the chain and re-locked the padlock.

"Forward, James," Garcia said to Gus, as he climbed aboard. For the first time that night, a small smile flitted on his lips. Gus didn't notice.

In the dark exhibit hall of the museum, Fred the parrot shuffled on his perch and uttered, "Uh-oh."

Chapter 47

Brian slept restlessly in the cabin. He kept waking up during the eerily quiet night. Maybe his urban-tuned ears just weren't used to such silence, the lack of traffic noise, the absence of human voices. He mused that city dwellers idealize the undisturbed peacefulness of a rural setting, until they actually experience it. Then they go bonkers from the eeriness of real quiet. Yet, he thought he could get used to this sort of tranquility. Maybe living in a small town like Clarkville would suit him better, though—quiet, for sure, but with a little more activity and background noise than this isolated ranch.

His thoughts turned to Carol Jensen. They were developing a closer relationship. He knew where he wanted it to go, which would be nice, but with significant complications. His principle residence was still in Chicago. With Carol acting as guardian for her teenage nephew Jerry, it was likely the boy would be living in her house until he went out on his own. In a couple of years, he'd probably go to college and be home summers.

As a single man approaching forty, Brian guessed he might not ever be a father, which was…okay. Jerry and he had bonded over a couple of fishing outings. Being the boy's co-guardian, in effect, could be satisfying. But he was getting way ahead of himself. He and Carol hadn't yet come close to being intimate. He still had his successful investigations business in Chicago. And, Michelle? He'd work on this current gig for Art Sands, see Carol for sure, then head back to Chicago and sort things out. Meanwhile…he drifted off to sleep again.

He thought about Sands and the assignment the billionaire had given him. Brian had not made much progress on his hunt for the kidnappers of Barbara Hardy. He'd meant to confront Gus Delmer today, but hadn't been able to find him. Oh well, it would have to wait for daylight.

In the early hours of the morning, Brian awoke again suddenly, certain he'd heard some peculiar sound. He listened carefully. Nothing. But as he wakened fully, he realized the sound had been a vehicle moving slowly in the near distance. Sound carried for miles in the stillness of a windless night at this secluded mountain place. A road ran along the west border of the ranch, about a mile from his cabin. This road stretched north for several miles, ending at the William Old Horn Dinosaur Museum in the northeast corner of the ranch. Art Sands had donated the twenty-acre parcel of land for the museum and had hired legal expertise to set up the nonprofit for its operation. The main purpose of the museum was to house the magnificent *T. rex* skeleton found two years earlier at nearby Bone Mountain The idea was to enable the public and the scientific community to have access to that tremendous cultural resource, and to provide employment for locals, especially members of the Crow nation.

Brian decided to check out the unexpected vehicle noise. He quickly put on a shirt and jeans and stepped into his boots.

As he did so, another sound intruded: rain pattering on the roof. He threw on his hooded rain jacket. He grabbed a flashlight and his Sig P226. He boarded his rental pickup and began to roll down the lane along the row of cabins, using only parking lights for illumination.

As Brian passed the cabin housing Darcy and Becky, the door opened, and Darcy stepped out onto the porch. She flagged him down and ran up to his side window.

"Where ya going?" she said.

"I heard a vehicle go by, heading north. I'm gonna check it out."

"I heard it too. Weird. I'm coming with." Without waiting for a response, she yanked open the passenger door and climbed into the truck. Darcy's t-shirt and jeans were already speckled from the steady rain.

"The museum's up there," Darcy said.

"Yep, and it's been closed since five P.M. What are you doing up at this hour?"

"Studying. Working on the dig all day, I'm falling behind. Don't like it."

Brian switched on the headlights and they rode in silence up the narrow gravel road. The windshield wipers slapped back and forth rhythmically. The headlights occasionally illuminated an animal, but the glowing eyes would dart away in a flash, making identification difficult. Once, a mule deer buck jumped from the roadside to the right of them and was gone in the darkness on the other side in a second's time.

"Whew," Darcy said.

Shortly, they arrived at the dinosaur museum. Floodlights lit up the parking lot and large identifying sign out front. Through the entrance door, the interior looked dark.

"Seems like they'd have lights on inside," Darcy said.

"Yeah, let's have a look."

They got out of the truck. The rain began to let up, a typical northern Rockies summer storm—in quickly and gone just as fast.

They found the front door locked, as expected.

Brian switched on his flashlight and led the way around back. No vehicles in sight. They noticed the big rollup door at the loading dock was securely closed. Brian tried the knob of the pedestrian door. Surprisingly, it opened. They went in. They noticed a security system screen aglow in the darkness to the right of the door. The green text indicated the alarm system had been disarmed.

"Strange. Where's the night guard, I wonder," Brian said. "Let's check out the rest of this place."

They went into the main exhibit hall, where the mighty *T. rex* skeleton loomed twenty feet above and covered thirty feet of the marble floor. But the separate skull box had been smashed open. The box yawned empty. The huge fossil skull was gone.

"Holy crap," Darcy said. "Whoever did this must've been in the vehicle we heard a while back. They grabbed the skull, loaded it up and split. We must've just missed them. But where's the guard?"

As if on cue, Robert Wolf groaned loudly and slammed his feet against the door of the closet in which he'd been imprisoned.

They tracked the sounds to a door at the rear of the cavernous room. Brian opened the door and trained his flashlight on the figure of Robert Wolf, lying on his side, mouth gagged, wrists and ankles secured by duct tape.

Brian used his pocketknife to cut through the tape. He untied the gag and helped Wolf to his feet.

"Jesus. Am I glad you guys came along," Wolf said. He struggled to his feet with Brian's help and wobbled unsteadily on his legs as blood began to circulate. He stretched his stiff limbs and seemed to be regaining his composure.

After quick introductions, Brian asked. "What happened?"

Wolf gave them the short version. The two thieves' faces had been covered by ski masks. They wore gloves. Dressed in work clothes. He had no idea who they were. He had stupidly turned off the alarms and opened the rear door when he heard noises outside. There had been no image on the monitor. The perps must have blocked the camera outside the rear door. And no doubt turned off the inside ones as well. The rest was obvious. They'd driven away in what sounded like a light truck.

"Can you turn on the interior lights?" Brian said.

With the help of Brian's flashlight, Wolf led them to the electrical panel, where he switched on the cameras and interior lights.

Brian opened his cell phone. No signal. He went to the reception counter in front and found a landline phone on a shelf under it. He called the sheriff's department and reported the theft. The fellow on the line identified himself as Deputy Jason Cowen and said he'd swing by the museum. He sounded tired but concerned.

Brian, Darcy and Wolf looked around the disaster area that surrounded the skull box. Whoever had wrecked the box had obviously not had a key. But they had otherwise known what they were doing.

"They must have rolled the skull platform out the cargo door and into a vehicle," Wolf said.

Brian figured the thieves had scouted the place ahead of time. Perhaps the staff on duty during daytime hours or the cameras in and about the building would have spotted something. At Brian's request, Wolf went to the rear of the building and buzzed open the rollup cargo door. Brian pointed his flashlight at the ground outside. There were fresh vehicle tracks, clearly visible in the mud created by the recent rain. He took some photos of the tracks with his phone.

"Where would they have driven to get out of here?" he asked Wolf.

The guard gestured to the nearby fence that formed a corner at the perimeter of the ranch. "See that gate? It's locked. I'm guessing they somehow got through it and took off on that road. At least, that's what it sounded like to me. That goes off the ranch. It leads to another crossroad that eventually goes to highway 89."

Brian frowned. "I'm gonna look at the gate. You guys better stay here in case the deputy shows up."

The rain had let up. There were scattered puddles outside the rear of the museum building. Brian carefully examined the hefty chromed padlock securing the heavy gate chain. It was locked, but there were faint scratches around the keyhole that told the tale: the lock had been picked and then re-locked. The tire tracks in the mud disappeared in the distance. They were beefy tracks, like what might be mounted on a heavy duty van or pickup. He guessed high-roof cargo van, so the looted fossil would fit. A commercial van would not have windows behind the front seat, ensuring privacy. At the rear of the building, he looked up at the camera above the cargo door. It had been smashed to bits. Pieces lay on the ground. As he stepped back through the pedestrian door, the sound of a vehicle pulling up in front came to him.

Wolf unlocked the front door to let the sheriff's deputy in. The tall young man wore a name badge reading "Cowen." He approached the empty *T. rex* skull display case and scratched his head through his Geyser County Sheriff's Dept. ball cap. "This sucks," he said.

"C'mon back here. I'll show you where they rolled it out and where they headed," Brian said.

After examining the tire tracks and gate outside, Deputy Cowen got his phone out. Finding no signal, he said, "I'm going out to my truck to radio in. The Sheriff's gonna love getting waked up for this news." He sighed and trudged toward the front entrance of the museum.

Chapter 48

In the cargo van, Garcia and the Delmer brothers rode in silence. The van jolted along a lumpy gravel road through Forest Service land. Blackness flowed by outside. The sky was full of clouds and moisture. No moonlight, no stars. The windshield wipers tracked back and forth rhythmically until Gus turned them off.

"Where we going with this thing?" Gus said.

"The buyer's flying out. Arrives soon. We'll meet him at his place. Not far from here. Meanwhile, we need to lay up for a couple hours."

"Where?"

"Seth's place is as good as any," Garcia replied.

"Bullshit!" Seth's voice came from the rear of the van, muffled by the huge dinosaur skull between him and the front seat occupants. "No fuckin' way do I want that thing on my property."

Garcia spoke slowly, as if addressing a slow child. "We've gotta keep the thing under wraps until we can get rid of it. Where better than your place? It's close. Gets us off the road while they're out searching. If they can't find any trace, they'll back off. Gives us a little breathing room. Anyway, we can't access the buyer's place until he's there."

"Shit," Seth replied.

"Relax, it's gonna be fine," Garcia said. He took Seth's silence as reluctant acquiescence.

Once they hit highway 89, Gus continued for a few miles and then steered the van onto the winding gravel road leading up to Seth's property high in the mountains.

The dashboard clock showed a little after three in the morning when they arrived. Gus stopped the van on the compacted gravel surface near the cluster of log buildings. He said to Garcia, "Wait here. I need to talk with Seth about uh, logistics."

At the rear of the van, Gus pulled the twin doors open. Seth glared at him as he jumped to the ground, and said, "Well?"

"How about we put the van in your barn?" Gus said.

"But what then? We try to drive this thing to some rich guy's house, we could get stopped by the sheriffs. They'll be out in force looking for anything capable of carrying that damned skull. They search this stolen truck, game's over. Next stop Deer Lodge for you and me, bro."

"I've got an idea." Gus said. "What about your dump truck? We roll the skull into the bed, strap 'er down and put a tarp on top. Nobody's gonna suspect a dump truck, right?"

Seth shrugged. "Better than that fuckin' van. Good thinkin'."

"What about this guy?" Gus said quietly as he nodded over his shoulder in the direction of Garcia.

Before Seth could reply, Garcia was suddenly at Gus's side. He'd somehow silently exited the passenger seat and crept over to the Delmers without being detected.

"I like the dump truck."

"The guy will have our cash, right?" Seth asked.

"Of course."

"Exactly how much?"

"Three million, split three ways. Sound good?"

"Sounds a little light," Seth said. "I saw online some dude paid eight million for a skull in South Dakota recently."

"Yeah, but that was a public auction. Our transaction is confidential. The buyer's gonna have to keep the skull under wraps, maybe just look at it by himself. Word gets out he's got it, he's gonna be going back to prison."

"Whaddaya mean *back*? He just get out?"

"Maybe. Doesn't matter. He's got the dough and we get it when we deliver the skull."

"You try anything cute, you're dead," Seth said to Garcia.

Garcia frowned. "Hey. Don't get salty with me. We're all on the same side, right?"

"We damn well better be," Seth said.

Gus stood shoulder to shoulder with his brother and said, "Damn straight."

Now Garcia grinned. He held his hands up in front of him, palms out, a placating gesture. "I've gotta use the bathroom and so forth. Why don't you guys get going with loading the truck?"

"C'mon then," Seth said to his brother.

As they watched Garcia make his way to the guest cabin in the distance, Seth said, "Are you thinkin' what I'm thinkin'?"

"That dude has gotta go," Gus replied.

"Correct. We get the cash and he's out of the picture."

"I wouldn't underestimate him, though. He's small but strong. Told me he was a Navy Seal, for what that's worth."

"Google says he was. But I've taken out a little insurance, so to speak."

"Good."

While the Delmers were plotting, Garcia got in touch with Massey. He'd brought an InReach Mini along. The small satellite communications device worked through an app on his cell phone. No cell signal necessary. Standing outside his cabin, with an unobstructed view of the clearing sky, he texted Massey with an update. He was happy that the Delmer brothers were limited by the sporadic cell coverage up there. "Item at D place. Confirm pmnt."

"3 mil plus 2 mil for minus 2." Massey texted that he was ready for delivery and gave Garcia directions to the home he'd recently purchased and now occupied nearby. Garcia was satisfied. Massey had agreed to pay him five million dollars—three for the skull (to be split three ways) and an additional two for eliminating the McKays. If he chose to complete the second task.

Garcia's thoughts turned to the man with the dough. This Massey guy liked his secret baubles, ergo the skull. With the McKays, it would be Massey's hatred, vengeance for the grief they'd caused him a couple of years ago in Chicago. The man had built up a white-hot loathing toward the two who'd cost him his job as exalted Chief Financial Officer of a large company and sent him to a prison cell. The Delmers, they were a wild card, one that could be discarded from his hand. Garcia liked safe bets. And he had other priorities.

Chapter 49

Brian, Darcy and the deputy exited the museum through the rear door and went to the gate in the high fence at the corner of the Sands property. They noted the hefty lock on the gate and the vehicle tracks in the mud on the other side.

"I reported the theft to the sheriff," Cowen said. "He says we'll be on it at sunup."

"Okay. In the meantime, I'm going to check something out," Brian said.

"Well, I'll secure this building and provide first aid for the guard, if he needs it. Then I'm gonna take off. Nothing more I can do until it's light out," Cowen said, as he pivoted on a boot heel and strode toward the museum.

Once Cowen was inside, Brian turned to Darcy and said, "Stand between me and the door over there, just in case anyone's looking."

Darcy shielded Brian's hands from view of anyone in the building as he extracted a lockpick kit from his pocket and got to work. First, he inserted a tiny tension wrench into the bottom of the gate lock's keyhole and applied slight pressure. Next he inserted his pick tool into the top of the keyhole. While applying a little twisting pressure to the wrench, he slid the pick back and forth in the hole. After a few minutes of maneuvering the two tools, the pins inside the lock moved into position, releasing the lock mechanism. The lock popped open.

"You missed your vocation," Darcy commented.

"I know my way around a snake rake," Brian said.

She opened the gate so Brian could get the truck from out front and move it through the gate. Once he'd gotten through, she closed the gate. They studied the tire tracks on the road with the aid of a flashlight.

"I'm thinking van," Darcy said."

"How so?"

Well, the tracks look like a big car or crossover tires, but they would have to be sturdy to carry a heavy load. They're smoother than most pickup tires, which are kinda knobby. Like the ones on that truck."

Brian swung the light beam onto one of the Ford pickup tires. It had pronounced blocky segments, four across. The sidewall of the tire indicated "all-terrain."

"Good deduction."

They hopped back in their vehicle. Darcy said, "Hit it."

Brian grinned and then guided the pickup along the muddy track, heading north and away from the ranch. The headlights lit up the sprinkles of rain and the muddy route through the countryside. In a few minutes, they reached a crossroad. There was no sign identifying either road. He made a left. After a few more miles, they reached highway 89. By then, the rain had stopped. A typical summer storm in the Rocky Mountains, fast to come and even faster to dissipate. In this dry country, he knew, farmers and ranchers appreciated every drop of rain. He turned left and headed south toward the Sands place.

They arrived at the cabins where he and Darcy had been staying at 4:12 A.M. per the dashboard clock.

"Let's get a couple hours of sleep," Brian said. "Whoever took the skull probably delivered it to a buyer, or at least is on the way. I've got an idea, but nothing we can do until daylight."

"Okay. Let me know when you're ready to roll," Darcy said, as she reached her cabin door. Inside, she heard Becky snoring and tried not to wake her up. Her bunk was inviting—she'd had minimal sleep, what with the dinosaur dig and keeping up with her grad school studies. She set an alarm on her phone and tumbled into bed.

Brian returned to his cabin, stripped to his underwear and lay down on his back. He'd long ago acquired the ability to fall asleep and wake up at will. He settled in his bed and was out within minutes.

When he came to, the first rays of sunlight were brightening the eastern sky. Birds were communicating raucously from perches near the cabin. He knew they made a hardscrabble living in the dry terrain among the junipers, cottonwoods, aspens and sagebrush. Not much different than humans who worked for a living around here. A few minutes later, he'd dressed, eaten an energy bar and was in the F-150, rolling toward Darcy's cabin. There were signs of life among the employee cabins, people getting ready to go to work at their jobs on the ranch.

As before, when he got to Darcy's cabin, she was out the door and into the truck in a flash. They set out toward Seth Delmer's property.

Chapter 50
(Day 14)

It was dawn when the Delmers carefully rolled the skull platform down the ramp at the rear of the cargo van. They were slow and cautious, not wanting the awkward load to get away from them. Finally, all four wheels cleared the ramp and rested on the ground. Seth backed his huge white tandem axle Mack Superliner dump truck up to the platform. The engine, revving fast, made the ground around them tremble. Seth seemed to relish causing a commotion, perhaps for the benefit of Garcia, who stood with hands on hips, watching.

The brothers unlatched the two-way tailgate on the left side and swung it open. They placed a solid metal ramp from the rear edge of the dump truck's bed to the ground twelve feet behind. With that short distance, the angle of the ramp was steep. They carefully maneuvered the wheeled platform holding the gape-mouthed dinosaur skull to the end of the ramp. The rear of the skull pointed toward the truck cab. Next, they began to walk the platform up the ramp and into the dump bed. This part was hard labor. At one point, the rear wheels of the stand rolled backward onto Gus's toes.

"Goddammit!" he screamed.

Garcia commented, "You guys are pros. Maybe I can finagle a bonus for ya from the buyer."

"How about finaglin' some help, so we can get this piece of rock loaded?" Seth said.

Garcia went to one side of the platform and halfheartedly helped the Delmer brothers push it upward. Finally, the skull platform was on the more or less level surface of the rusty dump bed.

Seth got a heavy gray waffled shipping blanket from the storage shed. He and Gus flung it over the top of the leering stone skull. They secured the wooden rolling platform with ratcheting cargo straps. Next, they got to work chocking the wheels of the platform. Satisfied it was secure, they placed a faded blue vinyl grommeted tarp over the blanket and attached it to the side hooks of the dump bed with bungee cords. The top of the cargo protruded above the edges of the side walls by about two feet.

Seth and Gus jumped down to the ground and slid the metal ramp into the dump bed behind the skull. They slammed the truck tailgate closed. From the ground, the load in the truck could have been anything.

"I'll put the van away," Gus said.

While he was doing that, Gus asked Garcia, "You got the location of this buyer dude?"

"Yep."

They stood in awkward silence, waiting for Gus to return.

After five minutes. Garcia said, "What's he doing in there?"

"Maybe calling his girlfriend. Ya know, some people have lives."

"I thought the cell signal was iffy here," Garcia said.

"Depends on the weather and also your carrier. If it ain't Verizon, ya might be outta luck."

In fact, Gus was calling Josie Wilshire at the Sands ranch to let her know what he was doing.

As soon as Gus returned, Garcia spoke: "Let's head out."

Seth got behind the wheel of the hulking Mack, while Garcia took the middle seat and Gus piled in at shotgun. It was a tight fit for the three men. The middle seat was an afterthought, just a lumpy torn vinyl surface with a joint down the middle, separating the two wide outboard seats. Garcia didn't complain. This would not be a long ride.

"Cozy, isn't it?" Seth said, as he rolled down his side window.

Garcia gave general directions to Seth, who eased the big truck out onto the road leading down to the highway. The clattering diesel engine seemed at ease, effortlessly propelling them along the rough road. The smokestack above the truck body on the passenger side belched black exhaust as Gus downshifted to slow their momentum on the steeper downhill stretches. Adding to Garcia's discomfort, the long floor-mounted gearshift lever with a large knob on top was situated in front of his crotch. Every time Seth shifted gears, the lever moved within an inch of his genital region. Seth made no effort to telegraph the shifts, seemingly oblivious to any potential discomfort to his middle passenger.

"How many gears has this rig got?" Garcia asked.

"Enough," Seth replied. "Thirteen, if you gotta know."

They rode along in an uneasy silence. Seth piloted the truck past the town of Clarkville and continued south on highway 89 along the Yellowstone River. An hour into the journey, Garcia said, "Turn left at that next road."

Chapter 51

Brian braked the F-150 to a stop outside Seth Delmer's cabin. He and Darcy got out and stood waiting for a moment, listening and watching. Silence. A slight breeze riffled the cottonwood leaves. A redwing blackbird trilled from its perch on a nearby tree. The place felt abandoned. Brian stepped up on the cabin's small porch and rapped on the door. No answer. He tried the knob. It turned easily in his hand. He pushed the door open and entered the front room with Darcy following.

The place was a mess. Two people had slept here, one on the unmade bed and one in a sleeping bag on the wood floor. A pile of candy bars and bags of corn chips sat in a heap on the small dining table.

"Munchies," Darcy said.

"Yep. Let's look around outside."

They moved among the small compound of buildings. The other log cabin was empty. There were a couple of discarded Kleenexes on the floor. The bed had mussed up sheets and a fleece blanket on top. The toilet lid was up. The sink was full of water splashes.

They went to the nearby outbuilding, some sort of storage shed. A big one. They rolled open the sliding barn door. With no windows, the interior was a pool of dark shadows. Something large and white glowed, filling about half the interior space. Darcy groped for a light switch. Once she'd found it, the space was bathed in pale gold light. A high-roof commercial cargo van hulked on the near side of the building.

Brian placed a palm on the van's hood. A small trace of warmth. He went to the rear of the vehicle and swung its side-by-side doors open. The cargo area yawned empty like a toothless mouth. He noticed a few small shards of dark stone on the rubber floor surface.

Darcy stepped in, gently pushing Brian aside. "Those rock bits look like my area of expertise." She picked up a slim shard of dark gray stone and studied it carefully for a moment.

"What we have here is failure to protect a *T. rex* skull," she said. "Though these bitty fragments can easily be glued back on." She swept her hands across the rubber floor surface, scaring up a few more shards. She put them all in a shorts pocket.

"So, what did they do with it?" Brian said.

They searched the area outside the shed. On the ground were tracks of narrow smooth wheels spaced about three feet apart. They figured the tracks matched the wheels of the rolling platform the *T. rex* skull had been mounted on at the museum. The wheels had dug down about an inch in the rain-softened soil. Much wider dual tire tracks of the type at the rear of heavy duty trucks covered the ground nearby. The narrow tracks disappeared abruptly where a ramp had apparently been placed on the ground behind the large truck.

"I've gotta admit, these guys planned it out pretty thoroughly," Brian said.

"Must have been three of them, judging from the cabins. The Delmer brothers and somebody else," Darcy said.

"My guess is the third person is the brains of the operation. From what I've seen of the Delmers, they wouldn't have the mental firepower to come up with a heist like this."

"They transferred the skull to…what? A dump truck? Drove it out of here, possibly to the buyer."

"But they're not home free yet."

"Had to go down to 89. But then where?"

"Dunno. But I have an idea, a long shot…"

They boarded the rental pickup and headed down to the highway, where Darcy jumped out. She squatted low to study the dual tire tracks from the Delmers' truck. They turned left, south toward Clarkville. She hopped in and reported her findings.

"So, we're going into town," she said.

"Yeah."

It was now after eight A.M. The sun shone brightly on the two-lane blacktop. With almost no traffic, the driving was about as easy as it gets. Brian switched on the cruise control and pondered the possibilities as they loped along at eighty. They arrived in Clarkville around a quarter of nine.

"I'd kill for a cup of good coffee," Darcy said.

"Me too." Brian parked the truck in a diagonal space on Main Street, near a coffee joint called MT Lava Java.

They got three large paper cups of black coffee to go.

"Why the extra cup?" Darcy asked.

"You'll see."

They sat on a wrought iron bench outside the coffee shop for a moment.

Brian said, "Here's what I'm thinking. The buyer of the skull is someone with a great deal of privacy. You don't have a stolen *T. rex* skull worth millions delivered to your house in a place where the neighbors might find it just a tad unusual."

Darcy took a sip of coffee. "So you're thinking some rich dude living out in the sticks."

He shrugged. "Maybe a brash newcomer. Somebody who buys a Montana ranch property thinking it's beyond the view of snooping locals. Which no place is, really. The time I've spent around here, I've learned that everybody watches everything. True of small towns and even truer of rural areas. Betcha there's a pair of binoculars on a windowsill in every house in Montana. Just look at Arthur Sands's mansion. And every cabin on the ranch."

"Yeah, I've noticed that. So, a private spot. But where do we start looking?"

"First, let's check in with a local real estate lady I happen to know. Her office is just down the block."

With a coffee in each hand, Brian led the way, walking four doors down to the real estate office of Norah Spivey. Before they entered, Brian said, "This woman's a friend of Barbara Hardy. I spent some time with her the other day. She happens to be the ex-wife of our very own Seth Delmer. She's smart and she's plugged into the local market. Little rough around the edges, but don't let that fool ya."

As they entered, a husky voice came from the interior of the office, beyond the front desk. "Hey, it's my newest best friend Brian." The owner of the voice trotted out to greet them. A short woman carrying a few extra pounds came toward them with a wide smile on her face. Brian carefully set down the two coffees and was embraced in a hug evoking a boa constrictor.

Coming up for air, Brian said, "It's great seeing you again, Norah. Meet my niece, Darcy."

Shrewd eyes appraised Darcy as they shook hands. "Well, c'mon in, you two."

Brian quickly grasped the unopened coffee and handed it to Norah. "Thought you might like a fresh cup."

She accepted the gift with a wink. "Just so happens I'm ready for a fresh one. Thanks. How can I help?"

"We're interested in recent purchases of upper bracket properties in the area. Probably five million dollars plus and in a desirable location, along what the state lawmakers call high-quality water."

"Funny, there's been one of those, very recent. Guy from Chicago bought a humongous house on just under a thousand acres up Andres Creek."

"Who's the buyer?"

"Lemme check on my computer. C'mon back."

They followed Norah to the rear of the office space, passing three unoccupied desks along the way. She sat at a desktop computer and gestured to the two visitor chairs across from her.

After manipulating a mouse and tapping a few keys, Norah said, "Fellah name of A. Hamilton Massey. Paid cash. Little over fifteen million bucks. I know that place. House is twenty thousand square feet. New construction about two years ago. Fellah owned it from Texas, died recently. Was only on the market for a week when this Massey guy snapped it up. Gray stone walls. Kinda looks like a castle. Sits on East Andres Creek. Thick line of trees blocks the view from the

Forest Service trail next door, which is designated Wilderness. Perennial fishing creek and ponds. Tons of wildlife. Super place. Real private."

Brian disguised his surprise at hearing Massey's name. "What's the word on Massey? Anything personal about him?"

"All I know is he's reclusive. Nobody's met him in person, including the broker who closed the deal. Heard something about him being involved in a scandal. Somebody said he's dirty. Maybe did some time. Wouldn't be the first guy with dirty money's bought himself a slice of paradise in our fair state. Who am I to judge?" She shrugged expansively.

Silence ensued for a moment as all three of them sipped coffee. Brian tossed his empty paper cup into a nearby waste basket. He stood and said, "Norah, you're a doll. I owe ya."

She smiled. "Yep, and I'll collect someday."

They said their goodbyes and the McKays left Norah sitting at her desk.

Out on the street, as they walked to the truck, Darcy said, "She likes you. You're turning into a regular babe magnet."

He shrugged. "Pays to make friends."

Chapter 52

The towering Mack dump truck churned its way up the narrow forest service road, belching black clouds from its upright exhaust pipe. Thick stands of coniferous trees walled off the road on the right. On the left, a tumbling mountain stream cascaded down through a boulder-strewn bed. The three occupants of the truck rode in tense silence. Each man was concerned about what would transpire when they reached their destination at the end of the road. Each anticipated a sizeable payday, quite possibly accompanied by violence. The buyer waiting for them was not someone to trust.

Seth was familiar with this road. He'd hunted elk up here on the public land adjacent to the skull buyer's house. He figured there was about a mile to go. He remembered an imposing gate of black steel bars blocking the driveway leading into the property recently acquired by the buyer. A tall barb wire fence blocked access to the place on both sides of the gate. Just in case the message of the gate and fence was unclear, a large orange and white sign affixed to the gate declared, NO TRESSPASSING. VIOLATERS WILL BE PROSECUTED TO THE FULL EXTENT OF THE LAW.

Just before reaching the gate, a lane branched off to the right and into a public parking lot where hikers and hunters could drop their vehicles before setting out on the forest service trail up East Andres Creek. If you took the trail, you'd climb several thousand vertical feet, deep into the Absaroka Beartooth Wilderness.

Finally, the dump truck rolled to a halt outside the gate. The air brakes chuffed loudly as pressure escaped from the braking system. Seth rolled down his window and waited to be acknowledged by somebody inside the barricaded confines. There was a keypad on a post to the left of the opening, but he ignored it.

A couple of minutes passed. Then, a deep voice boomed from a speaker box mounted on the post. "Yeah?"

Garcia yelled past Seth, "We're here. Open up."

The heavy steel pivot gate swung upward like an executioner's blade, until it pointed skyward on the right side of the opening. Seth let out the clutch and gave the rig some throttle. The truck thundered forward, the occiput of the tarp-covered skull brushing against the underside of a cottonwood branch.

"Careful. Take it slow," Garcia said.

Seth shook his head. "You want to drive, hotshot?"

They'd gone about a hundred yards when a sportily dressed giant appeared, walking toward them in the center of the narrow gravel road. The man went about six-six, three hundred. Bulbous belly of hard fat. Tan skin. Untucked sport shirt, shorts. His hair was trimmed close and his ears protruded like jug handles. A mirthless smile revealed pointed yellow incisors.

He held up a hand, clearly signaling STOP RIGHT NOW. Seth braked the dump truck to a standstill. Dust blew up from behind the vehicle, right in the face of the giant. He didn't blink. Just stood there motionless as a continent while the air cleared. The big man sauntered to the driver's side window. He bent his head and looked into the interior of the cab, registering the face of each of the three occupants. Then he straightened and addressed Seth. "You can pull your rig up ahead and around to the rear of the house. There's a place to back in and unload there."

"Yessir," Seth said. Then he snapped off an ironic little salute. Gus was surprised at the impertinence of his brother. Normally, Seth was cautious with strangers, especially ones who could flatten you like a flapjack in a frying pan.

They followed a paved driveway until it terminated at the rear of what could be described as a gray stone castle. Three stories loomed above. A slender figure regarded them from a window on the second floor, but they did not notice.

Garcia remained silent. He'd recognized the Brobdingnagian gatekeeper. The fellow had been a middle linebacker of great renown with the Chicago Bears for a ten-year period ending when Garcia had been about fifteen. Jake Pasciewicz made All-Pro six times while leading the Bears to a Super Bowl championship, he'd been frequently penalized for unnecessary roughness. Made the Tribune police blotter in the off-season one time when he'd beaten a man nearly to death in the parking lot of a north side bar. The victim had dared to honk his horn at Jake for blocking the exit. The charges of attempted manslaughter had been quietly dropped when the Bears' front office interceded. Bottom line, Jake P was an animal both on and off the field.

A four-car garage featuring gray paneled doors abutted the north-facing edifice of the grand building. Seth executed a turn and backed the rear of the truck up to within a few yards of the nearest garage door, following the hand motions of the mountainous man. The overhead door slowly eased up, revealing an empty garage space with a spotless concrete floor.

"You can roll the merchandise right in there," Pasciewicz said, pointing with his chin.

"Whoa. What about the cash?" Seth said.

"Let's get out of the truck," Garcia said.

The Delmers exited the vehicle followed by Garcia. They stood side by side on the asphalt surface, facing Pasciewicz.

"Okay, gents, here's the deal. You're gonna unload the thing. Mr. M will then inspect it. If it passes muster, he will give you guys the agreed-upon remuneration. You will then immediately depart the premises. Fair enough?"

Garcia addressed Seth. "Let's unload the thing."

Seth and Gus undid the tailgate latches, allowing the heavy steel panel to swing open. They removed the ramp from the dump bed and maneuvered it into position, spanning the gap from the edge of the bed to the ground, just outside the garage opening. The brothers ascended the ramp and detached the cords securing the tarp and blanket over the skull, as well as the compression straps and chocks securing the rolling platform. The rough stony head was unveiled, staring mercilessly forward. The dagger-like teeth seemed to menace the nearby men. Gus shuddered involuntarily.

"C'mon. Time's wasting," Garcia snapped.

The three men slowly worked the wheeled platform down the ramp, until it sat level on the ground. Then they wheeled it into the garage.

Pasciewicz regarded the process impassively. Then, as if addressing a well-behaved dog, "Very good. You're gonna wait right there. Do not touch anything." He pivoted on a heel and disappeared through a door at the far end of the garage.

They loaded up the shipping materials and closed up the truck bed. Then they waited nervously.

"He'd better deliver that cash pronto," Gus said. "Or I'm gonna…"

The others were silent. Seven minutes elapsed.

The huge man emerged through the doorway at the far end of the garage space. A. Hamilton Massey followed in his wake. The tall spindly ex-con's prison pallor overlaid his face like white talc. He blinked into the glaring sunshine like a domestic bird whose cage shroud had been suddenly lifted off.

"Uh, hello," Massey said. "Just let me have a closer look at the cranium." Without waiting for a response, he donned a pair of readers and began to inspect the fossil skull with the intensity of a jeweler examining a rose cut diamond in a platinum setting. After a few minutes, he said, "There are a few small chips from the stone. Looks like it happened recently. Any idea what caused the damage?"

The others remained silent.

"Well, it'll do," Massey said.

Garcia cleared his throat. "All right then. We've done our part. We're ready for our uh, remuneration."

"Hold on, hoss," Pasciewicz said. "The man's got to assemble the bank. Wait outside the door." The overhead door rolled down to the ground. Silence fell on them like the interior of an ancient sarcophagus.

"What the hell?" Gus said.

"Hang on a sec," Garcia said.

The Delmers' faces darkened with doubt, but they held their ground without further comment. A few minutes later, a sound from above caught their attention. They looked up as an open double-hung window on the second level slid open. The head and massive upper body of Pasciewicz appeared. Suddenly, a large black duffle bag was pushed from the window opening to crash to the ground inches from Seth Delmer's boots. He bent to pick it up.

"Not so fast. Let's have a look inside that bag before we do anything else," Garcia said.

"What the fuck you think I'm doing?" Seth said. He unzipped the duffle and pulled it open to reveal banded stacks of hundred dollar bills. He pulled a few stacks out to verify the contents appeared to be bundles of hundreds. "There's dozens of stacks in there," he said.

"Do the math, man," Garcia said. "Bank cash comes in a hundred bills per packet. So a packet of hundreds is ten thousand. So it takes a hundred packets for a million and three hundred for three million. That duffle is big enough for three hundred packets, so it might be okay. Let's not stand here counting it."

"Yeah, what if that monster comes out and tries to take it back?" Gus said.

"C'mon, let's get the fuck out of here," Seth said. He grabbed the duffle and lifted it off the ground. "This sucker weighs as much as a sandbag."

"Should be close to seventy pounds," Garcia said.

Seth grunted as he lifted the duffle and placed it in the dump bed.

"Whoa," Garcia said. "Make damn sure that thing is zipped up tight."

"It's tighter than a nun's pussy," Seth said. He got behind the wheel as the others jumped in. He executed an awkward turn and eased the big vehicle down the driveway, through the open gate and onto the road. He'd barely cleared the barrier when he noticed in the side mirror the gate slamming down like a scythe. He accelerated and soon they were exceeding thirty miles an hour on the narrow gravel lane. After about a mile, he spotted a light-colored pickup slowly making its way up toward them.

"See that truck?" Garcia said.

"Fuck 'em." Seth shifted into the next higher gear and increased his speed.

As they neared the smaller vehicle, Seth pulled on the lanyard activating the air horn. A deafening blast split the air as the dump truck passed the pickup in a tsunami of dust. Seth glanced at the rearview, noting with satisfaction that the oncoming vehicle they'd passed had been forced off the road and into the shallow ditch.

Chapter 53

Earlier that morning: Brian backed out of the diagonal parking space on bustling Main Street in downtown Clarkville. He turned to Darcy. "I've gotta make a couple of phone calls. Let's find a quiet spot."

He drove south on Main toward the Absaroka mountains. In a few blocks, still within the town limits, they entered a large park full of trees and grassy expanses. There were four softball diamonds, a pair of tennis courts and a soccer field, but nobody was playing. He parked at the side of the road and they walked to a gazebo sheltering a brown picnic table made of recycled plastic. No one was around except the occasional runner, dog walker or mom pushing a baby in a stroller.

He called James St. Claire in the FBI Chicago Field office. He got him right away. After a minute of chat, he asked, "Anything on Massey?"

"Damn, he's an elusive son of a bitch. Must have ditched his phone. Probably got a burner. In any case, nothing on Sensorvault and nobody's seen him physically in a coupla days."

"There a watch for him at the airports?"

"All the commercial ones. But not the private."

"Car rentals?"

"Sure. Nothing there,"

"What about Garcia?"

"Like I told ya, he flew to Bozeman. I texted Thorsten to keep an eye out but haven't heard back. Ya gotta realize, I'm up to my ass in white collar crime. Latest is pig butchering."

"Pig what?"

"Our term for fake crypto sales to dumbass suckas."

"Lovely."

"Yeah. Anyway, you might get in touch with Thorsten."

"I'll do that. Got a theft he'll be interested in."

"What's that? Cattle rustling?"

"Dinosaur skull lifted from the museum on the Art Sands place."

"Oh man. That's over the edge."

"Yeah. And a regular crime wave for Sands. First, his ex is snatched. Now, this dinosaur thing. I'm thinking they're connected."

"Prob'ly right. Hey, Darcy still workin' on that bone dig there?"

"Yeah, another day or two. Then back to MSU."

"Take care a that girl. She gets all swaggeroni."

"Watch what you say. She's sitting right next to me in my rental. We're gonna follow a lead on that skull."

"Jesus, man. Get Thorsten involved. No tellin' what shit's gonna be comin' down. Market for them dinosaur artifacts is off the hook. And that's based."

"I know. We'll take precautions."

"Okay, man. Hollaback."

As he hung up, Brian mused about James's speech patterns. The man could speak like the king of England if he wanted. But conversing with a friend like Brian, he'd often revert to the vernacular of the street. He'd grown up in a rough neighborhood on the South Side. And he was a few years younger. Anyway, he'd developed into one of the savviest FBI agents Brian knew. Brian was proud of his mentoring of James as a new recruit.

"So James said to take care of delicate little me," Darcy said with a frown.

"Only because he loves you." Which evoked an eyeroll.

His luck held. He caught Thorsten, the Bozeman FBI resident agent, straightaway.

"Yeah, I'm on the skull heist," Thorsten said. "Salt Lake City's involved, of course." As Brian knew, Bozeman was one of seventeen satellite offices under the FBI regional office in SLC. The satellites were scattered across Utah, Idaho and Montana.

"What's *your* interest?"

"I'm still working for Sands, trying to get a bead on the guys that abducted his ex."

"You at the ranch?"

"I'm sitting in my rental pickup in Clarkville. Darcy's with me. We're about to visit a new Montana landowner, a man you might remember from that Belcoe scandal last year."

"Massey. Read about the pardon. Couldn't believe it."

"Sucks, right?"

"How's he a Montana landowner?"

"Bought himself a trophy home on hundreds of acres in the valley south of Clarkville."

"How'd he swing it? Had to pay fines. And restitution to the folks he defrauded. Went bankrupt, as I recall."

"He's as bent as a paper clip. No doubt he stashed millions offshore before he went away. We suspected it, just couldn't prove it. Seems like the kind of guy would commission a stolen *T. rex* skull as décor for his new rustic retreat. Just a hunch."

"He's gotta be an angry bugger, too. Blamed everyone else for his own screwups. Thinks he's God's gift to the financial world. I'll bet he's got a hard-on for the FBI, the judge and jury who put him away. And you. Darcy, too."

"And you too, for that matter. You helped bring down him and those schmucks at that 606 Ranch."

"Yep. That, and my official status as the government's lone badass lawman around here, means I should accompany you guys when you visit this trophy place."

"We're on our way."

"I can't get away until later, maybe an hour?"

"We'll tread carefully. If it's dodgy, we'll pull back and we can team up with you later."

"Okay. If there's cell coverage, give me a call when you get there. If not, call when you can."

"One more thing: James St. Claire said he told you to watch for another Chicago guy, Andrew Garcia."

"I checked flight records. He flew into Bozeman two nights ago. Rented a gray Bronco. Then disappeared. Hasn't incurred any credit card charges since. Nothing."

"Thanks. Talk to you later."

Brian spread out the map from Nora's office on the console between the front bucket seats. He noted the location circled in red ink. She'd jotted down the rural address as well. He dictated the address into the truck's navigation system, and they were on their way. The sun was blazing. Both Brian and Darcy wore sunglasses and ball caps. They pulled the truck's visors down as they left the town behind and rolled onto the highway paralleling the Yellowstone River.

A few miles south of town, the robotic female nav voice had him make a left onto a well-maintained two-lane blacktop county road. After another eight miles, pavement gave way to gravel. The truck juddered as they climbed steadily up a twisting road through the National Forest. The next turn was a left onto a much narrower route, a bumpy dirt-and-gravel way paralleling a mountain stream. A thick forest of pines and firs formed a wall to the right. After they'd gone a couple of miles, a cloud of dust ahead announced another vehicle coming their way.

A large dump truck appeared, approaching at a speed clearly unsafe for such a cramped space. An ear-splitting air horn cleaved the air. The huge eggcrate grill of the truck loomed and closed the distance in no time. A pulverizing crash appeared imminent. The air horn blasted again. Brian held his breath as he jerked the pickup rightward at the last second while applying the brakes. They careened off the road surface and into a shallow ditch. Branches scraped the right side of the pickup as it bounced over rocks and finally came to a stop. The dump truck thundered past and down the road in a tsunami of dust. Brian and Darcy exchanged a look of outrage. The seatbelts had kept them secured in their seats and neither had been injured. Thankfully, the front airbags had not detonated.

"Son of a bitch!" Brian said. He put the pickup in four wheel drive and slowly guided it back onto the road. Then, as quickly as he could, he turned around and sped back where they'd come from.

"So we're gonna bag visiting Massey?" Darcy said.

"He can wait. I have a hunch the asshole driving that dump truck just delivered the skull. Let's see where they go."

"The driver and the shotgun guy looked stocky. Both wearing caps. The one in the middle was smaller, with shades, no cap. None of 'em familiar," Darcy said.

"The smaller dude might have been Garcia, that prick."

He gave the truck plenty of gas and they hurtled down the narrow gravel road to the highway.

Chapter 54

By the time they reached highway 89, the dump truck was gone. Brian waited for traffic to clear, as a procession of vehicles, many tourists with out of state plates and travel trailers in tow, plodded by. As soon as there was a break in traffic, he accelerated onto the two-lane blacktop.   As they topped a rise, he could see several vehicles ahead. The dump truck tooled along at the speed limit, heading north toward Clarkville.

When they reached the entrance for I-90 eastbound, they could see the dump truck merging onto the Interstate up ahead. Brian followed, allowing three vehicles between them and the bigger truck. After a few minutes, the truck took the exit for highway 89 north. Once again, Brian kept well back. There was plenty of traffic, so he was confident of not being busted by the driver of the truck if he were examining following vehicles in his mirrors.

After fifteen miles, the dump truck made a right onto a dirt way with a sign, Shields River Road. Brian followed. This time, there was no intervening traffic. But the dump truck was stirring up a rooster tail of dust. Brian gambled that the driver would be unable to see the pickup. He hung back about a half mile. He could still easily track the dust cloud. He knew that Seth Delmer's place was up that way.

Another twenty-five minutes elapsed as the dump truck with its trailing curtain of dust worked its way north and east on a series of dirt roads. Finally, the dust dissipated. Brian stopped the pickup. The truck had gone up a lane through the trees at Seth Delmer's place.

"Let's get this vehicle under cover," Brian said. He drove up the road about a hundred yards past the turnoff to the rural property. A group of Douglas firs appeared on the right, sheltering a shallow turnout. He rolled the pickup off the road and behind the dense conifers. He was confident they could not be seen from Delmer's entry drive.

"We can hoof it from here," he said.

"Good thing I'm wearing my hiking shoes," Darcy said.

They set out at a steady pace, looking ahead to the spot where the dump truck had turned in. Bushes and trees blocked their view of the driveway. When they reached the drive, they moved off it and into to the bordering vegetation before walking up. They stayed alert for any sign of the truck or its occupants. After a few minutes, they heard male voices just ahead.

Chapter 55

Seth stopped his truck outside the cabin. The three men jumped down from the cab. Without speaking, the Delmers went to the rear of the truck bed and unlatched the tailgate. Seth grabbed the black duffle bag and wrestled it off the truck. He slung the canvas carrying strap over a shoulder and carried the bag to the wooden picnic table located to the south of his cabin. Dappled sunlight made its way through the surrounding trees to the weathered tabletop.

"Have a seat, guys," Seth said. "Let's count this dough and split it up. Then, you can be on your way," he said, looking at Garcia.

Seth chose a seat on the bench and Gus plopped down next to him. Garcia sat on the opposite side. As always, the placement of the men reflected the opposing interests: Garcia vs. the Delmers. Garcia felt he had the upper hand. He had an idea that he did not share with the brothers.

Seth unzipped the duffle and began pulling banded packets of hundred dollar bills from the bag. The unmistakable portrait of Benjamin Franklin regarded him impassively from the top of each stack. He stopped to count one of the packets, riffling the edges of the crisp bills with a calloused thumb. "There's a hundred bills in this one. Ten thousand bucks."

"Right," Garcia said. "So, there should be three hundred packets, all containing a hundred bills. Let's each grab a bunch and count each packet and the number of packets. Keep the money in sight at all times." Without waiting for a reply, he reached into the duffle and pulled out a few packets. Seth and Gus did the same. The three men were silent as they concentrated on their task. After a few minutes, they evened up the packets, so each of them had four stacks, twenty-five high.

"I'll take my share in this duffle, if it's okay with you guys," Garcia said. "I'm sure you can scare up a backpack or something for your shares." He quickly shoveled a hundred packets of bills into the duffle, grabbed it by the handles and stood.

The Delmers regarded him silently.

"Well, it's been a pleasure," Garcia said with a tight smile.

"Aren't you forgetting something?" Gus said.

Garcia lost his smile. "What?"

"We're the ones who provided the van and the dump truck. Put you up here while we got ready for the deal to go down."

"So what? Massey recruited the three of us and paid three million. We each get a third."

"Bullshit. You came in late on this thing. We did all the work. And we incurred expenses. We're deducting a hundred grand. Leaves you with nine hundred, and you're lucky to get that much," Seth said.

"Hold on, man," Garcia said. "I've got a better idea. Why don't I just take the whole friggin' shaboodle?" He drew the .38 revolver from the waistband at the back of his pants.

Seth smiled. "What are ya gonna do with that thing?" He pulled a Smith & Wesson revolver from a cargo pants pocket under the picnic table and got to his feet.

Garcia pulled the trigger on the .38. It refused to retract. In that instant, Garcia knew he'd been a fool for not test-firing the gun.

"Funny how modifying the hammer screws up a revolver," Seth said. He pointed his S&W directly at the smaller man's chest. "Now, we're gonna put you on ice, dude."

Garcia backed up a step and suddenly hurled the inoperable .38 at Seth's face. The gun caught him in the chin and distracted him enough that Garcia was able to turn and sprint away from the picnic table, clutching the duffle containing a million dollars. He disappeared into the trees around the clearing.

"Dammit to hell!" Seth yelled.

Gus scrambled up off the bench and he and Seth gave chase, leaving the two million dollars of cash in neat stacks on the picnic table. They made a beeline to Garcia's rental. Seth aimed his S&W at the gray SUV as they approached it. The vehicle appeared to be empty. To make sure, they opened the front and back doors and the liftgate at the rear. Then they fanned out in an ever-increasing circle. After a few minutes, they came to a stop, chests heaving.

"I'm not cut out for this running through the woods shit," Gus said.

"Tell me about it," Seth said.

"Dude's probably long gone."

"No doubt. Rental vehicle's small potatoes compared to saving his hide."

"He's got his million bucks, anyway. We 've probably seen the last of him. Anyway, he's about as useful as an elevator in an outhouse."

"I'm gonna disable this wagon, just in case," Gus said. He proceeded to pop the Bronco's hood and pulled a bunch of wires loose. "This thing ain't going nowhere."

"Ah, don't worry. The fucker knows we've got plenty of guns here, and he ain't got squat. Let's secure our money."

The two brothers returned to the picnic table. The stacks of hundreds were still sitting on top, as they'd left them. Seth went into the main cabin and grabbed a backpack. He carefully placed the packets of bills into the pack, counting it as he went. Satisfied, he proclaimed, "Two million on the nose. Let's keep it together for now. I've got a good hidey-hole. C'mon. I'll show ya."

Gus followed Seth to the nearby storage building. A wooden work bench with a plywood shelf under the work surface took up the entire space along the far wall. Seth got to his knees and looked under the shelf, which was about a foot above the concrete floor. He reached in and, with both hands, pulled out a square black steel box.

"This thing is fireproof." Seth said. "Weighs sixty pounds. Combination lock. As you can see, it tucks into the shadows under the bench. Invisible if ya don't know it's under there." He sat on the floor and entered in six digits on the keypad. The lock clicked. He opened the lid of the box and stuffed the backpack inside. It was a tight squeeze. To close the lid, he had to exert pressure with both hands. Finally, he locked the box and slid it back under the bench.

"Snug as a bug in a rug," Gus said with a smile.

"Let's celebrate, bro," Seth said.

They returned to the cabin, where Seth extracted his current bottle of Canadian whiskey from the cupboard. Sitting at the table with full glasses of amber liquid, Gus said, "We did it. Hey, I better give Josie a call."

Chapter 56

Garcia walked cross country from the place where he'd left the Delmers. He had a pretty good sense of direction and he put it to use, working his way down to the road below Seth's driveway. In about a half hour, he reached the road, really more like a jeep trail. He checked his phone: nearly three P.M. Should be light for another five hours. He didn't know whether there were other properties on the road above Delmer's. He guessed not. In any case, the area seemed deserted. He began to walk down the road, keeping to the right. The route twisted around rock formations and old growth trees. If a vehicle were to approach from either direction, he'd probably hear it before it the driver would be able to see him, so he'd have time to get off to the side and hunker down, out of sight. As he walked, he reflected that the fiasco with the Delmer brothers had been a SNAFU—Situation Normal, All Fucked Up. He'd been inexcusably careless with the gun given him by Seth Delmer, not test firing it. Couldn't afford any more such carelessness. But this could still work out okay.

He walked for a little less than an hour, making good time, losing elevation gradually. Finally, he heard traffic noise below. Must be highway 89. He kept going until he could see the paved two-lane thoroughfare. Traffic was sporadic.

Looked like lots of tourists heading south. He knew Massey's place was to the south as well. Must be thirty miles. He'd need a ride.

Garcia went to the far side of the highway, faced the direction of oncoming traffic and stuck out a thumb. He hadn't hitchhiked since college. One thing he'd retained from his days as a Seal: when your plans go to shit, improvise. What was the quote by some English rock star? *Life is what happens when you're busy making other plans.*

The important thing always was to accomplish the mission. At this point, the first step in achieving the mission was to get his ass to Massey's place, where he should be able to get some wheels. Then he would have a decision to make. Should he complete the final assignment from Massey—killing McKay and his niece? An additional two million was at stake. But participating in a heist as a means of entrapment was one thing. Murder another whole thing. He didn't know whether he had the stomach for it.

Chapter 57

Brian and Darcy crept slowly through the grass and brush, stooped to present a lower profile. The voices ahead of them were louder now. They could not see the men speaking. They stopped to listen.

"Now, we're gonna put you on ice, dude." Sounded like Seth Delmer. Agitated.

A grunt of exertion. An exclamation from Seth: "Dammit to hell!" Then the sound of men running, heavy footfalls receding into the distance.

The McKays continued forward until they could see the cabin and other buildings. A weathered picnic table came into view. Banded stacks of paper money packets were arranged neatly on top. Nobody in sight. They waited. Voices and crashing around in the trees nearby. The Delmers chasing somebody? Garcia?

A few minutes later, Seth and Gus Delmer walked into view. Brian and Darcy stayed hidden in the small trees off the edge of the clearing. The Delmers' breath came noisily as they slogged to the picnic table and slumped down on benches across from each other. A discussion about the money ensued. Brian and Darcy could hear most of what was said, missing only the occasional word. Clearly the brothers were discussing what to do with the money. They arrived at a decision.

Seth got up and disappeared inside the cabin and then returned carrying a dark green backpack. He riffled through each packet of bills, apparently verifying the denomination in the corner of each one. He counted the packets as he placed them in the backpack one by one. His lips moved as he counted.

"Two million on the nose. Let's keep it together for now. I've got a good hidey-hole. C'mon. I'll show ya." Seth shouldered the backpack and led the way to the storage shed.

The brothers passed through the doorway and out of sight.

Brian and Darcy stayed put, awaiting further developments.

Chapter 58

Massey and his aide-de-camp, Jake Pasciewicz, sat in the office room in the massive stone and glass residence.

"I need to make a private phone call. If you'll excuse me…" Massey said.

Pasciewicz got to his feet. "No problem. Let me know when you're free. Something we need to discuss."

When the door had closed, Massey called Scooter Berman, the lawyer in Illinois who'd acted as his agent on the governor's pardon transaction.

"Mr. Massey, good to hear from you," Berman said.

"I am concerned that law enforcement people are after me. I saw men on the street near my Chicago residence who seemed a bit out of place. Here in Montana, I am experiencing unusual background noise on my phone. Even now, as a matter of fact."

"That could just be the remoteness of the location. Those cell towers are few and far between out there."

"Hard for me to know, since the device and location are both new and thus unfamiliar, but still—"

"I wouldn't worry. You've fulfilled your obligations to society and are clean as a baby's butt right after a diaper change, so—"

It was Massey's turn to interrupt, and he did so with his usual gracelessness. "Not an apt simile, Mr. Berman. At any rate, I know the mentality of the people with the FBI. They are no doubt resentful of my abbreviated term of incarceration. They will be attempting to maltreat me with any possible trumped up accusation. This despite the fact that nothing could possibly merit charging me with a crime. I intend to remain scrupulously honest and aboveboard in any detectible way. I am seeking your counsel as to proactive steps I might take to forestall any potential interference with my well-earned freedom."

Well paid-for, at least, Berman thought. What he said was, "I'll give the matter some serious thought. Meanwhile, stay alert. Have you considered the services of a bodyguard?"

"Actually, I have engaged one. He's with me now at my new pied-a-terre here."

"Anyone I might know?"

"Jake Pasciewicz."

Berman whistled. "Holy crap. You don't mess around. The man's one of the most fearsome creatures on earth."

"Yes. Well, let's keep in touch. If any overzealous officer of the law dares to breach my private space, I may wish to pursue bringing suit."

"Very good. Thanks for calling," Berman said.

Massey knew he'd been dismissed. He clicked off the call.

Without knocking, Pasciewicz opened the door to the office room, strode in and dropped into the chair he'd occupied earlier. Massey frowned, but said nothing. He suspected that the huge man had been listening to his conversation with the lawyer through the wall.

Pasciewicz had remained with Massey in the main house after the *T. rex* skull was delivered and the three men who'd schlepped it into the garage had been paid. Massey had JP, as everyone called him, roll the skull on its platform into the office room on the first floor of the massive house, where it now resided. The window blinds in that room were closed, protecting the skull from prying eyes, though the only likely eyes belonged to birds in the trees outside and the occasional deer that might wander by.

JP observed that Massey was a fearful man, seemingly worried that some physical harm might befall him at any time. He clearly depended on the big man both for bodyguarding and for reassurance. JP was fine with that—he was highly paid and so far, there had been no extraordinary demands. It had been mostly accompanying the disgraced executive wherever he went, helping him move stuff into his new Montana manse, taking delivery of furniture and then today, the dinosaur skull. He thought of Massey as an entitled dork, but that was not unusual in JP's line of business, personal protection.

"What's the plan, boss?" Pasciewicz said. "You mentioned being here a few days. How long we talkin'? A week?"

"We'll be here for a couple of weeks. I intend to enjoy my new home and the other uh, purchase."

The big man frowned. "Longer than I expected. I've got commitments—"

"But you agreed to accompany me until I'm settled in here."

"Okay, but, as a practical matter, what about food, supplies, contact with the outside world? I mean, this is a nice place to hang, but—"

"As part of your responsibilities, you will shop for supplies in the nearby town, Clarkville. I will remain here. I must keep myself to myself for a while. Though I am a free man, there are individuals who would deprive me of my liberty on the slightest pretext. You will be my bodyguard as well as my eyes and ears. You will be alert for any undue interest in me, any apparent attention from law enforcement. Of course, there's wi-fi here and cell coverage. We can both be in touch with the outside world—"

Pasciewicz cut him off. "Hmm, that's a wider scope than we discussed before. I get the bodyguard part, but—"

"Don't worry, I will double your rate of pay for the time we spend here."

A series of sharp beeps came from Massey's phone sitting on the table at his elbow. Simultaneously, the same alarm sounded from the phone in JP's shirt pocket. Both men grabbed their phones. There'd been a security breach. A motion detector outside had been tripped. Someone or something larger than a small animal was approaching the house. The camera near the main entrance of the house displayed the image of a wiry man of medium height making his way up the drive. Both men inside recognized him: Andrew Garcia.

"You expecting him here?" JP asked.

"No, but let him in. Might as well find out why he returned. He's yet to complete a task I've assigned him."

"Last time I saw him, he was a passenger in a dump truck. Now he's wearing out his shoes. Doesn't the guy have his own vehicle like normal people?"

There came a sharp series of knocks on the door, like a tool or weapon being rapped upon the heavy wood panels. JP tucked his phone away and went to answer the summons. As Massey sat in his high-backed chair, he heard the buzz of conversation in low tones out at the main entrance. He yelled, "Bring him in."

A moment later, Garcia strode into the room, followed by JP. The smaller man displayed a cocky grin on his lean face as he dropped into a chair near Massey. JP remained standing.

"Well, what brings—"

Garcia broke in. "Let's not waste time. I need a vehicle to complete the mission regarding the uh, matters we discussed."

"Don't you have a rental car?" Massey said.

"Had to leave it behind at the Delmer place...temporarily. The double-crossing assholes tried to kill me, but I made it out of there on foot."

"How did you get here?"

"Thumbed a ride. Don't worry, I got out a ways down the highway. Nobody knows I'm here except maybe a local grizzly bear or two."

Massey grimaced. "Where are the McKays currently?"

"He's staying with Sands, and the girl's digging dinosaur bones on some college project there."

"Why didn't you get dropped off in Clarkville and rent another vehicle?"

"The last thing I want to do is incur a credit card charge. People are no doubt trying to locate me."

"I suppose." Massey's voice was dry as an autumn twig.

"I need to talk to you. In private," Garcia said, with a glance at the gigantic former football player standing impassively, filling the doorway.

"JP is a trusted associate. Anything you say to me is fair game for him as well." Massey figured he should throw the big man a bone after banishing him when he'd called Berman.

Garcia hesitated, formulating a response, then said, "Okay, here's the deal. You're a man who knows about minimizing expenses, right?" Without waiting for an answer, he continued, "My plan would be to pay a visit to the Delmers and retrieve the two million you paid them for the skull. Those guys would both disappear, thus minimizing potential exposure of you to scrutiny. Plus you'd save a million."

"But, as you just said, I paid them *two* million."

"Correct. But my commission in this case would be fifty percent."

"I see. And of course, your commission regarding the McKays remains as we agreed."

Garcia hesitated, then replied, "Correct."

Massey shrugged. "Done. C.O.D. of course. JP will give you the keys to a suitably anonymous vehicle. Anything else?"

"A handgun."

A few minutes later, Garcia was behind the wheel of a late-model Toyota Highlander. A Kimber Ultra Carry II .40 caliber semiautomatic sat on the passenger's seat. He headed for the highway that would take him back to Seth Delmer's place.

Chapter 59

Brian and Darcy watched the Delmers move from the storage building to the main cabin. Once the men were inside, they moved up the driveway until they were almost to the cabin. The small trees and bushes hid them pretty well, but they remained cautious as they crept forward. They'd both silenced their phones. Voices came from inside, clearly audible through an open window.

The Delmer brothers were discussing their recent successes. Darcy turned on the audio recorder on her phone and then opened the home screen, so it wasn't obvious the recorder was on. The men got louder as they consumed more alcohol. Unaware that there was an audience, Seth boasted of how easy and lucrative it had been to kill Patchett at the upscale development in the valley—ka-ching! And how the kidnapping of Barbara Hardy for a hefty ransom had the law enforcement dudes scratching their heads—ka-ching! The icing on the cake was the sale of the stolen dinosaur skull for mucho dinero—ka-ching! All of these deeds had been at the behest of "the weird dude from Chicago," Massey, who'd paid them plenty.

Gus stroked his red beard nervously. "First I've heard about Patchett. Sometimes, you surprise me, man."

"Yeah, that just sorta popped out. Hadn't meant to bring it up. Oh well, don't worry. What's done is done."

"I'm thinkin' we should get away from here while the gettin's good," Gus said.

"Whaddaya mean? Run? Nobody knows shit."

"Except Garcia."

"He's in deep on the dinosaur thing. Gotta keep his mouth shut. Anyway, you can go to work for me on the woodlot. I could use the help. You can live in the other cabin long as you like. Bring Josie with you."

"That's tempting. But the sheriff's no dumb monkey. And those fuckin' McKays are snooping around. Kidnapping's a federal offense." He shuddered. "I understand you've got a business to run, but me, I'm free as the wind. Maybe Josie and I'll take off, move someplace where it never snows."

"Hah. I can just see you in a Hawaiian shirt and flip-flops on some beach. Nah, you're a Montana boy."

Brian and Darcy circled to the rear of the cabin to see what was going on inside. One of her running shoes inadvertently landed on a fallen tree branch outside a rear window. A loud SNAP sounded. The conversation in the cabin stopped abruptly.

Brian held a finger to his lips. They stood still, silent as smoke. Next came the sound of the cabin door opening and closing. Two sets of feet tromped down the wooden steps. Then nothing. They knew they were at a disadvantage. Seth Delmer would know every square foot of his property, while they were outsiders with no clue of what lay around them. Even in their inebriated state, the brothers would be able to thoroughly search the property. They had to hide, but where?

Darcy began to ease into the trees, slipping her phone into a jeans pocket. Brian stayed with her, head on a swivel. The weight of the Sig in the pancake holster at his back was reassuring. He wanted to text Bill Thorsten in the Bozeman FBI office, but his phone showed no signal. They moved to the north, arcing away from the cabins and deeper into the woods. Now they were among old growth Douglas firs, towering like massive green pyramids upwards of sixty feet. Interspersed among the trees were stumps, some bright as gold coins on top, indicating the evergreens had been cut recently. The turpentine smell of sap permeated the air. The terrain was lumpy, with random drop-offs and potholes. Some sort of tracked equipment had crisscrossed the woods, jumbling up the surface between stumps. They made slow progress, constantly checking the ground at their feet so as not to stumble.

They noticed some large pieces of equipment in the distance, partially obscured by intervening trees. Curious, they moved toward the machines, which were bright red and emblazoned with the name ELTEC on the sides. There was a sort of oversized tractor with a plow blade at one end and large curved steel grappling hooks at the other. Must be for picking up and moving logs. The beast's chunky rubber tires exceeded six feet in diameter. Nearby was a colossus unlike anything either of them had encountered in their lives: a red metal cube about twelve feet on a side sat atop a set of huge bulldozer tracks. At the front of the cube, where the operator's windshield looked out, was a monstrous contraption: a stout column of steel attached to a goose-neck boom. The stanchion rose about ten feet tall and had two sets of outstretched curved metal arms, one set on top, the other on the bottom.

For Brian, it brought to mind some sort of deadly sleepwalker. He imagined what those arms would do to a fir tree, encircling it and clamping it in an inescapable embrace. But the most frightening thing was at the bottom of the steel column: a disc-shaped saw blade about two feet in diameter sporting chunky teeth that looked capable of easily cutting the thickest tree around in seconds.

"It's a feller-buncher." A brassy baritone split the thin mountain air.

Seth Delmer had come up behind them and was now only a few yards away, holding a revolver in his right hand. He'd gotten close enough that he could hardly miss if he shot at them and yet far enough away that neither of the interlopers could lunge and reach him in time to avoid being hit. Brian began to slide his left hand behind his back toward his handgun. Before it had traveled two inches, a shot rang out.

"Don't fuckin' move! Hands above your head." Seth yelled. "The both of you. That was a warning. The next one'll be lights out for ya."

As Brian and Darcy complied, footsteps came from behind Seth. Gus Delmer appeared, circled around behind Brian, plucked the Sig from Brian's holster and stepped back quickly. Neither brother showed signs that they'd been imbibing like fish a few minutes earlier.

"Saw ya admiring my logging equipment. Don't blame ya. That little baby there is capable of grabbing and felling a tree up to twenty-two inches in diameter, easy as slicing bread. See, the arms squeeze a tree nice and tight while that blade revolves near the ground and cuts through it at the bottom. Sap oozes out like honey. That gizmo lifts up the tree and carefully deposits it on the ground with a bunch of other trees, ready for limbing, trimming and loading." He smiled like a new father in a maternity ward.

Brian and Darcy exchanged a glance. These guys seemed hyped, alert. It would not be easy to outmaneuver them. But they'd have to, or it could be, as Seth had said, "lights out."

"Hey, I can understand you being pissed off. We're trespassing," Brian said. "But we were just out hiking, exploring. Saw an elk off the road and walked over to get a picture. Meant no harm."

"Nice try, asshole," Seth said. He seemed to be the spokesman for the duo, Gus remaining silent. "My woodlot sets a quarter mile off the road. You didn't just wander in here like a tourist. In fact, I know who you two are. Brian McKay and the niece."

"The niece? I'm the friggin' niece?" Darcy's voice was indignant. "My name is Darcy McKay. I'm a grad student in paleontology at MSU. Who the hell are you guys?"

It was the Delmers' turn to trade a look. "Miss, you happened to drop in when we weren't expecting visitors. We don't mind a good-lookin' gal stopping by. But your uncle there is a whole nother matter. He's a meddler, trying to make us out as some kinda criminals. Which we aren't."

"Okay," Brian said. "That being the case, we have no interest in each other. So, we'll just be on our way." He started to lower his hands. Gus Delmer materialized behind him. Brian tried to connect with a back kick to the knee but caught only air. Next, he felt sharp pain at his left temple, then nothing. Gus stood over the unconscious Brian, holding a revolver by the barrel. He'd used the butt of the weapon as a club.

Darcy noticed blood on the gun and then on the side of Brian's head. She let her hands fall and leapt to her uncle's side. She dropped to a knee and cradled his lolling head in her hands. "Brian, say something."

Seth walked over and kicked at Darcy, catching her in the midsection with the tip of a steel-toed work boot. She fell over onto her side, clutching at her stomach.

"You asshole!" she screamed.

Seth shook his head as ruefully as a priest at a memorial service and turned to Gus. "I told 'em to stay there with their hands up, didn't I? Some people just can't follow directions." He shrugged. "Well, looks like we go to plan B."

"Wait a second. I don't—" Gus said.

"When things change up, ya gotta make adjustments. We let these two go, we're SOL. Go get a bucket of water. We've gotta revive this one." He nodded down at Brian's supine form.

Gus disappeared. By then, Darcy had gotten to her feet, livid with rage. She took a decisive step toward Seth, who stood nearby with his revolver dangling from a meaty hand. As she moved, he raised the weapon and clicked the hammer back.

"Hold it right there, girl. I *will* shoot ya, if you make me."

She stopped. This troll creeped her out. "Why'd that guy club Brian?" she demanded. "He might have a concussion. How about getting some medical help?"

"Not a chance. You two dealt your own hand. As you can understand, me and Gus enjoy being free men. You folks coulda stayed away from us. Hell, ya coulda even called the sheriff, who gets paid to go after the bad guys. Not that that woulda meant anything. But no, you hadda stick your nose in where it don't belong." He reflected for a moment. "Too damn bad, but it is what it is."

Gus returned, a galvanized bucket swinging from his right hand, water dripping over the rim. Without a word, he walked to Brian and dumped the contents onto his face. Brian remained motionless. Gus stood waiting, not sure what to do. As Seth and Darcy looked on, Gus bent toward Brian as if to check on him. Suddenly, Brian's eyes opened, and his arms snaked out, tackling Gus by the legs. He pulled the stocky man to the ground, got to a knee and cocked a fist as if to pop him in the nose.

Seth fired the pistol in the direction of the two men on the ground. The bullet tunneled through grass and stones near the pair, missing both of them. On the theory that a good distraction should be taken advantage of, Darcy charged Seth, tackling him to the ground.

By then, Gus had gained his feet and backed away from Brian. Seth rolled on top of Darcy, pinning her flat on her back. He outweighed her by eighty pounds, so she couldn't throw him off. Nevertheless, she got a good left jab off, catching the burly man in the eye.

Gus pointed his gun at Darcy's face and yelled, "You better fuckin' behave or I'll shoot ya for good." Darcy stopped struggling. She felt like she might have a broken rib. Nausea began to seep in. She took a deep breath. Seth got up, pulling Darcy to her feet. He roughly yanked her hands behind her back and fastened her wrists together with plastic zip tie hand cuffs. Then he shoved her over and repeated the process with her ankles.

Brian struggled to get to his feet and finally made it. His balance felt off. He staggered sideways and almost fell. Blood flowed from the wound in his temple in steady rivulets. Lying on the ground, Darcy desperately attempted to free her limbs.

Seth yelled, "Okay, you two have had your last warning. You try any more shit and I shoot to kill. No second chances. We clear?"

"Got it," Brian said between clenched teeth.

"Siddown," Seth commanded. Awkwardly and slowly, Brian managed to fold his legs and sat.

"Hands behind your back, buckeroo," Seth said to Brian. He complied and felt his wrists being pinioned together with a plastic zip cuff. The restraint was so tight, he began to lose feeling in his fingers. Seth did the same with a plastic cuff around Brian's ankles.

Brian's fingers grazed the phone in his right rear pants pocket. The Delmers had moved away and were now engrossed in conversation. Brian managed to extricate the phone from the pocket, hit the home button and then moved a finger to the upper left corner of the home screen, by feel. He pressed there, opening the messages app. By twisting his head to the right, he could barely look over his shoulder for a partial view of the screen. He found a recent text from Thorsten and tapped his thumb on it. He was able to tap the reply box, bringing up the keyboard. He attempted to quickly key in a message. He got only as far as "at d." Seth noticed what he was doing, marched over and kicked the phone out of his hand.

"No cell signal here, pal. Gotta give ya credit for trying. I've been thinking—"

"A new experience, no doubt," Darcy said.

"What I was about to say was, maybe we can let you guys go, after all," Seth said. "Tell us what you're doing here, who sent you. I've gotta know. It would make it a lot easier for everybody. You tell us everything and we send you on your way. How's that sound?"

"Like bullshit," Darcy said.

"You got some badass attitude, girl," Seth said.

"Up yours," she replied.

"I asked ya a question," Seth said to Brian.

"I'm with her," he replied.

"I've got an idea," Seth said. He looked at the buncher feller standing off in the woods.

Gus followed his gaze.

"You thinking what I'm thinking?" Seth said.

Just then, Gus's cell phone rang, belying Seth's claim there was no signal. Gus murmured, then turned and walked into the woods, apparently for privacy.

Brian hoped to God that his text had reached Thorsten.

Chapter 60

Bill Thorsten was uneasy. He hadn't heard from Brian McKay since their brief phone conversation that morning. It was now late afternoon. Brian said he and Darcy were about to visit Massey at his new place in Montana and promised to check in later. Thorsten sat at his laptop and began a search for Massey's property south of Clarkville. There was no such information to be found, either on the public Internet or in the FBI databases. He remembered Brian mentioning a real estate broker he'd visited in Clarkville. He'd said the woman specialized in remote rural properties. After a short additional search, he found the website for Montana Untamed.

He glanced at the time. It would be tough to get there by close of business. He phoned and got the proprietor, Nora Spivey.

"How may I help?" A throaty voice, world-weary.

"Trying to locate an address for a property recently purchased by Hamilton Massey of Chicago."

"And you are?"

"Name's Bill. I'm a friend of a friend of Barbara Hardy."

"Oh yeah? Y'know, she went through hell when those dirtbags kidnapped her. How's she doing?"

"Pretty good, considering. Uh, could I get that address from you, please?"

"I guess. Hang on." A minute of silence ensued, then Spivey came back on the line.

"Just curious. What's your interest in Mr. Massey?"

"I'm an old acquaintance. Gotta get in touch with him, business matter."

She sighed. "Huh. Well, what the hell. Not like it's a big effin' secret." She proceeded to give him a physical address on Andres Creek Road in the valley, with directions on how to get there from the highway.

"Thanks, Norah. I appreciate it."

While Thorsten was on the phone, Josie Wilshire was calling Gus Delmer. He picked up, but the cell connection was shaky, and his voice faded in and out. Sounded like yelling in the background.

"We're goddamned rich," he said. His slurred words made him sound like he'd been drinking. "Hang on, lemme duck into a quieter place. Lotsa noise around here."

"You at Seth's?"

"Yep. C'mon over. We'll sleep in the guest cabin tonight, take off in the morning. After that, who knows? Maybe I'll get that place for us in Hawaii."

"Do I get a say in the matter?"

"Well, of course, babe. Why doncha c'mon over? We can figure out where we go from there."

"Okay. It'll take me a while to pack my stuff. But we'd best leave sooner rather than later. Where we go short term is not important. If Seth's got any brains, he'll bug out as well. The law's gonna be onto you guys like flies on horseshit. Know what I mean?"

"Uh huh, I do. Bring whatever you need for the road and a full tank of gas in that truck of yours. We'll be outta here in the morning."

Josie packed her belongings into a rolling suitcase and a duffle. She loaded everything into the bed of her pickup. She went back into the cabin and searched to make sure she'd gotten all the little stuff one scatters around a living space over the course of a year. She sighed. What kind of life is it when a forty-year-old woman can move her household in a pickup truck? She'd never married, never had children. Her relatives were scattered across several states—she'd lost touch with them long ago. This job working for Mr. Sands had been a pretty nice gig. In a way, she hated to leave. But she had no choice. Gus had hit the bigtime, at least for now with his half million share from the ransom. And she had the hundred thousand bucks he'd given her, from the same source. It was hidden in a toolbox in her truck. Plus, he'd mentioned some major theft that was going to net him another big haul. She was under no illusion that their money would last. But they could live well for a while. She loved Gus, though sometimes she wondered why. And he seemed to love her too, in his own way.

Damn it, she deserved to have a little fun. And over half a million bucks would buy a lot of it. But Gus, like his older brother Seth, had committed serious crimes. No doubt, they would be on the radar of law enforcement at various levels, if they weren't already. She'd try to get Gus to grab his stuff and head out with her tonight. No need to stick around. Let Seth make his own bed, she reasoned. But Gus would be drunk and tired. Best she could do would be to prod him into getting on the road before noon tomorrow. She prayed that would be soon enough.

One final look around yielded a small framed childhood dog picture that had slid off the edge of the little side table. She pocketed the picture and dropped the cabin keys on the table in the main room. She drafted a text to her boss, Ray Chaffee, explaining that she was quitting and would be in touch as to where to send her last paycheck. She saved the draft; she'd send it once she was away from the ranch. She sighed, got behind the wheel and piloted the white F-150 out the ranch entry road and toward highway 89. When she'd gone a few miles north, she stopped in a pullout, brought up the text to Chaffee and clicked the "send" arrow. That simple task completed, she felt cautiously relieved. This move would work out for her. It had to.

Chapter 61

Thorsten had driven over the pass from Bozeman on the Interstate and was now reaching the exit for the town of Clarkville. This time of year, it would still be light for hours. He got off the highway and filled the tank of his aging Tahoe. As he replaced the fuel nozzle, questions troubled him. Had Brian and Darcy McKay encountered Massey as planned? If so, had Brian's hunch about the dinosaur skull played out? Why hadn't they contacted him? Had they reached Sheriff Reid?

He went into the gas station and bought a CLIF bar and a bottle of water. He hadn't eaten since early that morning. In a parking spot away from the building, he ate the snack as he checked messages on his phone. A text came in from Brian. Rather terse, it simply said, "at d." He was puzzled. Why so brief? What could "d" mean? Not Darcy, since Brian and she were together. What location could it mean? Then, it hit him: Delmer. He must be at one of the Delmer brothers' places. The younger one worked at the Sands ranch. The older one, Seth, had a place in the Crazies.

He got on the Internet and, after a lot of searching, located Delmer's Wood Products with an address off of Shields River Road. He entered it into his vehicle's navigation system and drove out.

Josie drove up the driveway to Seth Delmer's place. Leaden clouds now dominated the sky. The wind had picked up and the tree branches were rising and falling like waves. As she reached the top of the drive, she heard voices through the open driver's side window—men and a woman in a heated conversation. She eased the truck to a stop next to Seth's cabin. Feeling uncertain, she simply wanted to get Gus into her truck and the hell out of this place. He was basically a good guy, but impressionable. His brother was another story, a guy who'd cut corners, steal and strike out at anyone who looked at him cross-eyed. She turned off the engine, released the seat belt and sat for a moment with the window down. Birds flitted about in the trees. A magpie let loose with a raucous complaint. A flash of iridescent blue tailfeathers caught her eye and the distinctive black and white bird alit on a branch nearby. She sighed. She'd better get over there to face the mess that Seth had no doubt created.

She was greeted by a bizarre tableau. Seth was struggling with a young woman while Gus looked on. Seth was attempting to tie her ankles together with a plastic zip tie. A few feet away, a man sat awkwardly on the ground, conscious but with blood on his shirt. He appeared to be handcuffed. Gus stood over the captive, pointing a handgun at him. Blood seeped from a gash in the man's head. Josie recognized him: Brian McKay, the detective from Chicago whom Sands had hired to find the kidnappers. Looked like he'd been successful. Probably why the brothers were messing with him and the girl. She hesitated, waiting to see how this would play out, unsure whether to just go back to her truck and take off.

"Keep an eye on these two. I'm gonna give 'em a demonstration," Seth said to Gus.

Gus grabbed Darcy roughly by the zip ties around her wrists and dragged her over by Brian, where he dumped her on the ground like a sack of onions. With her wrists and ankles pinioned, she lay awkwardly on her side.

Seth went to the logging machine nearby and climbed into the operator's cab. The massive diesel engine came to life, hesitant at first, then settling down to a steady thrum. Brian and Darcy watched as the huge red machine began to move forward. The steel column at the end of the long boom in front was raised to about a foot above the ground. The machine began a clumsy pivot, one caterpillar tread moving forward while the other reversed direction. The effect was to turn the thing so it was facing a large tree on the edge of the clearing. The engine revved, belching thick black smoke out of the upright exhaust pipe. The machine lumbered forward steadily, the massive steel treads clanking over the lumpy ground. Sharp cracking noises sliced through the air as tree limbs on the ground were pulverized under the immense weight.

"Watch this, you guys," Gus yelled.

As Brian and Darcy looked on, the machine stopped several yards from a fir tree with a trunk about a foot in diameter. The cutting column slammed swiftly against the tree like a striking snake, crushing the lower branches against the trunk. Two pairs of steel arms reached around the tree trunk, trapping it in a crushing embrace. A massive disc saw at the base of the tree screamed as it bit into the captive trunk. The unforgiving metal arms lifted the decapitated tree away from the fresh stump, as if taking a toothpick off a table. The machine cab swiveled around and set the tree on the ground almost gently. The entire procedure took only seconds.

The saw was turned off while the diesel engine continued to idle. "He cuts trees super quick with that feller machine," Gus said. "He'll cut several of 'em in one go, bunching 'em up in one set of arms while the other arms grab another tree and pull it in as it's cut. Sometimes, he'll get six trees bunched in that grabber thing. Of course, you've gotta have a ton of experience to do it as good as Seth does." He sounded proud of his brother's skill. He seemed to have forgotten that he was supposed to be intimidating the detective and his niece.

At this point, Josie had had enough. She strode into the clearing. "What the hell are you guys doing to these people?" she yelled, as she approached Gus. He jumped as if he'd sat on a hot coal. Seth remained in the cab of the feller-buncher. The sound of the clattering diesel engine drowned out her words for him, but her body language was unmistakable.

She poked Gus in the chest with a rigid forefinger. "C'mon, let's get out of here! Don't add murder to your list of accomplishments with numbnuts over there." she nodded toward Seth in the logging machine.

As Gus formulated a reply, a pistol shot cracked from close by. A flock of redwing blackbirds erupted into the sky. Andrew Garcia walked toward the people and idling machine in the clearing, a snide smile on his narrow face. His semiautomatic Kimber handgun was angled skyward. He walked over to Gus and pointed the weapon in his face, inches from his nose. "Drop it."

Gus hesitated. Garcia yelled, "Now!" He fired a shot just over Gus's right ear. Gus let his handgun fall to the ground and backed away toward Josie, as Garcia eyed him impassively.

Garcia turned to Brian and Darcy, his eyes blank. He muttered, "Hang loose. You guys aren't going to be harmed."

What did that mean? If the guy was working with Massey, wouldn't he be about to harm the bejesus out of them?

With Garcia occupied, Josie grabbed Gus's elbow and eased him toward the edge of the clearing. The couple melted into the trees. Garcia didn't seem to notice. They'd both realized the time to go was now. Gus was leaving a million bucks behind, his share of the ransom money, stored in the safe in Seth's storage building. That was okay. He and Josie had plenty. He just hoped Seth would have the chance to use the money.

Suddenly, the engine of the feller-buncher revved to a roar. The machine advanced steadily toward Garcia, the tree grappling column extended in front like a poisonous snake moving in for the kill.

Garcia stumbled as he backed away from the incoming menace. He fired twice at the hulking machine when it was only a few feet from him. One bullet missed completely, while the other hit an upper corner of the windshield. Bits of tempered glass fell like hail into the operator's cab. The contraption kept coming. Garcia darted to the side like a toreador stepping out of the path of a charging bull. The machine thundered by, narrowly missing him as well as Brian and Darcy. It slammed into a copse of fir trees off the edge of the clearing, snapping branches and finally coming to a halt against several thick trunks. The engine continued on and the massive caterpillar treads spun in an attempt to gain traction. Finally, the engine stalled and the tracks stopped. The abrupt silence stretched out like a membrane on the verge of tearing.

The only ones left were Brian, Darcy and Garcia. No sound came from the direction of the feller-buncher.

Garcia walked to the logging machine, climbed atop a tread and reached up to the door handle of the cab. He yanked the door open. Seth appeared to be unconscious, his head lolling to the side. There was no sign of blood, so maybe he'd been knocked unconscious when his head struck the cab interior. Suddenly, Seth's eyes sprang open and he swiveled and kicked Garcia in the crotch, knocking the smaller man to the ground. Garcia's head slammed against a rock, stunning him into oblivion. In a flash, Seth fired up the feller buncher and backed away from the trees. He rumbled the machine over to the fallen Garcia and stopped.

Garcia lay on his back, dazed, but slowly coming to, like a boxer down for the count. His boots were only inches from the huge steel saw blade capable of decapitating the largest trees in the mature forest. He struggled to his feet, staggered and nearly fell again. The steel column rose off the forest floor by a few inches. The articulating boom snaked forward with astonishing speed and the two sets of shiny steel tree-bunching arms wrapped around Garcia, trapping him in an imprisoning embrace. He attempted to get out of the steel enclosure, but it was no use. He stood on top of the terrifying circular saw blade, all too aware of its potential for mayhem.

Brian had continued to rub the zip tie encasing his wrists against the edge of a rock behind his back. Methodically, he sawed the plastic shackles against stone until finally, he was able to tear the edge of the plastic. By twisting his wrists in opposite directions, he quickly enlarged the tear. Finally, the thin plastic strap gave way, and his wrists came free. He willed his stiff legs into getting him upright, but it was slow going. He'd been listening and watching helplessly as Seth trapped Garcia in the tree buncher arms.

Brian picked up the handgun Gus Delmer had dropped. He raised it and fired into the glass panel of the operator cab's side door. A howl came from within the cab.

"You fucker! You shot me." Seth emerged from the cab clutching a hand to his shoulder. Blood seeped from between his fingers as he sagged to the ground.

Garcia remained trapped in the steel grappling arms of the feller-buncher, his body held upright. The image reminded Brian of Hannibal Lecter in his straight jacket, being wheeled out of prison in a hand truck.

Chapter 62

The aging Tahoe rattled its way upward, the road little more than a jeep trail. Thorsten swung the steering wheel to the right, narrowly avoiding a sharp-edged rock that could have easily sliced a tire open. He'd turned off 89 about twenty minutes earlier. According to the nav system, he should be getting to Delmer's driveway any minute. A sign on the right informed him, PRIVATE PROPERTY STAY ON ROAD. There wasn't a whole lot of choice, with ditches and barbed wire fences hemming in the road on both sides.

Finally, a gap about twenty feet wide appeared in the fence on his left. That had to be it. He eased his SUV through the open gate and climbed up a two track route barely wide enough for one vehicle. As he approached a wide spot in the road, the sound of an engine came to him from above. He steered his vehicle to the right a few feet. Suddenly, a white pickup came crashing down the road ahead of a thick tan dust cloud. Thorsten waited, expecting the oncoming truck to slow as it neared. Instead, it maintained speed and came right at him. Too late to move. He braced himself for a collision. The white truck barely slipped by on his left, its driver's side outboard mirror clipping Thorsten's. In a flash, the truck was by him and slaloming down the road below. Thorsten noticed his mirror now hung from a cable like a bird's broken wing.

His impression: woman driving, man in the passenger seat. Strangers. Late-model crew cab. The pair were in a hell of a hurry, enough so as to risk an accident. Either they were running from something or they were speed demons. He eased the Tahoe back into the rutted tracks and drove on. Coniferous trees and sagebrush flanked the road, forming a narrow green tunnel. In a few minutes, he reached a cleared area containing a couple of log cabins and a large shed. In the distance, voices shattered the silence. He heard a man yell, "You fucker! You shot me."

Thorsten left his vehicle in front of the first cabin and checked his Sig P226 handgun, making sure the magazine was engaged, racking the slide back, allowing it to return forward and pushing down the de-cocking lever. He proceeded on foot toward the direction of the voices.

At the sound of approaching footsteps, Brian turned, gun in hand. Bill Thorsten came into view, holding his own gun pointing straight ahead. As he recognized Brian, his face relaxed, but he noticed his friend's disheveled appearance and tense expression. Darcy stood next to Brian, looking nervous. There were angry red welts on her wrists. The two of them looked like they'd been tumbled in a cement mixer.

"Well, I guess I got here too late. Looks like the excitement's over."

"Not quite. We've got a gunshot victim over there," Brian said, nodding toward Seth Delmer, who lay on his side on the ground, clutching his right shoulder. Blood oozed between the stocky man's fingers. His eyes were inert black pools as he eyed Thorsten.

"But the real action is over there in that logging machine," Brian said. Thorsten followed Brian's pointing forefinger and spotted a steel column attached to a huge red cube-shaped machine hulking above metal treads. Held rigidly upright within two pairs of stout steel arms, was Andrew Garcia. His face twitched spasmodically, but his body was held immobile. He appeared to be standing on a flat metal disc about four feet in diameter. Blood splotched the surface of his shirt. He'd obviously been treated roughly before being seized in the metal embrace. He didn't look happy.

"Get me out of this fucking thing!" he screamed.

The diesel engine of the logging machine idled nervously.

A black Durango SUV roared into the clearing and skidded to a stop near the three in conversation. The crest of the Geyser County Sheriff's Department was displayed in gold on the sides of the vehicle. Sheriff Jim Reid and Deputy Ben Vaught emerged.

"What the hell is going on here?" Reid's face was crimson.

Garcia yelled again. Reid turned and regarded the trapped man as if viewing a butterfly pinned to an entomologist's display board. "Uh, Ben, you want to see if you can get that fella outta there?"

The deputy headed toward the logging machine with deliberate steps. He climbed into the cab and gazed at the controls blankly. He could hear the trapped man struggling, thrashing about to no effect. He was afraid to move any levers or press any buttons.

After a full minute had elapsed, Vaught yelled at the others, "Anybody know how to open up this tree grabber deal?"

Seth Delmer, lying on his side, his voice weak, said, "Tell ya what. Make the wrong move, that blade will start spinning at 3,500 rpm and you'll cut off his feet."

"How the hell do we open up that grabber?" Brian said.

"Go fuck yourself. All of you," Seth said. He dropped his head to the ground and closed his eyes.

Darcy had been fiddling with her phone. "I've got it…I think," she said." She looked up at the deputy sitting motionless in the cab. "I'll give it a try," she said.

She went to the cab and addressed the deputy. "Let me in there."

"I'll turn off the engine if I can find the—"

"No, no, it's gotta be on to operate the arms."

Deputy Vaught got out of the cab and dropped to the ground. "I don't know—"

Darcy motioned him aside, mounted the caterpillar tread and vaulted herself onto the operator's seat. "Hey, this thing's pretty cool," she said. "Joysticks and a screen. Just like a video game." Then, with her phone in her left hand and her right hand hovering over a joystick with five unlabeled buttons, she muttered, "Guess I don't want the saw. What's this?" She studied a video on her phone, while listening to a man with a southern drawl explain how to open and close the tree-grabbing arms with buttons atop the left and right hand joysticks.

Meanwhile, Andrew Garcia had quieted down, but was still twisting and jerking his body in a futile effort to get loose from the metal arms holding him securely in place. Watching him, Brian reflected that people securely restrained in bonds invariably struggled to escape, even when they knew it was no use. It was a natural phenomenon.

Brian, the sheriff and deputy all watched with keen interest as Darcy studied the controls of the feller buncher.

"I hope to hell she knows what she's doing," Reid muttered.

Suddenly, Darcy pushed a button in the second row atop the right hand joystick. The top pair of metal arms holding Garcia opened with a CLANG. She moved her left hand to the leftmost joystick and pressed the comparable button. The steel bottom arms swept open, freeing Garcia. He slumped down atop the vicious-looking disc saw and then rolled himself off of it to the ground.

"Thank God," he murmured before passing out.

"No, thank Darcy," Brian said.

Darcy turned off the engine and dropped to the forest floor. Silence fell over the clearing like a feather landing on stone.

Reid turned to Brian. "How about telling me what happened here." Reid said.

Brian, with contributions from Thorsten and Darcy, briefly related what had transpired before the sheriff arrived. In response to Reid's questioning, Brian and Darcy said they were both okay and didn't need medical attention.

"I'm curious," Brian said to Reid. "How did you guys know to come here?"

"A nosy neighbor 'bout a half mile down the road said all kinds of crazy shit was going on. Vehicles racing up and down, gunshots."

Thorsten and Reid conferred, the upshot being that Reid would call for a vehicle to take Seth Delmer to the emergency room at the clinic in Clarkville. Vaught and another deputy would guard Delmer in shifts. Once released by the doctors, the injured man would be transferred to the Geyser County jail pending processing through the legal system. Garcia was not a suspect at that point. He accepted a ride to Clarkville, where, he said, he'd find a hotel room.

Reid called his office and told the dispatcher to put out an APB for Josie Wilshire and Gus Delmer. He provided descriptions of the couple and their vehicle and told them to get the plate number of her pickup from the state motor vehicle division. He figured he must have just missed Josie coming down the road as he drove up. As he pocketed his phone, he noticed a Dutch Masters cigar wrapper on the ground, just like the one Richard Smith had found at the Paradise Preserve after a gunshot had been reported up there a couple of weeks earlier when Terry Patchett had disappeared.

Chapter 63

Without letting Reid know their plans, the trio of Thorsten, Brian and Darcy boarded Thorsten's Tahoe and took off. With Brian riding shotgun and Darcy in back, Thorsten maneuvered the vehicle down the tortuous two-track from Seth Delmer's place to the gravel public road, and then to the main highway on the Yellowstone valley floor. He took a left on the two-lane blacktop and punched the accelerator. They cruised south at ninety, passing every vehicle they overtook. At the winding road to Massey's property, they sped upward as fast as the twisting route through the trees would permit. They encountered no other traffic.

A security gate made of heavy steel bars would have blocked the driveway, but it yawned open. As they rolled through, Brian noticed a keypad to the left of the opening. They approached the imposing three-story house of gray stone and parked near the main entrance. The place was silent, but Brian felt the presence of someone inside. Over the years of his FBI career, he'd experienced an eerie sense when approaching a residence as to whether it contained human life. Nothing tangible, just a feeling. This time, he felt Massey, and perhaps someone else, was in the trophy home before them.

They got out and went to the wide oak entry door with hammered black metal hinges. Thorsten rapped on it with his keys. No response. He repeated the process. Nothing.

Brian reached over and tried the knob. It turned easily in his hand and he pushed the door open. He slipped inside with Thorsten and Darcy on his heels. They stopped to listen. No sound permeated the spacious living room. Deep pile, light brown carpeting covered the floor. Fitments were sparse, in keeping with a house of which the owner had recently taken possession and had not had time to completely furnish it. A pair of upholstered easy chairs faced an immense flat-screen tv mounted on the far wall. A big leather sofa sat like a movie prop under the big front window. A couple of modern floor lamps with off-white linen shades completed the front room décor. No artwork on the walls. The space had the sterile feel of a sitting room in an unfinished luxury resort.

Thorsten faced Brian and raised an inquiring eyebrow. Brian flashed to the comedian John Belushi on early *Saturday Night Live*. Belushi, playing a sword-wielding Samurai tailor, would raise one eyebrow in mock question: should he use his sword to cut a fly opening in the customer's pants while he is wearing them? Thorsten though, was dead serious. Brian nodded toward the entryway to the next part of the house. The three of them moved forward into a hallway with rooms along its length on both sides. The first room to the left appeared to be a guest bedroom. To the right was another room, empty except for a few boxes.

Darcy said, "I'm gonna take a look this way." She moved up the hall and found a kitchen. Though the room contained the usual appliances, it looked as if it hadn't been used much.

Brian and Thorsten meanwhile entered another room. Nearly vacant bookshelves covered one wall. A few hardcovers sat dusty and deserted at the ends of the shelves, as if the previous owner had cleared out the reading materials and missed a few items. A large old-fashioned walnut desk faced the door. Behind it, two double-hung windows overlooked the lawn and bordering trees to the east. An office or study, it appeared. But unlike any other office in the world, a massive predatory dinosaur skull mounted above a rectangular wheeled wooden cart held court next to the desk.

Brian recognized the boney cranium as belonging to a huge *T. rex*, tyrant lizard king, ruler of the late Cretaceous period. No doubt, the skull stolen from the William Old Horn dinosaur museum. But the really surprising thing was the lifeless body of A. Hamilton Massey lying impaled face up on the razor-sharp teeth in the mouth of the apex predator's skull.

Draped across the inward-pointing, daggerlike teeth of the lower jaw, the long slender corpse was dressed in a white dress shirt, dark slacks and highly-shined black lace-up shoes. The upper teeth grazed the man's belly. Hamilton Massey's face had been battered. Angry red lacerations crisscrossed his forehead, cheeks and jaw. His nose was slightly out of kilter, looking like it had been recently broken. Blood had seeped from the body, pooling on the floor below.

Thorsten approached the man and took hold of a dangling wrist, He held it for a moment, then stepped away, shaking his head.

"I'd liked to have seen him back in prison," Thorsten said.

Brian snapped a photo of Massey in the dinosaur's mouth. In all his years of experience in law enforcement, he'd never encountered such a bizarre scene. "We should leave him be."

"I'll call my boss and the sheriff," Thorsten said.

Brian was curious as to whether the immense dinosaur jaws could be moved. He placed his hand carefully on the nares atop the skull with his fingers curled through the twin nasal openings. He was loath to grip the banana-sized incisors, fearing they'd cut through his skin like steak knives. The upper jaw was rigidly fixed in place, as was the lower when he pushed it from below. He stepped back and examined the point where the upper teeth contacted the front of Massey's shirt. There was a small gap between fossil stone and paunch.

"For what it's worth, I think someone killed him nearby and then muscled him in there as a final form of disrespect," Brian said.

"Probably Pasciewicz, I'd guess. Beat him to death, looks like. I wonder what set him off," Thorsten said.

Suddenly, a rumbling voice came from behind them. "Hold it, guys."

Standing in the doorway, a hulking number with a blocky head above a gargantuan body regarded them. He had the look of a man trying to stay calm, but his face was hard as ice. The guy looked oddly familiar to Brian. TV personality? Pro wrestler? Then he got it: Jake Pasciewicz, All-Pro defensive linebacker who'd dominated Chicago Bears opponents for years. Retired for a decade or so but hadn't gone to seed. Biceps like coconuts and a gut of hard fat. He'd had a rep as a nasty drunk who'd pounded the shit out of several citizens over the years but had never served time.

"Hello, Jake," Brian said. "How's tricks?"

"You jamokes stay right where you are."

"How'd our buddy get jammed up here? Say something indiscreet?" Brian asked.

"Don't worry about that. You'd best take care of your own self, dickwad."

Brian raised open hands to shoulder level in a *who me?* gesture. "Hey Jake, no need to get prickly. We were just uh, discussing your boss. In fact, we—"

"Can it, pal."

Darcy heard voices from the front of the house. Sounded like Brian talking with a man with a deep booming voice. Clearly not a friendly discussion. She grabbed a sizeable cast-iron frying pan off the stove and crept back down the hall toward the voices. She saw a huge man standing in the doorway of the room Brian and Thorsten had entered a few minutes earlier.

Pasciewicz was so intent on the two men, he didn't notice that Darcy silently tip-toeing up behind him.

Chapter 64

Darcy wielded the heavy cast iron skillet she'd found in the kitchen. Grasping the handle with both hands, she swung it back and then swept it forward with all her strength, like Serena Williams executing a 130-mile-an-hour unhittable ace. The bottom of the pan crunched into the back of Pasciewicz's head at the base where it met his thick neck. He grunted and fell to the floor like a puppet whose strings had been cut. He landed on his side with one arm trapped under his body and the other draped forward on the floor. Unconscious, the giant's mouth gaped open.

Darcy leaned in the doorway breathing hard, her face red. She looked at the huge man on the floor and shrugged. "Had to do it."

Seeing Darcy's troubled eyes and trying to lighten her mood, Brian said, "Reminds me of a double you hit in your last game with the Illini."

Thorsten stepped to the fallen man mountain, took a knee and felt for a pulse in the carotid artery.

"He's breathing okay and the pulse is strong enough. He'll survive. I'll secure him." Thorsten pulled a zip tie from a pocket and struggled to push Pasciewicz onto his stomach so he could pin his hands together behind his back. The big man's eyes fluttered open. His face lit up with a frantic animal wildness. He grabbed at Thorsten and clamped his thick fingers onto the back of the agent's neck, pulling the smaller man to him. Pasciewicz head-butted his assailant in the forehead. There was a sickening cracking noise, like a melon being struck with a ball peen hammer. Thorsten sagged back groaning and slipped into oblivion. Pasciewicz got to his feet.

Brian, who'd been studying Massey's corpse, turned at the sounds of the struggle and saw that Thorsten was now unconscious on the floor and Pasciewicz stood over him. Darcy remained in the doorway, watching, ready to take action, but uncertain.

The huge man had seemingly shrugged off the blow to the back of his head with the skillet. He charged Brian, like the aggressive linebacker he'd been with the Bears. He tackled Brian and knocked hm backwards, the full three hundred pounds of weight pinning him to the floor. JP tried the head butt again, but Brian anticipated it and managed to jerk his head to the side. The blocky forehead caught Brian in the side of his neck, causing him to nearly black out. He tried to get up but could not move under the ponderous weight. Darcy approached, hoping to strike the gargantuan man again, but his reflexes were amazingly quick. Still astride Brian, he pivoted his upper body and backhanded her away as if shooing a gnat.

Pasciewicz got to his feet again and delivered a vicious kick to Brian's ribs. He turned and moved toward Darcy, who dropped the skillet to the floor, darted away and sprinted for the front door. She twisted the doorknob and tore outside with JP on her heels. Thorsten's Tahoe was only a few yards from the door. Darcy knew she didn't have time to open the truck door, get inside and close and lock the door. Instead, she dove underneath the high clearance vehicle and moved her body under the central driveline.

She eyed the ground around of the truck. A pair of enormous leather boots appeared on the passenger side.

"C'mon out." The deep bass voice. "I've got long arms. If I hafta pull ya outta there, it's gonna get ugly."

"Not as ugly as you," Darcy said.

She scrambled sideways as a hand the size of a catcher's mitt reached toward her, grazing a shoulder. She heard a feral grunt of exertion as the hand moved in again and grabbed at her tee shirt. A finger and thumb held onto the sleeve with a vice-like grip. She lurched toward daylight on the far side of the truck, leaving the sleeve of her tee-shirt behind in the grasping digits. She squirmed out from under the truck's undercarriage and took off toward the trees as if trying to steal third base.

Pasciewicz bellowed a raging collection of words unheeded by Darcy as she quickly disappeared into the forest. He sighed, turned and headed back to the big house. He continued around to the back, where his Suburban was parked. He'd loaded up his stuff and all the cash he could find in the house earlier. No need to stick around. Let the two dickheads inside sort themselves out. He climbed aboard, fired up the engine and headed around the house to the driveway. A few minutes later, he was on 89 headed north toward the Interstate.

Brian eased himself up, favoring the right side of his torso. A sharp pain below his armpit let him know that one or more ribs had been broken by Pasciewicz's brutal kick. He approached Bill Thorsten, who lay motionless on the floor.

The agent's pulse was strong, but he remained unresponsive. He'd better get medical assistance.

First, Brian called 911 and reported the emergency need for medical assistance for Thorsten. Then he called Sheriff Reid. The woman who answered the phone said he was unavailable, but she'd ask him to call back.

A few minutes later, Brian's phone sounded off with "Katmandu." Reid.

"Where the fuck did you guys go?" His voice rasped like the blade of a bulldozer scraping rock.

"We're at Massey's new place in the valley. He's dead. His bodyguard, Pasciewicz, put the hurt on Thorsten. He's injured, needs a doctor. I called 911."

"Where's this Pascy what's his name?"

"Took off in his white Suburban. I've got the plate number. And the damned dinosaur skull is here. And Massey's in it." Brian recited the license plate number.

"I'm on my way. Don't touch anything."

Chapter 65
(Days 14-19)

Thorsten finally came to, just as an ambulance from the Clarkville clinic arrived. They loaded the agent and carried him away.

Reid got there and grilled Brian. Next, he called the Montana Division of Criminal Investigation in Helena to report the Massey homicide. He spoke with the DCI's Investigations Bureau chief for a few minutes. Clearly, the state investigators would conduct the probe into the murder of Massey. The county detective, Smith, simply did not have the expertise to handle it. Reid knew the state folks would also take over the investigation of the events at Seth Delmer's place as well as the dinosaur skull heist. How the FBI might be involved he did not care. He'd let them sort it out with the state guys.

Knowing his own department's limitations was good judgement, Reid felt. He figured it would serve him well in the coming weeks, and in next year's election. County voters expected his department to handle the traditional crimes: domestic violence, drunken bar fights, traffic violations and accidents. There was no upside in getting enmeshed with high profile homicides and dinosaur skull thefts.

At the Clarkville Clinic, Bill Thorsten was examined by Doc Banham. He'd suffered a serious concussion from Pasciewicz's head butt. Banham prescribed pain killers and had him hospitalized overnight for further observation. He was somewhat better after a few hours and looked forward to a full recovery.

X-rays of Brian's ribs revealed hairline breaks in two of them. Banham recommended Tylenol and rest. He and Darcy were also treated for nasty abrasions on their wrists.

Medical staff also attended to the gunshot wound Seth Delmer incurred from Brian while rampaging with the logging machine. He was eventually transferred from the hospital to the Geyser County jail, pending indictment for murder, kidnapping, theft and related charges. The evidence was strong. Darcy's phone recording of the Delmers bragging about their crimes was extremely helpful. When the DCI's lead investigator, Martin Quigley, played it for Seth, he knew he was in deep trouble. He hired a lawyer who began plea-bargaining.

His best bet, Quigley told Seth, would be to come clean about the crimes he'd been contracted for by Massey in return for a possible reduced sentence. Seth would admit nothing about the Patchett murder or the kidnapping of Barbara Hardy, He said the dinosaur theft was all Massey's idea and that Garcia, on Massey's orders, initiated the theft.

Had he not been killed, Massey would have been charged with soliciting the murder of Terry Patchett, soliciting the kidnapping of Barbara Hardy and ordering the theft of the *T. rex* skull. The McKays both felt he should also be charged with being an all-around dick. That last inculpation, while not a legal matter, was self-evident.

Garcia had left town, destination unknown, without speaking with the sheriff or the DCI. He had not disclosed Massey's contract on the McKays—that was irrelevant now, he felt. Thorsten had inquired about Garcia with James St. Claire in the Chicago FBI office. James said he'd been told that Garcia was a government "asset," but that he had no further information. He reported that the U.S. Assistant Attorney General, Criminal Division, in Washington, had just interceded, stating that Garcia was currently on official government business, and no further action was to be taken re him by the FBI. That same day, Darcy received a text from Garcia: THX U SAVED MY ASS I O U AG. That was the last any of them heard from the man.

On a clear summer morning, Garcia sat in an aisle seat in coach, sipping a diet cola and chewing on the peanuts from the complimentary half-ounce bag the flight attendant had dropped on his tray table. He'd ended up physically unscathed from his experience in Montana, though it had deeply embarrassed him. The incident in the clutches of the logging machine was something he'd relived in nightmares, already. Should he see a shrink? Nah. A Seal works out his issues on his own, whatever it takes. You solve a problem by using your intelligence guided by experience. Fortunate for him, his new bosses had covered for him, so he faced no criminal charges. He'd turned in his million-dollar share of the proceeds from the dinosaur skull heist. He was on his way to a fresh start in D.C. He had no desire to set foot in Montana again.

Gus Delmer and Josie Wilshire were still on the run. Sheriff Reid had issued an arrest warrant for the couple labeled "top priority" in the NCIC system accessible by law enforcement officers nationwide. Tips immediately started coming in from citizens throughout the mountain west. The latest sighting had been at a shopping mall in Sedona, Arizona, but that remained unverified, like all the others.

The Paradise Preserve had been purchased by a pair of wealthy brothers who'd made their fortune oil fracking in Texas. They vowed in a press release to construct "the most luxurious and exclusive residential community in the United States…more appealing to the discerning connoisseur of upmarket real estate than the ultra-exclusive Yellowstone Club near Big Sky Montana."

Chapter 66

Darcy returned to classes at MSU. Having missed a number of in-person classes, she was behind and needed to work extra hard to catch up and stay on track for completion of her credit hours for the term ending the coming May. Plus, she needed to work on her thesis and make up material covered in a pair of missed seminar sessions. She and Russell Eagle Feather had started dating. Whether it would become serious was anyone's guess. Darcy's top priority remained her studies, but she admitted to her apartment mate Becky that she might occasionally spend a night with Russell at his place.

One morning, as Darcy was leaving a paleontology class, her phone rang. Looked like a local number, but an unknown caller. "Yes," she said.

"This is Chad Kolbert calling for Darcy McKay. I'm a reporter for KXLF TV here in Bozeman."

"This is Darcy. What's up?"

"I'm dying to interview you face to face. Could we meet up?"

"Are you talking on camera?"

"Of course. You're a celebrity. The public wants to see and hear you."

Darcy cringed. Celebrity? But, as she thought about it, she figured a little public exposure would probably not hurt. Down the road, as a paleontologist, she'd be applying for grants and publishing papers. Look at Scott Noble Stevens, a very image-conscious scientist…and a very successful one. "Okay, she said. Let's figure something out."

After some discussion, they settled on meeting the next morning at the TV station in Bozeman.

The studio was hot and cramped. The overhead lights were harsh. After a woman production assistant worked on her face with makeup, Darcy sat back to wait. She didn't feel comfortable under the glare and amid the cables snaking across the floor. Production people rushed around, ignoring her. She'd been interviewed on TV in Chicago a year earlier, in the wake of the "Dirty Money" adventure. So, though not an on-air virgin, she was still nervous. She quickly ran through the coaching she'd had last time: keep your answers brief, make eye contact, speak slowly and distinctly and just relax. Couldn't hurt to smile once in a while.

Darcy was dressed in an off-white cotton long-sleeve shirt, jeans and running shoes. The assistant had clipped a tiny black microphone to the placket of her shirt. Kolbert had thrown on a sport coat over a pale blue button-down shirt and the obligatory pricey jeans. His square glasses lent a studious aspect to his smooth and intent expression.

Kolbert gave a brief recap of recent activities involving the murder of Terry Patchett, the kidnapping of Barbara Hardy and the chain of violent criminal events at Seth Delmer's "compound." He described Darcy as an amateur detective who'd "triumphed over hardcore criminals involved with murder and mayhem in the Crazy Mountains, along with the theft of a world-class *T. rex* skull from the William Big Horn Dinosaur Museum."

His opening question: "So, Darcy McKay, how does it feel to have survived this recent round of criminal violence as a detective in a high profile case?"

"Well, actually, I'm a grad student, not a detective. And this case, as you put it, was just my being in the wrong place at the right time, I guess. My uncle Brian is the detective."

He smiled broadly. "But you were on scene when the ex-NFL star gone rogue attacked your uncle and Bozeman-based FBI agent Bill Thorsten."

"Yes, it was a scary moment."

"How did it feel to knock out the attacker by slamming him in the head with a heavy frying pan?"

"Felt good."

"Anything you'd do differently if you had the opportunity?"

She smiled. "I might have used a bigger frying pan."

Kolbert chuckled. "What about advice for women who may find themselves in a possible dangerous situation with a larger adversary."

"Use any weapon at hand, like your elbows, knees, fists or any handy object you can grab and swing. Pepper spray is good. But a lot of times, you can avoid trouble by projecting a confident attitude."

"At the compound where the dinosaur thieves were hiding, you saved a man's life by releasing him from the clutches of a massive logging machine designed to cut old-growth trees off at the feet. How did you manage that?"

Off at the feet? "Well I used to be a pretty decent gamer back when I had the time. Turned out the logging machine was designed like a game: joysticks buttons, a screen. Not that complicated. I'm just glad I had the opportunity to help out."

The interviewer lobbed a few more softball questions at Darcy. She answered easily and tried to inject a little humor. Kolbert played along. Time slipped by quickly.

An off-camera producer signaled for them to wind it up. Kolbert's smile widened. In his mellifluous announcer's voice, he said, "Thank you, Darcy McKay. You're an inspiration to young women everywhere. And now please stay tuned for this message before we move on to our next segment: why are so many rich folks moving to western Montana and what's it doing to our local economy?"

The camera and On Air red lights clicked off. Darcy emitted a sigh of relief and unclipped the microphone.

Kolbert strode over for a handshake. He held onto her hand for an extra beat. "You did great," he gushed. "I'd really like to talk with you some more. Uh, do you have supper plans?"

"Actually, I'm meeting friends. Maybe another time."

As Darcy's interview wrapped up, Brian watched from the couch in his cabin on the Sands ranch. He felt proud of Darcy, figured she had a hell of a great future…if she didn't stick her neck out too much. Once again, Arthur Sands had tried to hire him for a fulltime security role, but he'd declined. He'd attempted to keep up with his investigations work in Chicago, but it was impossible to do justice to clients who expected to meet with him in person, rather than phone, text or email. Clients were drifting away but he didn't feel like returning to the city.

For a couple of days, Brian caught up on reading, fielded messages and walked around the huge ranch on old trails created by the bison and wild animals. He met with Arthur Sands, discussing security issues such as gates, locks, CCTV coverage of the perimeter and structures on the ranch. He'd lost contact with Michelle Emerson, his now former girlfriend. He was restless. But he'd had one long phone conversation with Carol Jensen. They'd agreed to get together soon.

Seeing Darcy on TV reminded Brian that he needed to get back to her friend Natalie Katz, who'd been terrified of Massey. He got her on the phone.

"Oh Brian, thanks for calling. I've been reading about you guys online."

"So you know Massey is no longer with us?"

"Thank God. I mean, that sounds callous, but—"

"No need to explain. I'm with you on that."

"Tell Darcy I hope to see her soon. Vacation in Yellowstone this fall."

"Bring your bear spray."

"It'll be refreshing to carry it for bears instead of criminals."

Chapter 67
(Day 20)

Brian remembered the local private investigator in Clarkville who was planning on retiring and selling his investigative practice. More than two weeks had elapsed since Bill Thorsten had sent him an email mentioning the P.I., Arthur Braswell.

Brian called him.

"Yes, I'm still seeking a buyer for my practice," Braswell said.

"Well, I'm interested and qualified."

They agreed to meet at Braswell's office in downtown Clarkville the next day.

The office was on the second floor of a hundred year old stone building, above an ancient bookstore on Main Street. After introductions, Brian sat at a small conference table with Braswell.

"I've got six main clients representing eighty percent of revenues and about a hundred smaller occasional or one-shot accounts," Braswell said. "Most of that business is word of mouth." Braswell was a stout man about sixty years old. He wore a plaid button-down shirt and khakis.

"Tell me about the clients," Brian said.

"The big ones are two law firms, a bank and three wealthy individuals and their families. I've had the law firms for hmmm…about fifteen years, mainly providing evidence to help win civil lawsuits or finding exculpatory evidence on behalf of defendants falsely accused. The individual accounts tend to be looking for ammunition so they can sue over water rights, property disputes, sometimes divorce, alimony, child custody."

"What about the bank?"

"Had 'em from the beginning. Uh, twenty-one years."

"Which one?"

"First Intermountain Bank. Main contact is Carol Jensen."

"Ah, I happen to know her. She's on the board of the dinosaur museum."

Braswell smiled. "Yep. She mentioned that she knew you."

News travels fast around here, Brian thought. After some more discussion as to the nature of the various client accounts and some back and forth, the two men agreed in principle that Brian would purchase the right to do business with Braswell's clients. Pending references checking out on both sides, of course. The clients would be informed of Brian's taking over and they would individually either agree to continue with him or perhaps seek investigation services elsewhere, which would likely mean Bozeman. Braswell would try to steer them toward Brian, but there would be no guarantees. Brian would pay Braswell twenty percent of the fees he earned from said clients for the first year. After that, there'd be no obligations on either side. Brian would take over the lease for Braswell's small office in Clarkville, beginning the first of the following month. They shook hands and went out for a celebratory lunch down the street at the Cattlemen's Restaurant.

They took a booth at the Cattlemen's. Over beers, Braswell commented, "I expect you'll be able to develop some new business on your own. You seem like a thoughtful man, and then there's your local uh, notoriety."

"What?"

"Well, starting with the events at Bone Mountain and then that Chicago gang's shenanigans at the 606 last year, plus this Delmer and Massey stuff, you and that niece of yours have been in the local news for a bit."

"Our fifteen minutes, you mean?"

"Actually more like a half hour. Can't hurt. You know, they say any publicity is good publicity."

"Probably right. I don't mind, but I hope Darcy goes back to being just another graduate student."

"I'm sure you'll both do fine," Braswell said with a smile.

As they were finishing their beers, a news bulletin came on the large screen TV on the wall nearby. Brian was startled by the headline crawling across the screen below the face of a talking head with a mic. The TV sound was muted, but closed captioning related the story:

> The body of missing Bozeman developer Terry Patchett has been found in a makeshift grave on the property of local logger Seth Delmer in the Crazy Mountains. A DCI spokesman confirmed that they discovered the body earlier today through the use of cadaver dogs trained to detect human remains. Patchett went missing nearly three weeks prior to

the discovery. A metal box containing five hundred thousand dollars in hundred dollar bills was also unearthed within feet of the grave. Finally, the remains of a dog, were disinterred nearby. More details later.

"Well," Braswell said, "that about clinches the murder case against Mr. Delmer."

"Yes, it does. That and Darcy's recording."

A week later, Brian had moved into a rental house in town, an easy three-block walk from his new office. He'd met some of the clients and felt optimistic that they would stay in the fold. Many of them would likely dry up though, because they simply would not need a private investigator's services. Maybe he could hang onto a few of his current Chicago clients. The prospect of returning to Chicago occasionally was attractive. He'd keep his apartment and office space until the current annual leases ran out. Arthur Sands wanted to retain him for occasional security projects at his ranch, at least until he could hire a new fulltime security manager. So, he seemed to be set financially. But what about personally?

Brian and Carol had not seen each other since the dinner they, Darcy and Carol's nephew, Jerry, had shared at Carol's house more than a week earlier. In their phone conversation the day before, she seemed happy that he'd moved into town and would be doing business locally. Of course, she'd see him on the occasions where the bank needed investigation work, such as background checks on potential significant borrowers—he'd need to review balance sheets, verifying the reasonableness of asset valuations, for example. The bank had been stuck recently when they loaned a million to a local blowhard businessman who'd overstated the value of an out of state condo building at three times its actual worth.

As Brian entered his new residence that afternoon, his phone rang. Carol.

"Are you moved in?" she said.

"I am. Want a tour?"

"Yep. When?"

"Uh, how about tomorrow for dinner? We could order in, have a nice bottle of wine, make an evening of it."

"Any dress code?"

He laughed. "Montana formal."

"Right. I'll put on clean jeans."

Chapter 68

(Day 21)

Jake Pasciewicz rolled his Suburban into Clarkville as the sun streaked the sky orange behind the Absaroka Mountains. A week had elapsed since he'd left Hamilton Massey's house after killing the ex-financial executive in a boiling rage. Massey had tried to stiff JP on the extra pay he had coming for staying on as bodyguard after the initially agreed time had gone by. Masset had explicitly agreed to pay him, and then welshed on the deal.

Sitting calmly at the desk in the office room of the huge Montana house, Massey had said, "Yes, I may have said I'd pay you more. But after additional thought, I decided not to. Why? Because we had an initial agreement for a specific amount. I paid you that amount, and that's all there is to say."

At that insult, JP had lost it. He'd grabbed the spindle-shanked geek by the front of his shirt and threatened to break all ten of his skinny fingers. When that had not had the desired effect, he'd broken the asshole's neck, lifted him up and jammed him into the dagger-toothed *T. rex* skull on display next to the desk. The body lay there, limp and lifeless. Looked like something out of the first *Jurassic Park* movie.

After he'd killed Massey, three troublemakers had showed up: a private eye named McKay, a blonde girl, whom he'd later learned was McKay's niece, and a local FBI agent. The girl had sneaked up behind him and knocked him senseless with a frying pan to the back of the noggin. When he'd come to, the two guys had tried to subdue him, and JP had fought them off. He'd tried to catch the girl, but she'd run outside and eluded him.

Pasciewicz had then roared away from Massey's place in his truck, heading for the Interstate. He'd been on the run ever since. He knew he'd be the main suspect in the murder. He deeply regretted his giving in to his violent temper. It had always been part of him, an asset in the brutal world of the NFL. Not so much after he'd retired from the sport.

He'd been staying in cheap motels in scattered mountain towns, biding his time, keeping out of sight. His disguise of straw fedora, thick-framed eyeglasses and monochromatic clothing, way different than his normal look, had been surprisingly effective. Plus, his vehicle sported the California license plates he'd stolen along the way.

Pasciewicz wanted payback on the two McKays, especially the girl. Never in his adult life outside of football had he been knocked to the floor by any man, let alone a wisp of a female. He'd leave the FBI agent alone—too much risk. According to a rental real estate site online, a house in the small town of Clarkville, Montana had recently been rented by a McKay, first name not indicated. Could be the meddling folks at Massey's place. He put the address in his phone and had the navigation app in his truck guide him to the building.

As darkness fell, Pasciewicz parked a block away from the rental place and went in on foot. He passed through the alley and approached the rear of the two-story house. At the back door, he could hear voices inside, a man and a woman. The latter did not strike him as the voice of a youngster like the one who'd brained him at Massey's house. The male sounded like the guy who'd laid hands on him at Massey's, the girl's uncle.

He pressed his ear against the door in an effort to better hear the conversation inside. Yes, it was definitely McKay speaking. Pasciewicz unholstered his Colt .45 automatic.

Chapter 69

Brian and Carol lingered after supper in his newly-rented house in Clarkville. It was located in a neighborhood of modest frame houses, with both mature and recently planted trees lining the street. The residents of his block were middle class, a mix of families with kids, couples and singles. That cool evening, there were a few kids outside, tooling around on bikes and scooters, and a sprinkling of adults out for a walk or coming home from work. He guessed most people were inside, having the evening meal, reading their screens, or both. The atmosphere seemed a bit bland on the surface, when he compared this place to his Chicago neighborhood full of a densely packed people of every ethnicity. In the city there was plenty of noise, nonstop activity and, yes, crime. This seemed a safe haven, especially after the violence of the past couple of weeks.

They sat on stools at the counter dividing the kitchen from the front room. Dinner was delicious, buffalo burgers and oven-roasted potatoes delivered by a local restaurant called Jill's. He'd snagged the bottle of Malbec from the dining table and poured glasses for both of them.

"Okay, you've told me some of it, and I've read the news reports. A lot of conjecture. And I know how it ended up. What I don't get is how on Earth you and Darcy got yourselves in the middle of it. I can understand *you* getting involved because Sands hired you to solve the kidnapping of his ex. So, okay. But Darcy?"

"We both happened to be close to the spot where the dinosaur skull got ripped off. We were asleep in our respective cabins, or at least I was. Darcy later told me she was awake. She's been studying nights after working the dinosaur dig during the day. Anyway, I heard a vehicle driving by at a time and place where it seemed weird. So, I got up to check it out. When I got wind of it that rainy night, she did too. As I drove by the cabin she was sharing with her friend Becky, she came running out, jumped in my truck and off we went. I didn't have any choice."

"Uh huh. But how *is* she? That was a hell of an experience you and she went through when those lowlife Delmers beat on you and tied both of you up. You guys are lucky to be alive." She raised her eyebrows as she sipped her wine. Brian noticed her face had become slightly flushed, maybe from the alcohol. He felt a little buzz, himself.

"Ah, she'll be okay. See, like me, she's sort of an orphan. She's had to fend for herself a lot. I've tried to be there as support, but I'm living my own life. Anyway, she's tough. She'll be fine."

"I hope so." She sighed.

"Thing is, she's super motivated. Sees her studies as top priority at this time in her life. On track for her masters in a year and a half. Then, I'm guessing, her doctorate. She knows exactly what she wants to do in her career. Luckier than most of us at that age. Hell, at any age."

"She's seeing Russell, I understand."

"Well, yeah. They're in a relationship. I hear they went on a short road trip together last weekend. Up to the dinosaur center in Bynum, where the paleontologist gave them a behind the scenes tour of the exhibits and current field project. Stayed overnight on the way back. That's all I know." He shrugged.

"Cool. They've got a lot in common, both being dinosaur freaks. They'd make a cute couple. But how did that Massey schmuck get into all this murder and kidnapping stuff around here? I thought he was a white collar criminal in Illinois, and he was supposed to be in prison there."

"Right. You know about how last year he participated in a business conference for a few days at that ranch owned by his employer, the Belcoe Corporation. The 606 place down by Yellowstone Park."

"I happen to know it well. I worked housekeeping down there one summer as a high school kid, back when it was a guest ranch."

"Anyway, while Massey was there, the ranch manager hired Seth Delmer to supply lumber and firewood to the place and to do some carpentry work in the lodge. Massey, being the devious jerk he was, asked Seth to find him a quarter ounce of cocaine. Says it relaxes him in all those high pressure business meetings. Seth knew a guy and got the coke to Massey the next day in exchange for a thousand cash. Next thing, Massey gets discussing other possible projects for Seth. But nothing materializes at the business meet and Massey goes back to Chicago. I got all this from an employee there who overheard the conversation."

"So Massey goes back to this Belcoe place, where he cooks the books and goes to the hoosegow."

"Correct. And even before he buys a pardon, he's giving Seth the order from his prison cell to kill Patchett so he can take over the Paradise Preserve. After that, Massey hires Seth to snatch and ransom Barbara. Unfortunately, Seth enlisted Gus's help. If little brother'd been just a bit smarter, he'd have stayed clear of it. As well as the next Massey brainchild, the great *T. rex* skull heist."

"You're still plugged into the investigation?"

"I'm in touch with my FBI friends, Bill Thorsten and James St. Clair. Thorsten knows the Montana DCI chief. They've been the main investigators. I understand Seth's lawyer is working on a plea deal, a reduced sentence in exchange for spilling his guts about everything."

"The whole thing sounds like a murderous crime spree based on Massey's twisted greed."

"Twisted. Yeah. Some people are born that way. Playing by the rules is for suckers. Lying to get an edge is second nature. Massey was one of those guys would sell his mother out for a few bucks."

"But he also spent a lot, getting the Delmers and Garcia to do his dirty work. He must have expected to come out ahead — right?"

"In the long run. He paid Seth some amount, I'd guess less than a hundred thousand, to off Patchett. And he must have paid for the pardon from prison — we'll never know how much. Then he received net ransom of a million in the kidnapping, after the Delmers got their shares. Next, he paid Garcia and the Delmers three million for the *T. rex* skull. So he was underwater on the crime spree when he died. But he no doubt expected to make millions off the Paradise Preserve.

And he could have easily unloaded the skull to another private collector, probably for a lot more than he'd paid."

"So what happens to all that money now?"

"The legal system and the courts will be unwinding it all. The feds will continue to investigate Massey's offshore assets. The DCI found two million of apparent skull money in a backpack at Seth's place. Garcia turned in the other million from the skull. As for the ransom two million one, a million went to a Massey bank account, Seth got a half million, while Gus and his girlfriend, Josie, made off with six hundred thousand. As yesterday's news reported, the DCI found Seth's share buried in the ground near his cabin, next to the grave of Patchett and a small dog. By the way, Norah Spivey told them the buried dog was a mutt named Whiskey."

"How did Gus and his girlfriend get away"

"You know about the chaos at the woodlot. One minute they're standing there on the sideline. People keep arriving: Me and Darcy. Then Josie. The party's almost complete when Garcia strolls in. Showing some intelligence, Gus and Josie quietly slip away. Gus leaves his million-dollar share of the dinosaur skull loot behind in the backpack with Seth's share. But they have their six hundred thousand. They nearly run Thorsten off the road as he's driving up and head down the highway before anyone even knows they've bailed. Their timing was good—they must have reached the highway just before the sheriff got to the road leading up to Seth's. Warrants are out for them nationwide. They're either smart or incredibly lucky. Maybe they're lounging on a beach in Mazatlán."

"You know, I kind of hope so. After all, neither of them participated in the murder."

"But legally, they aided in the kidnapping and Gus helped cart the skull away. Plus, Gus helped Seth rough up me and Darcy at gunpoint. They'd face felony charges and a good chance of spending years of their lives incarcerated."

"What's aiding actually mean?"

"Aiding's helping commit a crime by supporting or assisting. Abetting's encouraging someone to commit a crime, which Massey certainly did."

"Got it."

"What's the status of the skull?"

"It's back home. Dave Bakeno and a lab tech from the university cleaned it up. Had to get the blood stains off the teeth. What a mess. We've got it locked up in storage, pending completion of a new heavy-duty display case. Art Sands is footing the bill for it, along with a cutting edge security system for the museum."

"Good idea. What happened to the guard who let the thieves into the museum?"

"The board considered letting him go, but we decided to keep him on. He's been a great employee from the start. He's undergoing additional training in security measures. Plus, we didn't have the heart to keep his profane parrot Fred away from his nighttime home."

"Makes sense. I'll bet that was the last time the guy opens the door on his shift no matter what."

"What was Garcia's role in all this?" Carol asked. "Seems like he abetted like crazy on that skull caper."

"I'm still not sure. He resented my screening him for the job with Sands. He followed me in Chicago. Acted very suspicious. I don't know if he actually wanted the job with Sands or blew his chances intentionally. Maybe he wanted to size me up. Spied on Darcy, too. He really egged on the Delmers. But he said a funny thing to me as I was trying to escape from Seth: 'Hang loose. You guys aren't going to be harmed.' Thorsten told me Garcia supposedly has some connection to a federal government agency."

"Like Homeland Security?"

"Dunno. There are seventeen intelligence agencies in the U.S. Let's say he was undercover. Could he get away with leading the dinosaur skull theft? Undercover agents can entrap others. Maybe he was trying to get the Delmers in trouble. Or Massey."

"But where does the line get drawn?"

"Depends. If he were participating on the skull heist to nail down a conviction of Massey or the Delmers, it might be acceptable. Especially if he helped get the stolen goods back. His mysterious government employer would likely make the call. I hear he turned in the million dollars Massey paid him for the dinosaur skull heist to the FBI. Far as I know, he hasn't been charged with anything, and rumor has it he's in D.C. now."

"What about that man that's accused of killing Massey? Pasciewicz?"

"He's still out there. A guy like that, he's really distinctive. He's on the BOLO list for law enforcement nationwide. And the FBI ten most-wanted list as well. His mugshot's been posted all over the country and online. Just a matter of time before somebody spots him and calls law enforcement."

They talked about Carol's job and her nephew Jerry's high school triumphs and traumas. As with most teens, the traumas loomed large. At least he shared close friendship with fellow self-defined outsider, David Big Hair. The boys' strongest interests seemed to be sports, social media, trout fishing and recently, girls.

"He's rocketing up so fast. Fifteen, and he's already five eleven. We co-exist. He tolerates me. I'll never replace his mom."

The mood became somber as their thoughts turned to the memory of Carol's sister, Laura, who'd been murdered by an evil thug two years prior, leaving Jerry an orphan. After a brief stint with his grandparents, he'd come to live with Carol. She felt she was more like a big sister than aunt to the teen. Brian had had feelings toward Laura, who'd reciprocated. They'd been in the early stages of what might have become a serious romantic relationship, when she'd been cut down in her prime. Brian hoped Carol didn't associate him with the tragedy or somehow hold him responsible. He and Darcy had been directly involved in bringing the murderer to rough justice.

He tried to lighten the mood. "With your job, the museum board and Jerry, how do you manage? Me, I'm constantly making to-do lists on my phone and never seem to get it all done."

"One thing: being under time pressure allows me minimal room for morosity."

"Huh. Is that a word?"

"Yeah, little known."

A barely perceptible creaking noise came from outside the back door off the kitchen. Brian heard it first and then Carol suddenly stiffened.

"What was that?" she said.

"Sounded like something at the back door. It's locked. I'll check."

Chapter 70

Brian walked through the kitchen and approached the door silently. He pressed an ear against the wooden surface. He stayed that way for a whole minute. At first nothing. Then he heard a faint squeak representing someone or something putting considerable weight on the flat deck boards right outside the door. There was no window with a view of the deck. He stepped to the side, so he was not in line with the door and put his hand on the knob. He turned it as if to open it. The door latch mechanism rattled slightly, but the deadbolt held it closed.

Suddenly, a gunshot cracked, and a ragged hole appeared in the center of the door. One of the panes in the front window in the living room shattered. Glass tinkled to the floor. Brian could see daylight through the hole in the door. His heartbeat skittered like a restless puppy. He'd been lucky he'd moved aside in time. No room for any more rookie mistakes.

"Get down!" he yelled over his shoulder at Carol. She dove to the floor and moved to the far corner of the living room, behind a couch. She grabbed her phone and dialed 911.

Ducking low, Brian made it to the front room. "Wait here." He began to move toward the front door.

"What are you doing?"

"I'm going to just have a look outside."

"What? Are you crazy? Stay here and wait for the police. The dispatcher said they're on the way. Should be just a few minutes."

Brian's Sig Sauer was upstairs in the bedroom in the nightstand next to the bed. No time to retrieve it. He knew Carol was right. The smart thing would be to stay put and wait for the police. But he was pissed off. Someone had attempted to kill him in his new home. The least he could do was to find out who was out there. Anyway, they were probably gone by now. He went to the front door and eased it open. "I'll be right back," he said.

Trying to make as little noise as possible, he walked quickly to the side of the house and around the corner toward the back yard. At the end of the cedar-sided wall, he slowly eased his head forward enough to look around the corner toward the back entryway.

Jake Pasciewicz, all three hundred pounds of him, stood peering at the bullet hole in the back door, a pistol hanging from his right hand. Intent on his spying, he didn't notice Brian as he crept forward and came up from behind. Brian carefully considered the physics of the situation. He knew he couldn't overpower the vastly heavier man. But he could sure try to make use of gravity. Bent forward at the waist, he silently approached Pasciewicz. He extended both hands and grabbed the front of his quarry's ankles. He pulled back with all his strength, causing the giant to pitch forward and land on his face. As his nose hit the wooden deck, the cartilage was crushed. Blood gushed forth and stained the deck boards next to his head.

But Pasciewicz had endured an NFL career of violent collisions. He managed to get to his hands and knees, blood dripping steadily from his nose like a leaking garden hose. He still held the pistol loosely in his big right hand. He began to raise it toward Brian, who kicked it out of his hand. The gun clattered across the wooden deck, off the edge and into an adjacent lilac bush. Enraged, Pasciewicz struggled to his feet. As he approached Brian, a siren resonated in the distance. The gigantic man stopped to listen. Brian scrambled for the gun on the ground. He managed to grab it and aim it at Pasciewicz.

"You think that'll stop me?" Pasciewicz demanded. "I'll ram that gun right up your—"

Two police officers ran into the yard from the gap between houses. The first one held a revolver straight ahead and trained it on the two men in the yard.

"Hands up, both of you," yelled the young policeman.

The second cop, slightly older, moved in, gun in the two handed Weaver Stance.

Brian dropped the gun and raised his hands. Pasciewicz was having none of it. He rushed the second cop and seemed shocked when the man calmly pulled the trigger, resulting in a rapidly growing red splotch in the towering man's midsection. He fell to the ground screaming with rage and pain.

More sirens. Then came the sounds of car doors opening and footsteps rushing into the back yard.

Chapter 71

It took hours to sort it all out. Brian and Carol gave statements to the Clarkville police, who seemed sympathetic. Pasciewicz was taken away to the trauma unit in town, pending arraignment. Police officers examined and photographed the crime scene at the rear of the house as well as inside. Brian patched the bullet holes in the back door and front window temporarily with scraps of cardboard and masking tape he'd found in a closet. The police visited the house across the street, where Pasciewicz's gunshot had ended up, slamming into the concrete foundation in front. Fortunately, no one had been hurt.

The senior police officer asked Brian and Carol to come into the department later that day to give statements and answer additional questions.

Finally, all the law enforcement people left. Now, it was just the two of them. They returned to their abandoned glasses of wine in the living room. Getting late. Close to dawn. The end of a chaotic night. With the adrenaline rush they'd been through, they were jazzed. Sleep was now out of the question.

It was quiet for a moment. She went to the front window and he followed. Side by side, they peered out of an unbroken pane at the street. In the glow of a lone streetlight, the lindens recently planted along the block by the town's tree committee swayed like dancers in a ballet. The window was blurred into an impressionistic haze by the light rain that had just started.

"We're fortunate," Brian said. "Both of us. I mean, our lives. Lucky, I guess."

"Yes," she said. A faint mysterious smile played on her lips.

"As for us, well—"

She silenced him by grabbing the back of his head and pulling his face to hers. The kiss lasted a good ten seconds. Carol never made it home that night. She knew that her nephew would pretend to be scandalized.

ACKNOWLEDGEMENTS

Twisted Greed sprang from my previous novel, *Dirty Money*. My thanks to recurring characters who seem to tell the story as I look on. Brian McKay and his niece, Darcy McKay, outsmart the bad guys and solve the crimes in all the McKay novels. *Dirty Money* naturally flowed from *Bone Mountain*, the first installment of the McKay series. The main villain in *Twisted Greed*, disgraced executive A. Hamilton Massey, slithered from the pages of *Dirty Money*.

Writing *Twisted Greed* would have been impossible without the able help of my uber-alert partner, Sally Hughes, along with loyal and capable fellow writers, Mary Jane Corrigan and Dave Hayes. All three of them paid eagle-eyed attention to every word of the preliminary manuscript, correcting faux pas, spotting grammatical and logical errors and tightening the prose.

I offer my sincere thanks to you for reading this third novel of the Brian & Darcy McKay series of thrillers. I hope you enjoyed *Twisted Greed*. If so, please check out the previous McKay books, *Bone Mountain* and *Dirty Money*.

To learn more about Brian and Darcy McKay and other stories of mine, please stop by my website: robertdhughesauthor.com

ABOUT THE AUTHOR

Robert D. Hughes is the award-winning author of *Bone Mountain* and *Dirty Money*, the first two books in the Brian & Darcy McKay series of thrillers. His short stories of crime and mystery have appeared in numerous anthologies and magazines, both print and digital. He earned an MBA from the University of Michigan. As a financial professional in Chicago, Bob investigated white-collar crime, bringing several embezzlers to justice. He has a special affinity for the works of Lee Child, Michael Connelly, Thomas Perry and John Sandford. An Active Member of the Mystery Writers of America, he lives in Livingston, Montana.